WE GO AROUND IN THE NIGHT
AND ARE CONSUMED BY FIRE

WE GO AROUND IN THE NIGHT AND ARE CONSUMED BY FIRE

JULES GRANT

First published in 2016 by

Myriad Editions
59 Lansdowne Place
Brighton BN3 1FL

www.myriadeditions.com

First printing
1 3 5 7 9 10 8 6 4 2

'Renegade' taken from *Everything Speaks in its Own
Way* by Kate Tempest © Zingaro Books, 2012.
Reproduced by permission of Kate Tempest

'When I Remember Your Love I Weep' taken from
Selected Poems: Rumi translated by Coleman Banks,
Penguin Books, 2004 © Coleman Banks, 1995.
Reproduced by permission of Penguin Books Ltd

A CIP catalogue record for this book
is available from the British Library

ISBN (pbk): 978-1-908434-86-9
ISBN (ebk): 978-1-908434-87-6

Designed and typeset in Sabon LT
by WatchWord Editorial Services, London

Printed by CPI Group (UK) Ltd, Croydon CR0 4YY

*For my father, who believed in me always,
even when the facts clearly mitigated against it.*

So come here
Give me your hand
Because I know how to hold it
Look, I will write you a poem
And I'll set it on fire

Kate Tempest, 'Renegade'

Prologue

I'm trying to remember it now, because that was when everything changed. When I saw her go down, all I really remember is the pain like my heart was crushed, and me not able to breathe. Slow motion, a dream, I can see myself punching through the crowd, legs giving way when I got there. Then kneeling, all blood, her head on my knee.

Carla. My light, my soul.

1

November 2008

I'm not gonna fool you because like the man says, there's nothing shabbier than those farewell fucks. And I still feel pretty bad about it if I'm honest, Louise still sobbing on the comedown and me, I'm already half out the door.

I hit the street and just as I'm breathing back out, slow and careful, Mina legs it up from the ginnel, grinds her tail to a halt as she reaches me.

Hey Donna, how's it going?

I keep on walking and try for polite, Hey Mina, what's going on girl?

All the time I'm walking fast, past the burned-out Fiesta on bricks, dodging the broken glass, but she just follows me, hanging on to my arm. Not that I mind, maybe I even think she's cute, looking up at me like that with those big storm eyes, but she goes with Carla, on and off, and that's way more woman problems than I need right now.

I'm trying not to look over my shoulder just in case Louise is watching but already I'm feeling pretty good, like something brand new is about to happen, cold air hitting my lungs like menthol poppers. Mina smiles and I like the way her top teeth show, even and white. I grab on to her hand. C'mon, I says, let's get outta here.

OK, it's not clever, but now we're in the yard behind Fozzie's between the bins, underneath the ice-blue neon EXIT and I got her pushed up against the wall, biting her lip like I can't get enough of her smooth sweet skin. Then I'm just thinking how I should stop now before it all gets way too messy, when she pushes my hand between those creamy soft thighs, my gut falls out through my knees and I'm gone.

After, she lights up a cigarette, leans on the wall, buttons still all undone, my arm numb from holding her up and the salt of her still in my mouth. Don't tell Carla, she says.

As if.

And it's not like I owe her an explanation but I gotta punch this day back into shape somehow, so I look at the ground, stay away from the eyes. Don't worry baby girl, it's not like this is gonna happen again.

Then I look up and she's looking straight back and the storm's all backed up right there on the horizon, heading right for me.

Yeah right, she says. Then she gives me those teeth.

It's only later with Carla in Fozzie's knocking back Gold Label and eating fried chicken and laughing, watching Marta working it up with some babe from the Gooch, when Carla looks at me, So?

And I know she means Hey c'mon tell me what happened, I'm just hoping she means with Louise. It's over, I go, mouth full of dumpling.

Ahh jeez, goes Carla, I bet she took it bad.

I shrug, but then I'm thinkin' about Mina how slick she was and how she shuddered so long and how I put my hand over her mouth to stop her crying out. I kick against the boards. I don't wanna talk about it, I say.

Carla smiles and winks past me and I follow the wink. Marta's leaning in, her back to us, new girl trapped between herself and the bar. Girl catches the wink, smiles right back.

Carla peers at me, What's up with you, mardy?

Before I can answer she slaps a hand to my shoulder and I follow her eyes to where Fatboy and that lardarse Mouse are just filling the door. I check out my blade and I know Carla's the same. What the fuck?

But Carla's not listening. What's the score, motherfucker? she says under her breath, never takes her eyes off the door.

That's when Fatboy strides over, hands in his jacket, looking like someone just fucked his old lady in the tail. I look sideways at Carla, Aw, tell me you didn't?

Anyway there's not much time for conversation and I'm just trying to figure out what's with the jacket, when Fats leans down with one scrawny hand, grabs Carla by the scruff of the T. I'm up fast, reach for my blade.

Carla pushes back and her chair goes over, Sonn an' Lise come outta nowhere, then it's the four of us, facing him down.

Then Deej jumps the bar, Hey hey c'mon now ladies, just take it outside.

Fatboy throws her a look and it's just enough for me to grab his hand and twist it up behind him, slickety-dick, then I got one arm over his shoulder, blade pushed in right under his eye. I kick his blade away with my foot, then I'm in at his ear and I'm grinning. Someone's a long way from home, I say.

Most times if something kicks off girl on girl me and Carla both got stripes so we pretty much get to say what goes. Other times we let the boys do their thing. And apart from us and the Darts who stick together since Operation Balboa went down we don't mess with each other. That's the rules and mostly they work out fine. So two Cheetahs walking smack into a Darts bar with no pass is bang out of order. That happens and it's pretty much fair game to us, no comeback. Even if someone *did* tup your old lady behind your back, and by now I'm wondering just what the fuck Carla was thinking.

Anyhow, Fozzie's is Ashton which is deffo our patch, so Fatboy musta known what he was getting into when he came looking for Carla. I think about nicking his face, right under the eye, just so he's got a reminder. I sneak a look back but the door's just a wide hole now right into the night, and that fool-boy Mouse is nowhere to be seen.

Who says you could come over here? I say.

Then I know by the silence, just by the fact he says nothing. Zilcho. Nada. He's got no pass, and now he knows that I know. So now I'm laughing, Hey girls, it's playtime.

Up the Old Road and there's the car park by the mill, wet with the rain and all covered in weeds. The van bumps over the potholes and Carla pulls up by the doors and I'm out. I can see the street-lights winking from the road and hear the faraway sound of cars whishing by in the rain. I put my face up to the night, the raindrops fall soft, taste smoky.

By the time we get Fats up the stairs he's cursing. We stretch him out flat, tie his hands to the old radiator, tie his feet together. Sonn sets up the light, one of those big arc things, runs off a battery the size of Yorkshire. I go over to the boards where the window should be, peek out through the gaps. The sky's wet velvet, clouds scudding, no stars. I get out the phone, try Mikey again, no answer.

Then behind me I hear Fatboy hawk-up and spit.

I look over and Carla's sitting right up on his chest, wiping her face with one arm, blade up under his chin. She rips open his shirt. Best gag him, I say.

Lise takes off her pants, red with lace edges, stuffs them in his mouth to shut him up. Then Carla takes off her belt, the one with the Diesel buckle, wraps it right round his face to keep the gag in, clips it tight.

Yay, let's stick him, goes Sonn.

Carla nicks Fats on the chest, not deep, but he squeals. Then she reaches back, slaps her arse Asda-Price, turns on the charm.

What you think she wants with you, beast-boy, when she got all this?

You tell 'im honey, says Sonn.

I sit down by the window for a cig, let Carla get on with it.

After a while she sits back, points the knife at his belly, looks round at us, Well?

We all traipse on over for a look. Fats is squirming like a taddy, great big letter C carved right on to his belly.

Man, that's a fucking work of art, says Sonn.

Lise squints at the C. That for Carla?

Carla grins. Nope, it's for Cunt.

I hand her the biro. She breaks the ink with her teeth, spits on the cut, rubs the ink in with her hand, like polish. Then she pulls out the gag, leans right down to his face.

You beat her again, fuckwit, I'm gonna kill you, she says.

Fuck you lesbo-cunt, goes Fats. And that's his second mistake.

Carla rams the knickers back down his throat. In your dreams. She grabs for his fly. Hey, you even got a dick?

Fats is bucking now, eyes like saucers, trying to throw her off.

That's enough now, I go.

Carla lets go and Fats goes all limp, tiny flash at the corner of one eye, looks wet. And that's about the long and the short of it round our way, you could string up a homey's grandmother and he wouldn't shed a tear, but go anywhere near his dick and he's blubbing like a girl. Time for his goodbye present, I say, looking at Lise.

Carla puts the knife at his neck, Close your eyes.

Fats just opens them wider.

She reaches down, grabs his crotch, I said close them, fuck-head.

So now Fats got his eyes squeezed tight, looks just like he's praying, and that's got to be a first. Carla gives his dick an extra squeeze, You open those eyes, boy, you're dead.

Lise walks over, one six-inch stiletto each side of his head. Then he's thrashing about, choking, as a hot stream of piss hits him right in the face.

Lise shakes and steps off, dainty, grins down at him. Water-boarding, fuck-face, a-la-dyke.

After a while we drop him off, way out on the East Lancs, him still screeching like a girl, hands backed right up to his feet.

Sonn opens the back doors of the van, rolls him out on to the hard shoulder with a thud. Carla does a yu-ey, drives back straight towards him, swerves at the last minute and then we're back off towards town.

Lise hangs out the window, Hey Fats! You can keep the knickers.

Then everyone's laughing fit to shit, because a few pokes with a blade got nothing on sheer out-and-out humiliation, anyways not where a Cheetah's concerned.

Never liked those keks much anyway, says Lise.

Carla's got this look like she's flying. I hope he fucking chokes on them, she says.

Then we're laughing so hard the van hits the pavement, drags the bollard right along the wet tarmac, throwing out sparks. Till Carla puts her foot down, drives up and over some old-boy garden, scrapes it off good.

Towards town up the parkway and we pass the park. Everyone knows the Alex is the line between the Doddington and the Gooch, always has been, and back in the day that was pretty much it for South Manchester. Used to be the park was just another rec, scrubby grass full of dog shit, old settees, broken swings, somewhere to dump your empties after a weekend, but that was before they knocked down the Crescents, and long before the council knocked down Gooch Close and Doddington Way and the Pepperhill, sent everyone spinning right out to Hattersley and Wythenshawe, mixed them all up, wondered why when they got them all out there there was hell on.

Operation China took out most of the Gooch way back in the '90s. I guess the council was feeling all puffed up with themselves after that, went on a roll thinking if they knocked all our places down, moved in some yuppies, somehow we'd be gone. You don't have to be Yasser Arafat to know things just don't work that way, never have. Knock people's places down, just makes them cling on harder. Then you got people clinging on to dreams, and you can't ever fight that.

The dib have another go every five years give or take, take out the top tier. Cut something back just makes it grow thicker and faster, Carla says, but I guess no one ever told the police that. So now instead of one lot in the south there's the Young Gooch, the Mad Dogs, the Bloods and a dozen others, all hanging together. Makes no odds what you call them, never will. Go west from the Alex, scratch the surface, you'll always find Gooch.

Follow the A57 east out of town and you're in Darts country, God's Own, we're the grown-ups. Take my word for it, it's not just estates full of hoodies on mountain bikes shooting at anything that moves, postcode boundaries and such. Sure, we got all that, but they're just bangers, the youngers, don't really belong to anything much. Just kids running round like headless chickens getting under everyone's feet, out to get noticed, no controlling them. Gets everyone a bad name.

These days it's about business. Across the east there's maybe half a dozen shotters, including White Mike who heads up the Darts. Shotters are free-floating businessmen, don't get mixed up with the street stuff unless they have to.

The Brontes we're Darts but we're not if you get me, special status, on account of we're dykes and we're smarter than most. Me and Carla started it off, pretty much, back when I was in the hostel and Carla lived in Bronte Close with her mam. Never looked back since then.

Don't get me wrong, there's always been women hang around with the Darts or on the street, but used to be either you're someone's old lady or a fish looking for a barrel to get shot in, and that's about the long and short of it if you're a girl. I got no time for it, you-are-who-you-fuck and all that cat-fighting stuff. Don't need some gang-banging dickhead to cover *my* arse.

Time was, everybody hated each other but now we all just get on with it. Mike reckons it's better for business and I reckon he's right. And as long as there's enough to go round and no one takes the piss, I guess it'll stay that way. Mind you, anything ever happens to Mike and we'll have that psycho Tony Maggs to work with, and he's a crazy homophobic bastard, which is rich, considering. A real fruit-loop and I got no time for that rent-boy thing. He was anyone else and people would call it what it is, put some lead between his eyes, put him out of his misery.

Go north up through town and you got the Cheetahs and Salford. Salford never really been touched, run a real tight ship, been in business since Adam was a lad. Tiny Stewart's been tried three times for murder so far, walked every time. Lives out in Preston now, got a pool and everything, did that TV thing last year, told the world he's gone straight. My arse. Award-winning documentary? Award-winning piss-take more like. I even felt a bit sorry for that BBC tosser.

The Cheetahs run on families, always have. Got some real mad fuckers and they're all related to each other like the Queen and the Royal Family, so they're tight. Big Tommo McVey is in charge. He's a brutal bastard and you wouldn't cross him, but he's not stupid and he gets on with Mike okay, so we're sound. Mike says it'll all change when baby brother

Mad Daz takes over, anything happens to Tom. That's the trouble with doing things by family, see. You know what's coming next but fuck all anyone can do about it.

What I'm saying is they got a real steady ship in the north on account of never being taken down by the dib. To my mind it's stale though, all of them past thirty. One thing Carla says about pruning is it keeps all the new shoots coming, keeps everything fresh.

Bang on the border, we get to the bridge. Looks good, the tag, even in the dark.

Hey look, whoops Lise, that's us.

Read it me, says Sonn.

I read it out.

What the fuck does that mean? says Sonn.

How d'you get it up there? goes Lise.

I point to the metal ledge over the carriageway. One hand, hang on with the other. Took four cans, I says.

Tricksy, says Lise. Shouldn't that be 'We Are Consumed'?

Sonn snorts. You wanna swing from that bridge, Lise, make some alterations, no problemo, she says.

So we're still laughing when Carla pulls us up sharp. Then we're just staring down the Cheetah border, and it's silent as a grave. Carla's chewing on her lip like she does when she's thinking. Then I'm on it, No way.

I'm going in to get her, says Carla. Not loud, like when she wants me to talk her out of it, just dead quiet like when she means, you say what you want but I am.

Are you mad, bitch? goes Sonn. And fair enough, it's only what we're all thinking.

You wanna lose those stripes for some sugar, baby girl? That gonna be haaard candy girlfriend, I kid you not, she says.

Now we're all smiling. I swear, ever since she got Sky Plus she's been talking like that.

Carla just shrugs and I seen that look too many times before.

Anyone don't wanna come can get out now, she says.

Did I say that? goes Sonn, sulky. I'm just saying, is all.

I lean over and turn off the engine and it's like someone just switched the amp off. Just the sound of the rain and nothing moving, smudges of the street-lights all down the estate.

Then all at once I'm seeing it all stretched out in front of me and trying to work out who to call, trying to figure out what's gonna happen if Carla struts in there and takes a Cheetah's old lady, and what if it kicks off like a full-on war and who's gonna side with who if it does, and then who's gonna win. And whoever wins who's gonna get wasted because although it ought to amount to the same thing, it almost never does.

And what if the lads say sorry girls but you're on your own with this one, we can't be backing you up on this. Thinking if they did there'd be no end to it and then some Cheetah or Longsight dyke could shimmy up and smooch their missus right out from under their skinnyboy arse. Maybe they're right.

What you smiling at? says Lise.

Nothing, I says. What we got in the back?

She's up and climbs over and pulls up the floor, peeps back over.

Mac, the Glock, three bats and the tyre arm, she says.

Then I'm looking at the Mac and I'm shaking my head. The Uzi, I says, look under the seat. And I'm not being picky for nothing because I swear not one of them can hit shit on a barn door with a Mac-10, and one day the kickback's gonna take us all out.

Sonn leans down and she's scrabbling under the dash, pulls out the Black & Decker and grins. And you gotta hand it to her, she loves that fuckin' nail gun even though no one else with a gram of sense would touch it. God love her, chain of evidence means nothing to that girl.

Yo, Uzi! shouts Lise from the back.

I wedge my feet on the dash. Listen up now, I say, because this is the score. Darts to Cheetah, we got no problems, but Carla's not just dipping her swizzle in some other chick's sherbet so we got no real argument girl on girl. We go in now and it's gonna piss the Cheetahs off big-time, and then they're gonna come mob-handed, thinking we musta cleared it with Mike, which we haven't. Then we got us a war.

I'n't we supposed to ask before we kick off a war? goes Lise.

Don't get me wrong, I love Lise like a sister, and in a showdown there's no one I'd rather stand with, but for someone with all them GCSEs there's times she isn't that bright. Sonn's polishing the nail gun with the hem of her T now, and even though she's looking down I can tell that she's grinning.

You could say that, Lise, I says.

Now I'm looking over at Carla for some help. Well I'm hoping for some kind of back-down if I'm honest, but she's looking straight down the road into the estate like she's expecting the three wise men to rock up, do some tricks with a camel.

You sure about this one, Car? Because this could be a shit-loada trouble.

Carla looks straight ahead like she never heard.

I don't like the way this thing is going, so I got one more thing I can try. It's a low punch, but it beats a good kicking, which is deffo what we're all heading for if things don't slow down. What about Mina then? I says.

And right off I wish I hadn't, because maybe I'm imagining things but she gives me this look, What about her?

So that's it then, game on, because whatever goes down I've run with Carla for more years than I been without her, and one way or another she's like my sister, my blood. And maybe if we get out of this even half-alive I won't ever have to think about what happened with Mina, because Carla must want this new one pretty bad, so she's not gonna care about what we got up to.

Carla leans forward, and with the street-light on her and her mouth pressed together like that she's got the face to make a heart turn. She looks right at me. Girl, you coming or not?

Hey gorgeous, I says, you got it.

Then she starts up the van and turns off the lights, and we're moving slow across the border and down the estate. And it's dead quiet, except for the click-click of Sonn loading up the nails, and the thumpa thumpa thumpa of our hearts.

OK I don't know why but now I'm thinking about Aurora and I can't shake it.

I'm up to three god-kids now, counting Ror – four if you count the one on the way. Everyone knows Ror's my special one though because she was the first, and because she's Carla's if I'm honest, which makes her nearly mine. Not that I'm into all that Our-Lady-Of-All-The-Sorrows shit. I've got shit enough without having to kneel down for it.

When it comes to god-kids I only do girls. Lise says having only girls could be discrimination but I told her it's not, it's just putting the balance back. The way I see it, what a girl needs these days is someone to back her up. And round our way that better be someone who *can* back her up, not someone who's going to beat on her or fuck her or fuck her over, not someone she's gonna *owe*. A girl needs someone to tell her, look, just because you're a girl you don't have to take all the shit they throw out. Especially not lying down. A girl needs someone around who knows that when she doesn't want to do something it's most likely because she doesn't want to do it, not just because she can't piss standing up.

Lise says soon people going to only want girls and that'll be my fault. I told her, not before time. Truth is women are just catching on, being how boys are just grief. Every mam knows you can't just love them and let them alone to figure it out, think stuff out for themselves. You got to work on them, hold on to them, no let-up. Otherwise they're like those rat things that follow each other over the cliffs on Discovery Wild, just going to band together, get themselves killed.

Being my god-kid is an honour, anyone will tell you; it's a matter of protection when all's said and done. If she's my soldier she gets to use my tag when she hits the streets and then no one's going to shit on her. No wonder there's a queue. And it makes sense: what kind of mam wouldn't want the best for her kid?

Anyhow, like I said, Ror's my special girl, she's just gone ten now, born October 1998 just after me and Car left care. That was a good year all round. Sometimes I tag her up with mine when I'm passing the school. D-o-n-n-A-u-r-o-r-A. Link us up on the A just so's everyone knows she's my soldier, in case there's any of that playground shit. Other times I sneak into the yard, sit under the prefab window. Throw bits of gravel one at a time up at the glass, just to make her smile.

One time last summer, when everything smelled of hot tarmac and old cans, and Aurora got herself right next to the window so we could pass notes, we're just minding our own business when the window bursts wide open.

Old Wizeny-Cunt puts her head out, sees me, then slams it shut, hard.

I can hear the other kids laughing. Then, over the top, The Wiz starts shrieking,

O-Rora. Give. It. To. Me. Don't. You. Dare.

And then I knew, it was the note. My girl's gone and swallowed it, without me having to teach her, or anything. I have to tell you now, I was properly proud.

I pull the handbrake up hard, cut the engine. Carla slams her fist against the wheel, What the fuck now?

Don't get me wrong, Carla's a great mam. Probably the best, being how she never shouts and hardly ever hits out, how her and Ror are always laughing about some scam or other. And Carla's dead good at all that soppy stuff that I'd be totally shit at. But sometimes she gets carried away

17

with things, gives no thought to what might happen to Ror if she's left all alone with both of us gone. Lise says that's most likely because Carla's got a mam that would have been better dead years ago but just isn't. Anyhow, now and again I gotta do the thinking for all of us.

Get in the back, I says to Carla, you're not going. The rest of us, it's enough.

Now everyone's looking at me, thinking I've gone soft in the head. Maybe I have, but I'll get plenty of time to think about that later. Right now I gotta pull rank, just to get some control back, before we all get the jitters. It's a fucking order, I says.

Carla's looking down the street through the windscreen. I follow her eyes and see Fatboy's steel door glint in the street-lights.

It's too late, she says. And it is.

I look around, nothing moving.

It's too fucking quiet, I say. And it is.

Next thing, Carla whips the van round, puts her foot down, backs up the crescent quick-time, engine whining like a 747, it's a pure wonder they don't hear us in Hattersley. Before we know it, we're up on the pavement by the house. I give Carla a shove, Stay in the van then, keep her ticking. Just till we know.

Sonn's over the side gate and round the back before you can say commando. Knows her stuff that girl. Me and Lise are over the front fence, bank up the door on each side, Glock cold and sweet in my hand.

Then something makes me look back at the van and I can see Carla texting, the wink of her phone. What the fuck is she doing?

I'm watching Carla for a sign but she's leaning back now inside the van, in the shadows. I can hear my own breath, tight in my chest. The blood pumps to my knees and those tiny prickles creep up and all over my skin. I wait. The blood rushes to my thighs and I'm breathing shallow, hardly moving. Better than good.

I bang once on the door with my fist.

Seems like forever before I hear the grille-hole slide open, me and Lise sinking back into the wall, brick cold and wet against my cheek, everything smelling like bonfires and dog piss. I hear the bolts on the door slide back, one by one, sneak a look at the van.

Then bugger-me, like she's on a walk in the park I see Carla smiling as she slides out of the van, and I know it's not me she's smiling at. Course it's not. And right beside me the door opens, and this tiny cute chick with long black hair and a silvery holdall steps right out of the doorway like she's stepping on to the fucking red carpet, and I swear she floats to the van. No, Hi girls. Not even a, Ta then. Doesn't even bother to close the door behind her.

And Carla's standing there, right in the middle of the pavement, bang in the middle of a Cheetah estate like she's Mother Teresa, holding out her arms. Fuck's sake.

I try to work up some heat, but I know there's not much point, being how I've seen it all before. Flash Carla a new shade of lip-gloss and any discipline goes straight to shit.

Hey Donna, says Lise, sorta quiet.

I follow the look and then we're both staring back into the doorway.

Two round pairs of eyes, not three foot off the floor, Paddington duffel coats all buttoned up, staring back. The big one's got this Dora the Explorer pulley bag, the babba's got some kinda dog-cum-teddy thing, holds it out to me.

I look back at the van, but I can't tell where Carla ends and Fatboy's old lady begins, so I reckon any help from those two is out of the question.

We can't just leave them, says Lise.

We're not taking them, I says, or we're fucked.

On the way back, it's pretty quiet, Sonn driving, glasses slipping off the end of her nose, leaning over the wheel like Mr Magoo. Carla's got a grip of the new chick, cooing and shushing her all over the place. Then those two weird little kids, four eyes like saucers, sitting right up front in the middle, just staring out.

And all in a wunner I know things just up and got crazy. To be honest I don't know what I was thinking before. Like maybe if we get out of here with his woman Fatboy'd be glad to be rid? Or maybe he's got some other old lady lined up and won't even notice this one's gone? Or maybe he'll just wanna forget how we did him, so he'll pretend it all never happened?

Yeah that's right Donna, as if.

2

I wake early-doors, get my chuff round to Carla's soon as I'm up. I'll have to talk some sense into her pronto or we're all in the shit. God knows I'm no angel, but some day that girl's sheer appetite is going to be the death of us all.

When I get there, she's in the kitchen making a butty for Aurora for school. Hey there lovely, she says, want a brew?

I look round the kitchen. Where is she?

Kimmie? She's upstairs.

Kimmie? Do me a favour.

She curls a lip at me, Why you always gotta be like this?

Car, she's a Cheetah's old lady for God's sake. You tired of living or what?

Then her eyes go all bright and she laughs. Oh stop fussing, she goes.

She's cute, because that's where Aurora gets it from, but I'm having none of it. I tell her I want Kim out of here by tonight, before the Cheetahs come knocking.

Then she gets sulky. Where they gonna go?

I tell her Tools got a cousin got houses all over, owes me one. Got this two-bedder empty over Ardwick way, gave me the keys. I jingle the keys at her, smile.

21

They're going babe. Today. If I have to take them myself.

Carla's got that big fat scowl on, but someone has to think straight and I know she's going to thank me for it one day soon, no matter what she says. But for now she's whining, Aw, she wants to stay here.

Right, I say. She's gonna stay here. And what you gonna do when the next one comes along?

What next one? she says.

I look at her face, all flushed and warm, and I know we got big trouble ahead. I swear to God, sometimes she believes her own shit, that girl.

It's not like she's in love. No more than usual anyway. Carla's always in love with someone or other, see, but it never lasts. And when I think about it I suppose it must be hard, trying to stay ahead when everyone just wants to shag you senseless, and you can't trust anyone, nowhere to turn.

I've not got that problem myself. Not that I go short or anything, but Carla she just can't seem to help it. She walks into a club and I'm not kidding everyone just turns and stares, as if something comes off her people can't turn away from. Like making music or being a mam, loving's just in her blood. And when she turns and does that slow smile it feels like the sun just came out, all tingly and warm. Not that it gets me like that, but I can tell you, I've seen grown women weep.

What I'm really saying is, I get it. And hell, I wouldn't have her any other way. It's just the way it takes her over sometimes, makes her forget the important stuff, and that's when it gets me jumpy and shit.

Aurora stomps into the kitchen in her socks, leans back against the fridge, arms folded, in a right old strop. Maroon sweatshirt with the badge sewn on wonky, Clearwater Juniors.

I'm not bloody going, she says.

I smile. I wouldn't want to go either if I had to wear that sweatshirt.

Carla gives me the look, turns on Ror. Oh yes you are lady, get your shoes on, she says.

Ror stares back, chin out, Ricky Hatton style, tosses her head back towards the door. *They're* not going. Why do *I* have to go?

She means those two little fuckers of Kim's, and you have to admit she's got a point.

Get your Frosties, goes Carla, I'm not mucking about.

Ror's still there arms folded when those two brats come racing in, bump into Carla, make her drop the butter all over. Oi now watch it, she says.

See? I can't go, you'll never cope, goes Ror, sly. Tell her Donna, she says.

But before I can say anything Kim floats in, hair all messed up, wearing Carla's blue shirt. Bare feet and a toe-ring, tiny scorpion-thing etched on her ankle. And OK she looks pretty hot all undone like that, but she's not really my type. I like something you can get hold of with both hands, and Kim, she's got a look like she's fragile, as if you couldn't really love her, you'd be too afraid that she'd break.

Now Carla's all sweetness and light and she's smiling at Ror, but tight like a warning. C'mon love, get your shoes on, you don't want to be late.

Ror sees right through it, points over at Kim. And who does she think she is?

Carla's up and got Ror by the arm, frogmarches her into the hall. You're going, lady. And while you're about it, grow up.

I grow up any faster I'll overtake you, says Ror.

Well, you've got to smile, and now even Carla's laughing. I'm not kidding, sometimes that kid just makes us all howl.

3

Aurora: fed up
Geeta: wer r u?
Aurora: on bus wish this snow wd go
Geeta: me 2 wots up?
Aurora: i hate me mam
Geeta: i no i hate mine 2
Aurora: runnin away u comin
Geeta: cant 2day got kickbox at 6
Aurora: satdi then?
Geeta: safe

Even in the prefab, it's baltic. Old Wizeny-Cunt in that big red coat your Nan wouldn't even wear.

You can keep your coats on today class, goes The Wiz. Handy that, seeing as how me mitts are pure blue.

Aurora Borealis, says The Wiz. Now then, who knows what that is?

And straight off, I just know that's gonna stick. Like the time she made us do *Sleeping Beauty* for a play, just so I'd have to scrap anyone who called me Princess. She just picks on me like that.

Everyone looking. Oh go on then gog me whydontya? Starin' are we? U don't even no me. Even that sly one Sunita-kiss-me-arse-Clegg, and what she's got to laugh about, I dunno. If I had her face, I'd kill myself. I give her a wave. I'll see you at break-time, I says.

Me Miss! Oh I know Miss! Oh yeah, it's that lardy snitch Chelse with her hand up like usual. Someone wants to put that girl on a diet. Me, I don't know what geography's even for. I'm never gonna need it, am I, on stage?

Yeeaaahhs Chelsea, goes The Wiz.

Aurora Borealis, Northern Lights Miss, says Chelse.

Then everyone looks right at me, and laughs.

As if I care. Then I'm thinking about that *X-Factor* one, she's great. I got her going round in me head now off YouTube like Whass-uh-hup, Oh Ba-by Whass-up? I can see her going with her stick-legs all jerky. And one day, my fans, that's gonna be me.

I'm just looking out now on to the yard, and the snow's all shitty banked up at the edge, that Dale Smith who's only got his Nan, acting like he's not even late. Must be mint not having a Mam to drag you outta bed every day. Me, my life's shit, I never get to be late.

Half-ten and tac-tics is definitely called for, so by now I've got me hand up and I'm nudging Geet. Miss? Please Miss? Toilet Miss?

The Wiz shakes her head, mean. Only five minutes till break-time O-Rora, you can wait.

I'm not kidding but that's got to be against some rule I reckon, some human rule so there's got to be a Court for that, somewhere. Then I'm looking right at her, smiling, because now I can hear myself, dressed up all Judge Judy, sparkly earrings and that black cape, going Right You, you can't just Stop someone going to the Toilet when they Need, and now you're going to Prison for it Lady, for Life. So then The Wiz will be locked up like me Da and her hair will most likely go white overnight like in that film, and it just serves her right.

Yeah OK Miss, whatever.

Ten minutes later we're all in the yard for break, freezing our keks off. Geet's Dad says they make us stand outside in the snow for fresh air, but I know we're just being wronged when we've done nothing bad. It's A-Matter-of-Control Donna says, and the way I see it there's loads of those in our school. Mam always says I get me brains from her, but I know I gets them from Donna because she's about the cleverest person I know.

I'm just working up to giving that Sunita Clegg a proper battering, get myself warm. I don't have do it straight away, because everyone knows I've said it and they're waiting. Most times when someone needs sorting I let them wait, and then other times I trick them, don't do it at all. That's the clever bit, see? The waiting gets them worse than if I just went right up and did it, straight off the bat. I'm not telling you who taught me that, on account of not being a grass.

Let's just wag it, goes Geeta.

Hey I'm on it, I says. And it just serves Mam right.

Half-eleven and we're snug-as-two-bugs in the Arndale, squatting down behind the fountain on account of security. You can spot those plastic yellow waistcoats a mile off, it's mad. If I was the boss of the Arndale Centre I'd do away with the waistcoats straight off. How they're ever going to catch anyone in those things is way beyond me.

Let's go yours then, says Geet.

I can't let on to Geet but the actual thing is, Mam'd throw a hissy if she even thought I was wagging it. Which is a laugh, seeing how she didn't hardly go to school ever, at least from what Nan used to say. Then again, I suppose one of us got to be able to read.

I'm pretty good when it comes to reading, even though The Wiz does her best to put me off, sending me out half the time to stand by the door, fucking me up in geography so I got to batter someone and get sent to the head. I got a reading age of fourteen The Wiz told Mam no kidding, and that's way best in the class. Not bad for someone just gone ten. And I'm top except for Geet, but that's because her Dad makes her sit at the table, does stuff with her every night, two hours after tea and no messing about, which is about the worst thing I can think of. I'm lucky, being how me Dad doesn't want owt to do with me and Mam anyway. He's in Glasgow, some place called The Bar-L. Mam says it's like Strangeways only worse because it's full of Scottish. And that's just about the best place for him, Donna says.

You can see Strangeways from the snide market on Cheetham Hill Road. It's this big castle with towers like Shutter Island, only scarier. There's a massive wall and then curls of wire stuff on top, which looks like nothing much to be honest but Geet says it'll cut you to shreds. They have to have it though, to stop all the Dads getting out. Just looking at it makes me heart go like mad.

It's Friday so Mam's likely down the club setting up but I can never be sure, and there's no chance I'm letting Geet see The Other One, or she'll be asking questions forever. And well we can't go to Geet's, can we, because she's got it worse than me, being how she lives with her Mam and her Nan and Aunty Soraya who's just weird, and those two little shits that look through the keyhole when you're doing the toilet. Even her Dad lives there. I couldn't be doing with all that, dunno how she gets any peace. They got these carpets that don't go right to the edge and you can see all the floorboards, but Mam says there's nothing wrong with that it probably just means they can't afford ones that fit. I'm not so sure because Geet's got a whole bedroom with only her own stuff in, and there's always loads to eat and a proper table, and you gotta take your shoes off when you go in, for manners and that.

I got to check on Nan first, I tell her.

It's only half-one but it doesn't matter, mostly because Nan won't know what day it is, never mind what time, on account of the drink. I don't say that to Geet though.

We get there, curtains still shut and the gas fire on full, Nan fast asleep in her chair. I put Geet in the chair by the door, turn down the fire. It's roasting, and Mam says one day the whole place will go up.

Stay here Geet and watch her, I says. If she wakes up just shout me.

Why, where you going?

Just do it, I says.

I go into the bedroom and pull off the wet sheet, put it in the laundry bag for tomorrow, gather up all the tissues and stuff them in the waste basket, put on a clean sheet. The top sheet's a tiny bit wet but not enough to want changing, so I hang it over the bed-end to dry. Beside the bed, the ashtray's fallen on the floor and there's glass where Nan has knocked something over, so I scrape it all up with me hand then into the bin, cut me hand on the glass.

It's only a nick but I suck it hard. You Can't Be Too Careful, Donna says, not with cuts. Donna knew this girl called Sarah once, picked up a needle out the back, now she has to go to hospital every week get all the bad blood sucked out and some new stuff pumped in. Just one tiny prick, Donna says, and That's All It Takes.

Geet's sat straight up in the chair, staring at Nan.

What's up? I go. Is she dribbling?

Geet shakes her head, fast.

Don't worry she won't bite you, I says.

I go through to the kitchen, boil the kettle for the pots. There's not much in the sink being how Nan doesn't really bother with eating even when I make her stuff. There's some corned beef in the cupboard so I make her a butty. The bread's got those little spots of blue coming; I smell it though and it seems okay. I scrape them off for now. I'll get some fresh in the morning.

I get out The Complan. We always get The Complan because Nan never eats the butty, and Mam says we've got to get the goodness into her somehow, or it'll be The End. The milk smells okay so I do half and half, for protein. Mrs Shepherd in food hygiene says if you don't have enough protein you just Waste Away. Sometimes I wake straight up in the night just thinking about that, the Wasting Away and what it would look like, and what would happen if I get here one day and she's all gone.

Nan hasn't moved so I get ready to wake her.

You got to be careful with Nan, waking her up. Sometimes she wakes right up in a fright and once she knocked me clean over and I hit me head on the fire. Mam went mad when she saw the bump and they had a full-on screamer right here in the flat, even though I knew Nan was sorry and didn't mean anything by it. I told Mam it was an accident but she just went, Accident? I'll give her Accident. She's One Long Bloody Accident, that one. Hey Donna, I ever get like that, just shoot me, says Mam.

Mam stopped me coming to Nan's for two full days after that, it was the worst thing of me life, ever. I was so scared about the Wasting Away that I couldn't even sleep, until Donna tells Mam, Listen, you're going to make that kid sick, so in the end she gave in. And Nan was dead sorry, so even if it happened again there's no way I'd grass her up.

I stand well back, lean forward and poke at her arm.

Whaaa... hoozat...?

It's me Nan, I whisper, I done you a butty, corned beef. Make me a space, Geet, I says.

Geet clears the glasses and mugs off the table Nan keeps by the chair. Oh Nan, I goes, you knocked off that ashtray an' all.

I get down on the carpet to clean up the mess, feel Nan's hand on me head.

Hiya darlin, oh I'm sorry, she says.

By the time we get to Shah's it's gone half-two. The snow's all gone on the pavement, just dirty brown wedges each side on the kerb, being how Mrs Shah puts the grit out every day.

She's alright Mrs Shah, as long as you're not thieving her shop. I wouldn't nick off me own corner shop, that's just

31

low, Donna says. Their Nizam let me off with five pence one week, when I didn't have enough for the milk, but I know that's just because he fancies me Mam. We get loads of favours on account of the way she looks, which is well handy, and Mam doesn't even mind. Got good taste that boy, Mam says.

We're right up to them when I spot Donna up against the shutters in her parka, fur right up to her face, chips in her hand, talking. I turn back but she sees me. Donna's got eyes in the back of her head, Mam says, and I reckon that's true, though me Mam's one to talk.

Aw shit, I goes, under me breath.

Hey, says Donna, what you doing, lady, outta school?

Inset Day, I tell her, only don't tell me Mam.

Oh right, says Donna, and what kinda Inset Day's that, that I can't tell yer Mam? You didn't say owt this morning.

I told you she was smart.

Aww, Dee-Dee, I goes.

I got her now, because Mam says that's what I used to call her before I could even walk, and even if she doesn't want to, she loves it when I call her that.

She takes a swipe at me and I duck. Get outta here. I won't tell this once, but don't do it again. And don't be hanging about on street corners, either, now just get yourself home.

I lean forward, whisper so Geet won't hear. Not if *she's* there.

She's not. I dropped her off in Ardwick this morning. She looks at me hard, Hungry? And holds out the chips.

I tuck the chips under me arm, grab on to Geeta, and we walk to the corner slow.

Behind me I can hear them all laughing and snide, *Oh Dee-Dee.*

Yeah right shut it, she says, but she doesn't sound mad.

We get to the underpass. It's not warm exactly, but it's out of the wind and there's bound to be an earner. Soon as we're inside, I seen Space and Wheelie-boy, under the arch. Hold these, I tell Geeta, and I give her the chips.

Space looks me up and down, smiles. Alright Ro? Take this round to Danny at the Wheatsheaf, there's a fiver in it, he says.

I tuck the parcel under me coat first, then I'm shaking me head at him. A tenner I says, because it's only half-two. Yeah and by the way I've just gone ten, so now that's double the risk.

Space just smiles and shakes his head, not like Get Lost, but like Mam does, when she means Whatever-Did-I-Do-To-Deserve-All-Of-This. You get any sharper, Ro-girl, you're gonna cut yourself, he goes.

I've always liked Space, ever since he saw me being chased down by the garages, let me hide in his car, and I don't mind working. A job's a job at the end of the day, beats going to school. You never have to beg if you got your own money. Geet gets pocket money from her Dad but it's not really hers. She has to put half of it in the post office and she has to be good if she wants the other half. And she's not allowed to get sweets or snide DVDs. What's the point of having money if you can't buy stuff you need with it?

When you do a runner for someone you never get the money until you've dropped the package off in case you get stopped. Means you can say you just found the package, and I got let off twice already like that. Not like I'd ever tell anyway, I'm not completely stupid.

So by the time we've done it then been back to get the tenner it's nearly half-three and we're back in the clear, timewise.

Me and Geet go back to Shah's, get some toffees. I put two pound on the leccy, get me Mam some cigs and a *Heat* then we go back to mine.

The back door sticks, like always. I turn the key, give it a kick, and Sappho shoots out between me legs. Yeah, well, she can stay out. No way I'm going out after her shouting Sappho, have people thinking I'm tapped. She's like a man, she'll come back when she's ready, Mam says.

On the middle of the table there's a note, I can tell from here it's from Mam.

iT bEtA bE Hom TImE
OR ThEr bE TRubuL.
luv MAM. xx

Like I said before, I wouldn't swap her, but to be honest sometimes I could do with one of them Mams who give you a bit more, well, slack. It's not like I can't be trusted.

Geet's just stood staring, looking at the note like she's stuck to the lino. I scrunch it up quick, shove it in me pocket. It's not like Mam's stupid or anything, so anyone laughs at her, even Geet, and I'd have to go savage. But she mustn't have seen it, because she says nothing.

I get the bread out, root around in the back of the fridge for the peanut butter, Ta-raaahh!

I'll spread, you fry, goes Geet, and I can tell she's excited, because there's no way her Mam'd let her make anything on her own, let alone a fried butty. When I have kids I'm gonna teach them to fry stuff, right off the bat, then if anything happens they're not gonna starve. Or, worse, have to eat pasta which is pretty much just flour and water, the exact same stuff as the glue you make in the Infants, and how minging is that?

By the time Mam gets home I've got the fire on, one bar. She comes in through the back all soaked, snow melting, dripping little pools on the lino.

Hiya Geet love, she goes, does your Mam know you're here? She holds out her phone. Give her a ring then and you can stop for your tea. She reaches into her bag and gets out a bumper pack of Mars bars.

Then the three of us are down on our knees in front of the fire, I've got mine melted just right and I'm just about to lick it when Mam looks up, sees the cigs.

And where did those come from?

Oh, Mr Lowski, I says.

I don't even know why I said that, because it's just about the worst thing I could've said, but it's done now and I'll have to blag it.

Geet looks right at me, but it's best not to look back.

Mr Lowski? says Mam, in her dangerous voice.

Aw no Mam, I says, not like that.

Trouble is, she's red-hot, Mam is, on old men giving us money and stuff. The way she goes on, anyone'd think I came in on the last cabbage boat from Birkenhead. Any lad over twelve even speaks to me, she goes off on one.

Bags. I helped him back from the shops with his bags, I tell her. To be honest it sounds a bit much even to me, a tenner for that one tiny thing. You can get a taxi to The Housing for that.

Look Mam, I say, I got you a *Heat*.

She just bats at the *Heat* like it's nothing, which is well rude, especially when it's a present.

How. Many. Times. Have. I. Told. You? You. Don't. Take. Money. From. Anyone. Got. It? Truth now, did he make you go in his flat?

So by now I'm worrying about Mr Lowski, and if Mam gets it in her head he's a nonce, when really he's dead nice and gave me ten pence once when I shooed off that dog after it shat on his path, there'll be hell on. And then that'd be just one more thing I'd done that I'd have to worry about.

I never, he just gave it me, honest, he can't carry it himself. I got some leccy an' all. Please Mam.

Then she comes over all sorry. Oh God Ror, you're a good girl, she goes, and she gives me a hug. Don't you do it again, though.

Then she's got that singy voice going on, the one that means she's happy.

She puts on her music and kicks off her shoes, dances over to me where I'm kneeling, pulls me up and swings me right round. Oh TFI Friday, she goes.

4

I pull up outside the Darts lock-up, Tony Maggs and Danny waiting outside in Danny's black BM.

He's a big bastard, Tony, lardy as fuck. When he smiles only his mouth moves, gives you a real creepy feeling. It's the eyes, nothing behind them. When he looks at you they go dead, slide about like a snake.

They open up, hold the doors while I drive the van in. Inside, Danny walks over, looks at the side of the van, reads the sign out loud,

> ARTEMIS WOMEN'S CLEANING SERVICES
> Commercial and Domestic Cleaning

You can read, then?

He picks at the sign, Does it come off?

I grab his arm, What do you think, idiot?

I kid you not, if I had to rely on these lot for me cash I'd probably starve.

I go round to the back doors of the van, open them wide. Don't just stand there, I tell him. Then all three of us are unloading the buckets and mops, and the containers marked bleach. I get under the floor by the wheel arch, bring out the stash. Tony takes it off me, cuts right in, sniffs at the blade, licks it. Kosher, he says, and nods at Danny. Still, when Danny walks into the back for the cash I make sure I'm nearest the door, just in case.

Danny holds the bag open, lets me see the money.

You don't count the money at the drop, not when you got business with someone you know. It's a big no-no, a lack of respect, and it's not like you don't know where to find each other if someone's taking the piss. Don't get me wrong, it's not that we actually trust each other, and I always count it afterwards, just in case. To be honest, it wouldn't bother me if someone counted their money but it's a man-thing, like respect's all they got.

By now I'm loading the van back up, putting the mops and the buckets back over the floor. Danny starts to lift the containers of bleach.

Hey, don't touch those, I tell him. And I must've been a bit sharp because Danny and Tony are looking back at me now, and I got to think fast. Bleach, you know, it's toxic.

Oh yeah toxic, says Tony, of course.

Then they're both nodding like they even know what that means, and I've split before I spoil it all and laugh. I'm still laughing when I pull up at Shah's. I have a quick chat with the lads, bump into Ror. Little sod's wagging it, and I'm gonna have to talk to Carla if I catch her again.

Got time to kill so I head for Oxford Road and the bookstall beside the Met steps. Today there's a sign pinned to the table with a picture of that kid who got shot last month riding his bike: *All today's proceeds to Moss Side Mothers Against Violence.*

I pick up a book.

When I remember your love I weep and when I hear people talking of you something in my chest where nothing much happens now moves as in sleep.

I hold it out to the girl, turban wrapped round her head, tatty blonde dreads. Twenty pence, she says. Her fingernails are dirty, torn, so she's either straight or a minger, maybe both.

I put the book under my jacket, cross over the road to the Peace Gardens, sit down on the bench, watch the students messing around in the snow. Carla says it's just weird me coming here like I do, calls them wasters. Sends her mental, watching them marching around with those placards, Jobs for the Workers, then they all fuck off skiing for Christmas.

Me, I like the way it makes me feel when I sit here. Gives me a wide-open feeling, like there's no doubt about it, there's something beyond. I get the same thing at the airport, and Piccadilly station. Things moving, people going somewhere. Things rolling forward somehow. You can't beat it.

I turn the book, look at the cover. Some dude called Rumi. Beat that for a tag.

I must have forgotten the time because I look up and it's getting dark, sleet falling soft then melting away into wet on the ground. My shoulder's throbbing and tight, right down my arm.

Oxford Road is humming now, jammed, people running home, cars crawling bumper to bumper, chasing tail lights. Below the steps of the Met Union, a *Big Issue* seller is crouched against the cold, dog between his knees under the blanket. As I go past he looks up at me, holds out the cup.

Eat the dog, I says. He gives me the finger and a smile.

The bookstall's nearly cleared away, just the girl, packing everything away into plastic boxes. I give her back the book.

She smiles at me. Want your money back?

I tell her no, I've read it, she might as well sell it again. I don't tell her about the page I've ripped out and put back in my jacket.

She takes the book and looks at the cover, squints at me. You like poetry, then?

Poetry? Is she shitting me?

Do I? I says. I suppose.

On the way home and the A57 is rammed and there's a tailback, Friday afternoon, everyone heading out to the sticks.

I pull into the garage for petrol. Across four lanes there's the 24-hour Asda, old gaffer herding trolleys in the rain, looks like somebody's grandad. Poor bastard, no chance I'd want to be herding trolleys when I'm seventy. Probably worked all his life and paid all his taxes, now he's got to manage on sixty pounds a week or work till he drops. If I had a grandad, no way I'd let him eat shit like that.

Give nowt to the government take nowt back, Dad used to say, but then he was a real grafter, never paid tax or took a benefit in his life, made his own way. You get on that radar, girl, you're done for, he'd say. Next thing you know they know everything about you, got you tied up to the merry-go-round like a rat in a wheel.

Well Pops, times are more complicated now. I fill up the van, go up to the metal grille to pay, get out the Artemis card, give the taxman a nod.

I get to Lise's, park the van round the back and carry the containers into the house, two in each hand. It's heavy, and I wonder if this stuff actually weighs more than bleach or just feels like it does.

Inside, it's nearly dark, curtains drawn. Boxes of knock-off perfume and lipsticks everywhere, the whole house smells like a WAG's bedroom on Derby night. Don't ask me how I know, it's not something I'm proud of.

Jeez, it stinks in here Lise.

Lise is sitting at the table, cig in the corner of her mouth, squinting, bucket full of cheap perfume just by her chair. Uhmmmm, the smell of money, she says.

She's got the last of the old containers in front of her, nearly empty, and half a dozen empty perfume bottles waiting to be filled. About time an' all, she says, I'm about running out.

I put the new stuff down on the table, and she unscrews the top off one container, jams a funnel into an empty perfume bottle, starts to fill it with E.

Hey, empty the bucket for me will ya, she says.

I bend down to get it. Christ, don't put that bucket right beside you and smoke, I tell her. One day you're gonna flick some ash in there and it'll all be over. That stuff's flammable stupid.

She pulls her face at me.

I take the bucket into the kitchen, tip it all down the sink, gagging, the smell of cheap perfume knocking me sick.

All she's got to do is get the new stuff into the bottle, but I get back just in time to see her licking up some that she's spilled on the table.

Fuck's sake, I say, don't suck up all the profits.

Then she gives me this smile. I love you, she says.

I'm not fucking surprised, how much have you had?

You gotta keep Lise away from stuff, see, especially stuff like Liquid Ecstasy. The rest of us, it's no bother, but with Lise she's always on the edge somehow, mostly where drugs are concerned, and even though she knows the rules I still have to keep an eye on her.

Sonn thinks maybe that's what makes her so creative in the whole drugs department thing, how she gets her ideas: perfume atomisers filled with E, lipsticks with speed in, all the rest of it. And fair do's, the trips are a real money-spinner on a Friday night. I mean, no one checks a girl's perfume bottle, do they? We make a fortune at Heaven, a fiver a squirt.

I take the rest of the stuff off her, put the lid back on, get out the books to take home.

It used to take ages, doing the books, till I got a system going. Now there's one for the tax man, and one in code, just for us. Most of the boys don't keep books, but I figured out early on, if this was going to work, it better look legit. When Operation Balboa went down that's how they got them in the end, all that cash and nothing to show for it. You have to learn by mistakes, see, and it's handier if they're someone else's.

Just as I'm about to leave, Sonn turns up with Rio, asks how it's going.

Coolio, says Lise, smiling at Sonn, eyes half-closed.

Sonn looks at me, raises one eyebrow. I nod. Off her face. Then Rio jumps up. Rio's half pitbull, half Staffie, blind in one eye now, looks mean as hell. Sonn found him wandering round Lower Broughton with a firework round his neck, reckoned she'd keep him for a guard dog. Thing is, he's afraid of his own shadow. Has his uses though. You always know when things are about to kick off, on account of how fast Rio turns tail and disappears.

I ruff him where he likes it, round his neck.

I never used to be into dogs that much. But I've got to admit, Rio's kind of grown on me lately, and Sonn, well, she loves him to death. Aurora's been whining for a dog for ages and I'd probably give in if it was up to me, but Carla's not really up for it. Just one more responsibility, she says.

Sonn wants to know where Kim and the kids are. I tell her it's OK, it's sorted, they're in Ardwick. She doesn't say much, Sonn, but she's got a good head on her shoulders when it comes to what matters. I feel jumpy, she says.

It's a relief to be honest, knowing I'm not the only one with the jitters, even though I can't let it show. I've got that feeling I get, in the pit of my belly, like things just won't settle.

Don't worry, I say, we're on our own turf. Tonight it's Heaven, right bang in the middle of our own patch, and the club'll be full of Darts as well as us. Cheetahs are no match for all of us together.

She doesn't look sure.

I tell her I saw Tony today, and if he'd heard something he would have said.

Deep down I know for a fact that might not be true but I can't afford for them to all get nervy, and I don't want to even think about what it means if he does know and kept shtum. No harm in staying ready, I say.

Just then, I hear one of my phones go. I look at the screen, check it isn't Louise.

It's Mina. I pick up. Hey Donna, you wanna meet up?

I feel Sonn watching me. I take it you're joking, I says into the phone.

There's silence at the end of the line.

Yeah, I'll tell her, I say, and cut her off.

Sonn's still watching.

I shrug. Message for Carla.

Then Mina's face is right there in front of me, big storm eyes looking up, and I'm thinking maybe I'll ring her back in a bit, and explain.

I make my way to the lock-up to drop off the van. By the doors, Carla's new red Ducati winks smooth, right next to the old 950.

The answer-machine's flashing but it's just some old biddy from Chorlton Green, wants her office cleaned. I ring her back and tell her we'll go round on Monday to give her a quote, mark it up in the book.

I try Mike again, no answer. I could ring Tony, find out where Mike's at, but somehow I just don't want to.

I turn on the computer, go on to the web and log into Flyway. Nothing.

We got identity codes for Flyway after Xcalibre was set up. Serious and Organised Crime Unit, that's who they really are, and ever since they did that whole exchange thing with Baltimore they've been red-hot on tracing mobiles. Beats me why they need to make up pretend names for it, as if calling themselves Xcalibre's gonna turn them all into King Arthur. That's the way they like to see themselves, make up for them being total losers.

So now they got all that new tracer equipment, think we don't know about it. Emails are too risky, being how you can never get them off a main server, but messaging on Flyway's a breeze, no trails. One account between everyone; open a message and keep it in draft. Someone else goes into the account and when they've read it, they delete it. That way it never gets sent anywhere, leaves no trail. It's not rocket science. Finn's got it all down to a fine art now, B-Tech in computing from the Adult-Ed and everything, so now we just use Flyway and the codes.

I peel the plates and the sign from the van, put them in the bottom drawer of the filing cabinet, go over to the old Metro van. It's a shed now, but it was the first wheels I ever had, done just about everything in it over the years, can't seem to let it go.

The door creaks when I open it, needs oiling. I sit in the driver's seat, for a think.

Don't know why I still do that, when we got three leather armchairs and the old red sofa, even a proper swivel chair pulled up at the desk. But there's something about the old van, seats all cracked and torn and dust on the dash, driver's door hanging on by a thread, kind of makes me feel safe. The door hasn't worked properly since that time Keira left her old man that day over in Glossop. Us driving off, him hanging on through the window trying to grab on to the keys. Then I kicked the door open, him still clinging on to it, and if it hadn't been for that bollard he'd be hanging on yet. Then we were off, up and away, laughing, over Woodhead Pass at eighty, me holding the door on with one hand. Still makes me smile when I think of it.

I wind down the window, put my knees up on the wheel, lean right back. The seat fits round me like an old pair of Docs.

I turn the knob on the old CD radio. Key 103, old classic by Aretha, Respect. Sing to me baby.

I sit for a bit, staring out through the windscreen, thinking about Mike and where he could be and then what he's gonna say when I tell him about Kim, when something catches my eye.

The IKEA rug, the one we put down to hide the trapdoor, has got one corner turned up, like someone's been down there, didn't put it back straight.

I'm out of the van and over there before you can say Jack Shit.

I pull up the trap, climb down the ladder into the vault. The vault's just a concrete cellar really. In the far corner there's the old cell door blocking the hole we made in the bricks. Took Sonn two whole weeks and a Manchester City pneumatic drill to get through to the canal tunnel.

Door's pretty neat too. Paid a fortune for it, on account of how it's a Strangeways original. Some guy up in Radcliffe picked it up after the riots in the '90s, back when they did the big refurbishment, kept it in his hallway, been polishing it ever since, saddo. Story goes, it took ten lifers on E Wing to rip off the hinges. Then they dragged out the nonce, threw him over the railings, thirty feet straight down to the net. Then they threw the door right down on top of him, smashed his head open like a watermelon.

Solid steel, six inches thick, eight of us couldn't move it, until Sonn made a rope and tackle to get it down to the vault. Still got the cell number on the top. Local History that, Lise says.

Even Mike doesn't know about the vault, nobody does. Not many people know what's underneath Manchester, which is handy, from our point of view. It's a maze down there, all the channels for the old canals, the ones that aren't used any more, Spaghetti Junction in the dark.

Where we cut through the wall, looks like there was an old air-raid shelter, benches still along the walls, dry as a bone, sealed up where there used to be steps up to the street. Lise won't go down there on her own, says she hears things, babies crying and shit, but that's just Lise. As far as I'm concerned it's perfect. On the other side of the shelter we put a trapdoor, so we can always get out if we need to.

I get down into the vault and the hair on my arms starts up, tingles. You can tell when a person's been in your space, even if nothing's been moved. As if somehow something's been changed, the air rearranged.

So I'm looking round but everything looks like it should.

I check the safe. Money, snide passports, licence plates. Everything's still there. Then I get one of those shivers, like someone walked over my grave. I'm out of there pretty smart, put back the rug, lock up. Then I'm outside on the cobbles. Must be imagining things. Can't believe I got the heebies like that, feel like a right soft cunt.

5

By the time we pick everyone up it's gone ten, cars swishing past in the rain, air smelling like wet wood and tobacco, catches the back of your throat. We get to Sonn's last, on account of how she always takes the longest to get ready. I never known anyone as particular as Sonn when she's going out: irons everything, even her jeans, goes mad if she can't sit in the front, stretch out her legs, just in case they get messed. One time when she'd got in the back all squashed up with Marta and Lise we got all the way there and had to turn right round again, take her home to get changed. Kept saying we'd creased her, even though none of us could see it. Lise says it's some kind of weirdness comes from right down inside her, most likely from worrying and stuff.

I can't see it myself. Sonn's solid as a brick shithouse, never seems to worry about anything, just likes things organised. Now and again it can get you down, her going mad if someone's a minute late, or when she has to check all the plugs three times before going to bed. Sometimes it's just funny though, when you ask her what day we went somewhere, and she can tell you the exact date, time, everything, along with what we got up to, no kidding. Can be useful, that.

We crawl through Rusholme in the traffic. It's chucking it down and Wilmslow Road got a life all its own at this time of night, students pouring out from all over, the lights from the curry-houses and shebeens. I got my eyes everywhere seeing how it doesn't do to get caught mob-handed down Curry Mile without a pass or a nod from Tanweer.

Way back, when we was kids, before things got so hot, we used to come down on a Friday night, hang about outside Taj or the Asian Kitchen, looking for a free bag of pakora, jug of sweet lassi if we were lucky. Sometimes we'd offer to sit on the pavement, mind the punters' cars, in return for some scran. All the kids went down Rusholme on Fridays, and I swear, none of us ever went hungry back then. Me and Carla did better than most, on account of us having Samina whose dad worked at Taj on and off. Must be every kid's dream, that, have a dad who works on Curry Mile.

Eid was the best. Everyone down, three deep on the pavements, watch the Mile End boys, handsome as, doing their wheelies and handbreak-turns, spinning and whirling against the dark, sky all lit up by the fireworks. Then all the grown-ups would come out of the curry-houses, bring trays of food and them funny-shaped sweets, right out on to the street. Didn't matter back then, who you were or where you came from, everyone got fed.

Nice folks, the Pakis, Dad used to say. You want kindness, Donna? Find someone who doesn't have much, and had to risk everything just to get that.

He was right. Well, except for the Paki bit, but that was just ignorance, and I know he didn't mean anything by it. Nice folks. My mouth still waters just thinking about it.

We pass the turn-off for the Mancunian. Used to be the

Interstellar, best live venue in town. Cheetahs put paid to that, back in 2002, the day Marty Smith got sprung from Group 4 on his way to the court. Tiny Stewart's boys drove the prison van off the M602 and they were all in Liverpool before anyone could say Jack Shit. Things were humming for sure, something was bound to go down and that night the Cheetahs took out three Mile-Enders over some poxy door deal, caught two sociology students in the crossfire, gave them some free scrap metal to take back home to the south.

Back then I didn't know what sociology even was, and when Lise told me I laughed till I cried.

The Council closed the club down after that. Just goes to show, you can take out a dozen Mancs from Moss Side and no one gives a toss, but creep up behind a fee-paying student from Surrey and the whole place goes up. Don't teach that over at Owens Park, do they?

By the time it reopened it had given up on real music, given in to all that whiny-whiteboy singer-songwriter shit, and no one who's anyone goes there any more.

We drive up Oxford Road, under the Precinct walkway, past the student flats and the Rec. The Rec's just a flat piece of wasteland, between the flats and the road. It's what's left after the Council pulled out all the trees and the bushes, cleared all the rubbish; put some paths and a bench in, so mummy and daddy won't fret.

Across the grass the globe access lights stare like cold little moons. In the distance the halls of residence are all lit up, every single window with a light on. You can tell none of those bastards pay for their own electricity. In a couple of years they'll be squeezing us out all over Chorlton Green and Whalley Range, or piled up in some fancy loft apartment in Castlefield. Don't even have the good grace to fuck off back where they're from.

It's quiet, says Sonn.

At the G-Mex we turn right down Whitworth Street. I scan round. Sonn's right, dead as Southern Cemetery at Hallowe'en.

Not a sign of anyone, not the dib, no dealers, not even a mountain bike. Gives me the chills.

We pass the bottom of Canal Street. The rain's falling fine now, makes a mist over the cobbles. Even the working girls are hanging back, right under the doorways, keeping out of the rain. That must be the shittiest job in the world, especially on a night like tonight.

A tram rattles past all lit up, windows streamy, squeals to a stop on the metal tracks, just as I pull up at the junction. The doors hiss open, cast an oblong of light across the wet pavement, into an office doorway. On the step there's a girl all huddled up, wet through, hair like rat's tails, trying to get a cig lit with a damp lighter, must be all of thirteen. Makes me think of Ror.

We get to Heaven and Lloyd's on the door, lets us in past the queue. Lise blows him a kiss, raps him on the vest as she passes, cheeky. You know things are past crazy when someone the size of Lloyd wears body-armour under his Crombie. Built like a Sherman Tank, that fucker. Somehow you'd think the bullets would just bounce off.

Half-eleven and the place is kicking, Carla spinning up on the decks, floor heaving with sweat and skin. I look round for Mike, no sign. Not that the shotters come out on the scene much – too risky. Come to think of it, there's not a single Darts lieutenant here as far as I can see, not even Tony.

Then me and Marta are leaning on the wall by the bar, minding our business, just keeping an eye out, when Danny comes over, all Whaassup and shit.

I can't say I like Danny much, but he's baby-daddy to my girl Finn, and once, when it got tight way out on the East Lancs with a boot fulla snow and Lise off her head on brown in the back, well, he calls me right up, tells me I got a tail. You can't mess with that, so I ditched the car pronto. I musta walked ten miles that night, two kilos of coke on my back, dragging Lise by the hand, and all the while she's giggling and spewing and whining like a kid in Asda on bank holiday. But I tell you it beat the other options we had hands-down: a twenty-year break in Her Majesty's Pisshole or a bullet to the brain from some jumped-up gangbanger looking for an easy start-up loan. That was the last train I pulled myself if you get my drift. I don't mind saying I've made loads of mistakes but I make it a rule not to make the same one twice.

After I made the drop we stayed in the flat three days straight. Lise locked in the bedroom all screaming and crashing about, Mrs Giggs from Flat Three banging on the wall, Carla on the answerphone every ten minutes going Fuckssake Donna where *are* you girl?

No one else gets to talk to me like that, on account of respect.

Me, I was working it out in my head, and when Lise got clean I made her promise, no more H. Next day I tell them all, Listen up, we got to be clever, get organised, and if you wanna be in, you gotta be clean.

Lise looks at me as if I said we're giving up women for Lent, starts whining. Aw yeah Donna but why though?

Otherwise, we're all gonna be dead, dumbfuck.

I never found out how Danny knew about the tail, or why he gave us the heads-up that night. At the time I assumed it was on account of Finn. There's some things it's best not to ask, but still I'm pretty careful round him now.

But tonight Danny looks at the floor, says, Finn, she's not coming in. Got some stuff going on at home or some shit like that.

She coulda text me, I say.

Something doesn't fit right. I look at him and he can't look back, and, straight off, that feeling I got in my belly since last night gets way worse.

I flash a look across to Carla on the decks but she's just laughing, schmoozing it up for the dykes at the front. I do a scan, but the music's pumping and all I can see is skin. Arms, crop-tops, six-packs, all sweating, glistening then disappearing as the blue strobes go round. Now and then, little shafts of light shine down and light up a couple of dancers, making the darkness seem blacker and dense, making me squint.

I check out the queue to the bogs. It's still there, snaking right round the dance-floor and into the Ladies'. And I know Lise'll be in there, up against the mirror with the atomiser, straight to the tongue, a fiver a pop. Sonn keeping everyone right, patrolling the door.

By the length of that queue, we'll make a killing tonight.

You can tell if there's trouble on a dance-floor, just by the rhythms, the way the whole thing moves. Got this sway about it, like everything is attached to everything else – the whole thing flows, moves like a sea. If something goes down then the rhythm gets broken, like dropping a stone in a pool.

Then the ripples spill over, spread out, and if you know what you're doing you can follow them, trace the thing back to the source. I stand and watch it for hours, testing myself, keep myself from getting bored.

So now I'm watching but there's nothing doing. Then, as I start to relax, I see it, the ripple.

I trace it back to the door and see Fatboy and Mouse, and a couple of big Cheetah bastards I don't even know, pushing into the crowd from the top.

No fucking sign of that shit-eater Lloyd.

I whip round for Marta but she's on it already. Danny's nowhere to be seen, but I got no time for that now.

I'm looking for Sonn and then I see her and Lise, wading in against the tide, looking for me but heading straight for the decks. Then I'm pushing through bodies and swimming in treacle, trying to keep my head up, get Carla's attention, but she's got some girl against the decks between her arms while she spins so she's paying no mind.

I know I've got to get there fast but it might as well be the other side of Salford.

On the crest of a sway I see Carla turn and a speaker turns over.

Then there's people pushing, stumbling, coming towards me, shoving me back. Some arse-wipe knocks into me and I drop my blade, have to bend down to get it, lose sight of her.

The thing about firing guns in a place like Heaven, you don't hear it for the music. If it wasn't for the flash, you wouldn't know it happened at all.

For a second the room lights up, flicka flicka flicka, white-hot and blue at the edges. Then everything goes dark.

I've got a new strength from somewhere, pushing up against the wall of people screaming and running, punching my way to Carla. Then all of a sudden something gives, swings loose, and I'm out in front of it all.

Carla, lying on her back on the floor, a big space round her, everyone scattered, her lying there, all on her own. Blood all over her chest, the floor, everywhere.

I can't tell whether I slip and fall or my knees just give way, but next thing I'm down on the floor and I can hear a voice shouting Get an ambulance, Get-a-fuck-in-Am-bu-lance.

And then I realise it's me.

Then I can't shout any more and her head's in my lap, and her lips are still moving, the bubbles all frothy and pink with the blood.

Someone's grabbing at my shoulder and I'm shaking them off. And somewhere, way out in the distance, the sound of Lise, crying.

6

I start up, heart going twenty to the dozen, neck all dead from where it's been twisted in the chair, must have fallen asleep. Then they're wheeling her back into the room, people and tubes everywhere, so I jump to my feet.

They unhook all the stuff and link it up to machines by the bed. Stand back please, you gotta stand back.

Her face is all stained with the yellow-orange stuff from the op and brown smears of dried blood. I reach for her hand. I'm here babe, I say.

My phone beeps twice in my pocket and everyone looks at me, fierce; you'd think I'd just set off the clock on some Semtex. Some prick with a badge pushes me back out of the way and I bang my leg on the chair. Hey, you can't have that phone in here love, you gotta leave now.

Then I must have looked wild because he backs off a bit. You can wait in the day room, we'll call you, he says.

In the day room I can't sit still and my heart is squeezed, head spinning like a waltzer. Then I'm looking out over the city from the window, and everything's on fire, the dawn all coming up over the flyover and it looks beautiful. I remember what they told Ror at school, it's only pollution.

Then I'm wondering why teachers always have to go and spoil things like that.

Then I remember the text.

Lise: TURN ON THE NEWS.

Up on the day room wall there's a telly, high up, no knobs on the front. I turn the room over, find the remote shoved down the arm of a chair, turn the bloody thing on, turn to Sky News.

Bang in the middle of the screen there's that slaphead Gartside, our very own chief super, right in the middle of a press conference, flashbulbs bouncing off his baldy patch.

For a second I think it must be about Carla, try turning the sound up.

Just as I find the sound button there's a whole row of mugshots flashing up on the screen. I don't need surround-sound to tell me who those faces belong to.

Tanweer, Mikey, Tommo, Jason Uzumi, the whole fucking top tier of the Greater Manchester wedding cake – staring right back at me. Man, I got to sit down.

Gartside's beaming now, proper smug. Diligence and commitment of our officers... top tier of gangland criminals... culmination of years of police work... Operation Revive.

Operation Revive? You couldn't make it up. Dickheads.

Some bloke from News Corp, asking about informers, immunity or something.

Gartside beams wider. It is not the policy of the Greater Manchester Police to offer immunity to any criminal in return for information.

My arse.

Then this babe from the *Evening News* stands up. The camera zooms in so close I can see the notebook shaking in her hands. Won't there be mayhem on the streets now, aspiring leaders jockeying for position, as in 2001 and 1992?

Yo sweetheart, great question.

Gartside looks at her like she's shit on his shoe, when actually come to think of it she's pretty hot, and if I ever bump into her on Canal Street I'm going to snog her face off just for asking that question. He's rattled, but he's trying not to show it, trying to get a grip on the smile before it slides right off his face. No, no... come a long way... confident this time... yes, the root of the problem.

That's right Grandad. In your dreams.

There's a rush somewhere behind me and I turn round to see a white coat fly down the corridor towards the ICU.

I look out into the corridor. Doctor in glasses and green pyjamas is jogging down the corridor towards me, towards Carla.

I step out in front of him. What's going on?

He pushes past, doesn't even look at me. I'm sorry, he says.

I get to the door of the ICU. Can't see much for the curtains but there's a crowd of folk round the end of the bed, everyone flapping and moving around. I'm just about to go in, make them let me see her, when I see the two uniforms by the curtain, standing back, like they're waiting.

I should've gone in. I could have gone fuck 'em. Should have, but didn't. If it happened now I'd walk straight in, stab anyone who got in the way, do my ten years in Styal, just for the chance to hold on to her hand.

But it's not now, it's then. So I stand back at the door behind the curtain like a yellow-belly, rooted, just watching.

I think about praying, there's no excuse for it, I'm so freaked.

I try to remember the name of that one she made me take her to over Liverpool way, queuing for hours just to see some old bones in the glass thing and stuff. St Thérèse, that's it. So I make St Thérèse this promise, right there and then: if you bring her back to me it's all over, I promise. And just for that second I mean it as well. And that's how they get you I reckon, the God Squad, just creep about and wait till you're down.

I get a grip. Hey Thérèse you cunt. Let her die you useless bag of shit-for-bones and I'll bomb every Catholic church from here to Liverpool. Then I'll take all your bony bits and pieces to that glue factory outside Warrington, fucking melt them down myself. And then, I'll personally fuck the Pope with his own stick. That's right, the gold one with the ball on the end.

Then I start to feel better. They won't dare let her die.

So when it happens, I'm just not ready for it. It's like stepping off into nothing. Just the noise of the machine when it stops bleeping, does that long whine, thin, like a shop alarm going off in the night.

7

Carla's just standing there, smiling. That top she got down Ashton market last week is skin-tight and I like the way her belly dips and swells on the way to her jeans. I know I must have said this before, but she's got this amazing dip-thing going on, just about everywhere.

I love you, she says.

And somehow I don't laugh like usual, or grab her by the belt and jump on her back to make her yell out. I don't even tell her to shut it. I know it, I say, and my heart does a flip.

Then, she stretches her arms out, and I'm holding her. I got my lips on the sweet warm of her neck, and she smells like a memory, but more like herself than ever before. I can smell the vanilla she gets in that weird stuff from Lush, and the rose from the soap that she keeps on the sink. Underneath it all, the very best, the actual pure smell of her, like hot earth and summer, and cinnamon bread.

I breathe her in deep and all the tiny baby hairs that escape from her band are soft like they're silk. Then something inside me is melting, and all the bad stuff that's in me just drains away, Oh you smell good, I say.

Then she laughs, and it's like a hundred pure lines going off in my heart and every good feeling I've ever had comes tumbling down, to the one perfect place where she's touching my face.

Take me to the water and wash me down, she says, and I know I've heard that someplace, I just can't think from where. Yeah, I promise, I say.

Now I'm trying to lift her, but she's rooted somehow, my hands slipping, and I can't. I lift up my hands and the blood is all over, and she starts to slide down. Then it's like someone's knocked the breath clean out of me, and I know for a fact something bad's gonna happen, and then I know it's my fault.

I'm trying to shout but it's a whisper and she's falling, getting smaller, just slipping away. Don't leave me, I say.

I'm on my knees now just trying to stop all the sliding away but I can't make it stop and her lips are still moving, the bubbles all pink.

Aurora, she says.

I open my eyes with a start and there's Aurora, standing over the settee looking down at me, still in her jimmies, arms folded. Where's me Mam then?

It's like a CS grenade, going off in my chest.

And it's the way she says it. Not like she's bothered, but just the way she does when her Mam's out on the pull and I've got to stay over so she's safe. And even though she's acting big and she's got a proper strop on, she looks really small.

Get your clothes on, I'll tell you, I say.

Before I can get off the settee, there's Kim, standing

there, face like a slapped arse, in Carla's blue shirt. Carla must have let her back in without telling me. Makes me see red.

You better tell me where she's been all last night, because I'm gonna kill her, she says.

By the time I've ripped the shirt off her back, thrown her out on to the pavement, brats, clothes, tart's-make-up case and all, she's bleating. Aurora stands on the step beside me with a smug grin, lifts her hand for a wave, Ta-ra then. I tell her to get back in, give her a shove. She twists away, Hey give over pushing me, she says.

It's weird how you can practise saying stuff, over and over but then, when it comes down to it, things get their own head of steam and somehow the words get a life of their own.

She's not coming back, Ror. They shot her, I says.

To be honest I don't like to think of it now, how hard it must have been for the kid, but at the time it was the noise, got right on me nerves. There's me, trying to think about what to do about it all, keep me head straight, while Ror's kicking out at me, wailing like a banshee, and even though I'm trying to hold her I just can't keep a grip.

I fucking hate you. You killed her, says Ror.

Something white-hot shoots right up inside me, and I give her a slap.

Part of me can't believe I done it, not just because I never slapped a kid before, but because even if I did, the last one I'd slap would be Ror.

Lise is just coming in through the door, grabs a hold of Ror, looks right at me, What the fuck are you doing?

Now Lise is just staring and Ror's took to sobbing, holding right on to Lise when it should have been me. *Aurora.*

And then I can't hack it.

Fuck this, you sort it. I'm outta here.

8

I pick up the hire van and get my arse on over to Tony's. One of his boys opens the door, shirt open, skinny, bare chest smooth as the proverbial.

The place is a shit-tip, forty-six-inch flatscreen, Sky Sports. Five or six toe-rags, none of them a day over seventeen sprawled around watching, one perched on the arm of Tony's chair. He waves a hand and they scatter like birds.

There's Danny and Tools, monged out like two rag dolls at a jumble. Danny looks right across at me, takes a long toke. Toolie just smiles.

I try to smile back, but my face aches.

Toolie nods. Hey I'm sorry y'know, for your mate. Then he holds out the spliff. I don't mind telling you, it touches me, that.

Tony picks the wrapper from a packet of custard creams, nearly empty, holds it out to me.

No ta.

He looks down into the packet. Little twats. Eaten all me fuckin' biscuits. Eat me out of fuckin' house and home if I let them.

Hey, he shouts.

Three heads appear round the door.

Get Donna a brew. He shakes the packet at them. And who's eaten me fuckin' biscuits, 'cos they're dead.

The heads grin and disappear.

No respect, says Tony, shaking his head.

He picks up his phone, taps speed-dial. Mam? Yeah, me. I've run out of biscuits, it's them little twats. Custards. Oh and get me some Hobnobs as well will you?

He puts the phone down. She'll be round in a minute, he says.

I try to imagine what my mam would've done if she lived next door and I phoned her to bring me some biscuits, and it's not pretty.

When the tea comes it's the colour of pale piss. Tony waves a hand at the boys. Don't worry about them, they're sound. Then he shouts, A.J.!

Anthony Junior puts his face in the door and grins through his Curly Wurly, pasty and mean. For ten years old he's massive, no mistaking he's Tony's.

Tony slaps the arm of his chair. Come here son, gonna learn you something useful today.

You got to wonder what kind of weird arrangement must have gone down for Tony to end up with a kid of his own, wonder what the mam was like being how she never put in an appearance as far as anyone knows. Down the Feathers there's bets on: he got her up the duff when he was blind drunk then killed her to get the lad to himself, else she's some old slapper who did it for the money, happy to hand over the baby for some cash. No one's ever even seen him with a woman so I doubt it happened the usual way and I can't imagine him down the Fertility Clinic so she's probably propping up an underpass somewhere.

I'm his mam and his dad, Tony says if you ask him. He don't need no one else. Which is bollocks being how old Mrs Maggs next door does all the real work.

A.J. sits on the arm of his dad's chair swinging a leg. Looks up at me, proper basking in it, smug little fucker.

Tony gives his arm a tap, Don't forget what I told you. The kid nods.

Sit down, says Tony, but I'm still standing and to be honest I don't know how I'm gonna bend. There's a pain in my gut reaches right up to my chest and whatever I try I just can't get a handle on it. Like the time I got stabbed outside the Paradise, just a million times worse.

Thing is, when you get stabbed, you don't even know that you're cut. Like the biggest punch ever, takes your breath right out. It's only when you look down, see the blood, that's when you know, and then that's when it hurts. So I keep looking down, expect to see my guts hanging out like Mel Gibson in *Braveheart*, give me some kind of perspective. But there's nothing.

Forget it, I tell him, I'm standing.

He looks me up and down, starts to mess with his phone. Beats me how this useless turd got to be next in line, in fact why I'm even standing here asking him fuck all. Personality of a snail on Valium, Carla says. Then the thought of her makes my head spin and the edges go dark.

So now I'm looking right into those eyes, trying to work out why he's just jiving around. Hey, am I gonna do it or are you?

Then there's no sound in the room at all, just the hiss and plop of the gas, and I can feel something tight and hot coming up behind my eyes. And whatever it is, I'm shit scared it'll all spill out and I'll be scriking for England, right in front of these pricks.

Tony looks past me, does this thin kind of smile, Things have changed, Don.

Don? Now I hate the fucker. Name's Donna to you mate, I say.

I say what happens now, he says. So you better wind your neck in, you lot, stay low for a bit.

Now I'm the one staring. Wind your neck in? You lot?

They fucking killed her, I says. Man, she's *dead*.

I look over at Danny and Tools, and they can't look at me, so now I'm on a roll. OK, yeah, I get it, I'll do it meself then. Just don't get in me way, if that's not too much to ask.

Not on my watch you don't, he says.

Then he starts going on about Carla, how she was out of control, how it was my fault for not keeping her in line, oh she had it all coming and that. The fact that I don't do him right there and then I just got to put down to how I'm feeling. All spacey and shit.

As it turned out maybe it was just as well. Because even though I couldn't know it then, it was gonna take more than just me and a sorry nine millimetre to sort that fucker out.

Out on the pavement. I lean on the wall and my mouth's full of sour. Like that time I found me mam in the alley and I thought she was dead.

Then it's all over my boots.

9

When I get to Marie's she's just sitting there, wailing and knocking back the vodka, no sign of Ror. Aww, where's my Aurora? she says.

You can't be having her over here, I tell her, you're not fit.

Then she's wailing and scriking all over the place, Ah want my baby, she says.

First off, I don't know whether she's thinking about Carla or Ror. Then I get it, it's neither, it's all about herself.

And that's Marie all over, because it's always all about her, as long as I can remember. And all these years, while Carla's been wiping up after her, I can't remember one time when she was there like a mam. So I make the decision, and it's not even hard.

Funeral's on Tuesday. You're not having her, I say.

By the time I get back to Carla's, they're all there and there's people coming and going like Piccadilly Gardens in Wakes Week, Ror nowhere to be seen.

Locked herself in her room, best leave her, says Lise.

Sonn looks at me, face pinched like new concrete, What did he say? When we gonna do them?

The funeral, I say, let's get that organised first.

That's the rules, see. No one gets payback till after the family stuff's done, so the way I see it we got three whole days before we have to think about what anyone else is going to do, or justice and shit.

It doesn't do to mess with the rules. One time maybe last year when Leon Johnson shot some kid right there at his own brother's funeral, there was hell on. I'm not kidding, the gloves were well off, whether the kid deserved it or not. Next thing, word went out even from his own, no reprisals for a witness, fill your boots. And before you knew it there was a queue a mile long outside the pig-pen on Moss Lane, and that smug fuckwit Gartside thought his Christmases had all come at once. What I'm saying is, you don't break the rules whatever, and Leon got twenty-three years, and a haircut, to think about that.

We sit around for a bit, turn on the news. Finn's on her netbook, checking out Flyway. Seems like everyone's on there, on account of the police raids last night. Hey look at this, she says, looks like they've taken Mikey to Durham, gone and split them all up.

Lise brings toast, but no one eats anything. I'm gonna have to tell them something, some time, but not yet.

Sonn comes in with the new sim cards from the safe and then everyone gets to switch their home lines back on. Everyone got three sims, pay-as-you-go. One for between us and for business, one for legit, one for family and personal. How many phones they use is up to them, but most of us just use one or two at a time. I got an extra sim just in case, connects me to Mike, people further up the food-chain. I try not to use it though. Flyway's the best bet if you want to stay safe. Phones are things you got to be real strict about, and iPhones, well, they're just asking for trouble. One slip and the whole world can see where you are, what you're doing, who you've connected with, all that notification and location rubbish. You gotta smile when the numpties go flashing their new smartphones about. Finn can track any one of them, 24/7 on her netbook any time she wants to. Sometimes I wonder if people even realise how dangerous that shit is.

Use the codes, no one gets that number except us, I tell them. I look at Finn. Not even Danny.

I look up at the TV and Mike's mugshot is on the screen, one black eye and a long cut underneath, must have took a proper hiding on the way to the cells.

Motherfuckers, says Sonn.

I'm feeling pretty bad now, about earlier, so I go upstairs. Ror's all wrapped round in the duvet, puffa-jacket zipped right up to her neck, facing into the wall. Rio's curled up right beside her, one eye open, looks up at me. Don't you start, I say.

I sit down on the bed put my hand on her back, listen to the sirens up and down the estate. Ror, I'm sorry, come here baby.

Ror says nothing but she wraps herself tighter, so now I know for a fact she's awake. I sit for a bit, just listening to her breathing, and somehow Carla feels nearer now I'm here. Then I wonder where they've put her, and whether she's cold.

After a while I feel Ror go slack like she's fallen asleep. I reach over and push back her hair and there's no movement. Then a kind of calm washes all over me. It'll be alright baby, I say.

Downstairs and something's disconnected, like my body's not attached to my head. Lise hands me a can. Did you see her?

I guess she means Ror, but I'm seeing Carla, tubes everywhere, me stroking her head where the baby hairs are. Yeah, I saw her, I say.

Later, when everyone's gone, Lise and me are just sitting, watching the sky get dark. She wants to know what happened with Tony but I can't bring myself to say, don't want to make it all real. It's all cool Lise, don't worry.

Like I said, I got no real problem someone taking over since Mikey went down because someone's gotta do it and it's not my call who it is. And I'm thinking if I don't tell anyone what Tony said, maybe it'll all just sort itself out, like somehow he'll know that he made this mistake. Then he'll start doing normal stuff, like getting the plan together, calling in favours and calling the shots, just like Mike would have done.

I think about going up to Durham, see Mike, maybe get the heads-up, but I know that would be suicide for both of us, least till after the trial. Ten defendants, so there's got to be a chance he'll get off, and even if he doesn't he'll get moved to Cat. A, so then he can run us from there. It's the not knowing gets you down. Remand's a real bastard, nothing solid or finished, not like most people think. Could be a year till a trial, doesn't bear thinking about. Mike says in Scotland they got a hundred and ten days, the prosecution, to get their shit together. If they can't try you by then, you walk. Keeps everyone on their toes. In England they can just fuck around with you till they got nothing else on. I know people never been convicted of anything, still spent half a lifetime inside when you add it all up. And I've no problem seeing what a girl might see in Mikey, because he's got those crinkly brown eyes and he sticks by his word. I'm telling you, you can do business with a man like that. Then I think about Tony, and somehow I know things just slipped a mile sideways, and I remember those eyes.

After a while we stop talking, and I let Carla slide in. I can see her face, that crooked smile she does when she's done something bad. The smell of her rushes me, makes my throat hurt.

Then I'm thinking last summer, way up on Snake Pass, the day she got her new bike. In my head we're racing each other again, her taking the corners not using the brakes. Louise, clinging on round my waist, all scared but not wanting to say. And how even though I knew she was scared I didn't pay it no mind, because all I can see is Carla up in front, sun glinting off metal, me trying to catch her, and the roar of the bikes.

The radio grates on me, someone whining about summer and glory days, brings me right back.

Hey Lise. You don't turn that fucking radio off, I'm gonna smash it right over your head, I say.

10

I open my eyes just a crack. There's light coming through the gap in the curtains, and I can see Ror rooting through the drawer.

I sit up. C'mere love.

But the minute she hears me her spine goes up like a ramrod, won't even look round. You're in Mam's bed, she says, and you'd better get out.

She won't look at me, even when I go over, put my arms round her back.

I don't mind admitting I got no form for this, and things turn so fast that one minute I'm raging, then I just want to grab a hold of her, make it all go away.

Fuck off then, she says.

So now I'm raging. Now look lady, you just be careful.

Oh or what then?

She turns and looks at me, eyes hard, and it's a look I've never seen before in a kid. Then there's something about the side of her mouth, the way the crease is twitching, reminds me of Carla. Oh baby, I say.

But before I can reach her she's off out the door.

By the time I get downstairs Lise is making eggy-bread,

Ror pushing hers round on the plate. I tell Lise I'm going out.

Where to? says Ror.

Nowhere, I says, I just got things to sort.

Ror gets up from the table, stomps out. I hear the front door slam.

She's just frightened, says Lise. I'll go and get her in a bit, she'll be round at Marie's.

Sit down, I goes, you're not running after her. She's got to learn to behave.

Lise pulls a face but the way I see it Ror'll come back when she's ready, and I got way too much on my mind to go chasing about. I'll be honest, I don't know how I'm supposed to do all what needs doing, look after everyone else at the same time.

You can't just let her go, says Lise.

Just watch me, I say.

I put the plates in the sink. I'll see you down the lock-up at two, I say. Don't be late.

I get to the lock-up and Finn's on the door, lets me in with the bike.

I'm trying not to look at the Ducati, still right there where Carla parked it, up by the van. Got a polish on the hub you can see your face in, that bike, and sometimes she used it like a mirror just to do her lipstick. We used to laugh at her then, how she loved that damn bike.

I go through to the back and everything looks the same, feels different. Everyone round the table the same way they always are, Rio asleep with one eye open as usual, curled up on the red armchair, down by the desk.

They're all looking at me, waiting for me to tell them something that makes some kind of sense, and the screw in my belly does a hundred-degree turn.

Lise comes through the door at the back from the store, arms full of hardware, shrugs them out on to the table in front of me, Inventory, she says. And right enough she's bang-on, because there's nothing in the rules that says you can't plan, even before the family stuff.

Then there's a knock at the doors at the front and Finn slides the peephole, Hey-up, it's Mina.

And that's about all I need right now, just when I need to use all my wits, but I reckon it'll cause more ruck to shut her out than let her in. If I shut her out folk'd be bound to ask questions and I can't be doing with that. If I'd been thinking straight, I might have stuck my neck out on that one. That's the thing about some women. Got this way of fucking with your common sense, till you don't have a scoobie which way is up.

I look around. Marta, Sonn, Lise, Finn, Mina, and me. Six not counting the dog. Not exactly a full platoon, given what we're gonna have to do. Dad always said one volunteer with something to fight for is worth a hundred squaddies on a paycheque, and not just because of IQ. It's not about war, love, it's about passion, he'd say. And I dunno what place he got that from, I'm just hoping he's right.

Then, not for the first time, I wish he was here.

Hey, says Finn from the door with a grin, looky this!

I look up and there's Mel from the Pool striding in, with that Jen DeLaTorres from over Warrington way. Got a look of Grace Jones about her, that baby. Leave the door open, goes Mel, because there's more.

Then it's standing room only, and you just got to smile. I reckon Carla must've fucked her way round every dyke bar north of Watford, and this here's the payback. Man, she must have been good.

I feel the weight lift from my shoulders. Mel's solid as a rock, something in her you can trust, runs the Toxteth dyke scene pretty much, least since Teardrop McCarthy went down.

The first time we met was summer before last, one of those hot draggy days somehow play havoc with reason. We'd biked up to Dovestones for something to do, just messing in the rezzer and larking about. But Carla was bored, trust me I know the signs, scuffing her feet and pulling at the grass, her and Mina at each other's throats all damn day.

We stopped on the way home for a beer, no let-up in the heat. Let's go over to Liverpool for a mad one, goes Carla, wind up some Scousers. Seemed like a plan at the time.

Sonn was the driver – she's pretty much always the driver on account of she doesn't drink. Which is a bugger because she's a shit driver even sober.

Drink-driving is one of my rules and I'm dead strict on it. Chicken, Tony calls it, but that's because he's stupid. No discipline, that's some people's problem. Everyone knows the secret to staying this side of the wall is only break the laws you have to – anything more is just sloppy. Anyways we all pile into the van and head for Fiery Jill's over in Liverpool 8, Carla and Mina, me and Louise, Lise, Finn and Marta, Sonn at the wheel.

Saturday night and the whole place is heaving. Inside we split up, work the room. Everything's going nice, Lise and

Finn on the dance-floor showing off, when something makes me look round for Carla.

She's surrounded by Scousers, looks edgy. I get my arse over toot-sweet, come up from behind, polite because fair do's I'm a foreigner, What's going on girls?

None of your fucking business, says the one with tattoos.

I take a good look. Two of them look like they work out; the other one's skinny with Doc Martens and glasses but that means nothing. Sonn's got glasses and she could lay the whole of the Olympic hockey team out even on a bad day. But I can't let it go. Wrong answer, I say.

Forgot their manners, says Car, and shrugs. I only asked her to dance.

I look at the three women, none of them an oil painting, laugh. Are you kidding me? Which one?

A small round face with a bleach-blonde DA peeps out from behind Carla, ducks back again.

Who is she? I ask Carla.

Mine, says Glasses, that's who.

I'm not fucking asking you, I say.

Glasses reaches over to push Carla to one side, grabs the blonde's arm, twists and pulls, I'm so gonna batter you when I get you home.

I step in between, point at the blonde, Hey, she gets to decide who she dances with, it's 2007.

Not in Liverpool, says Carla, they're all behind in the head, comes of shagging their mothers.

Before I know it something hits me smack in the gut and I'm flying backwards, pair of somebody's arms wrapped tight round my waist. I crash-land backwards on a table, Glasses on top. Women, chairs and bottles falling everywhere. She puts her hands round my throat and I can't breathe. Then I see the chair coming down from behind, crashes down on her head. She slips off and down to one side in slow motion, out cold.

Carla looks down from above me and grins, pulls me to my feet with one hand. We turn, look back across a sea of arms and legs, kicks and punches flying where the dance-floor used to be. In the corner of my eye I see Lise out of the way against the pillar with the blonde.

Alrighty, nods Carla, let's do this.

We sprint across the room, together in perfect time, wade on in.

By the time the bouncers split us all up and chuck us all out we're battered and breathless but laughing. On the next street we sit down on the kerb outside a lap-dancing club to get our breath. I look round. At least everyone's here and alive.

Marta leans back, rests one elbow on the pavement, wipes blood from her nose with the back of her hand. She touches the bridge with the tips of her fingers, looks broken. Not again, she says, I can't be doing with all that packing.

Finn stretches her arms out in front of her, cracks her fingers one by one, lump the size of boiled egg coming up over one eye. Well wicked, she says.

Lise brushes a speck of dirt off her skirt, examines her hands. You're going to have to come out without me if this kind of thing goes on, she says, I've broke a nail.

I turn to Carla, Where's the blonde?

Sent her out the back exit with Lise, she says with a grin. Gave her money for a taxi, told her to get herself home.

Mina's mouth twists into her cheek.

I don't know her from Eve, Carla hisses at her, it was only a bloody dance.

Mina gets up from the kerb, goes to lean on the wall, lights a cig. I suck my knuckles, nudge Carla and grin, You satisfied now? This is your fault you pillock.

Yeah but you love me, she says, and crinkles her nose.

It's wearing off, I say.

I'm starving, goes Lise, gotta be a KFC round here somewhere. She walks up to the corner, disappears, and we're getting up to follow her when I hear a shout. Lise sprinting back round the corner, high heels in her hand.

I catch hold of her arm as she goes past, What you running for? How many are there?

Hundreds. She twists free, runs on past.

Don't be mad, I call after her. Lise is always exaggerating.

Uh-oh, says Finn, low.

Scousers pour round the corner towards us, maybe a dozen across, four-deep. I see a blade glint mean in the street-light. The front row see us and slow to a stop, back rows bumping into the front there's so fucking many of them. I spot Glasses out front, holding what looks like a chair leg.

Mina's looking the other way down the street. Ahh shit, she goes.

I swing round, another line of Scouse dykes strung out across the street, heading up towards us. Lise is turning one way then the other, nowhere to run. Oh shit oh shit oh shit, she says, why'd you let me wear these bloody shoes?

I back up to the black door of the lap-dancing club, bang on it with the heel of my boot, keep my eyes on the corner.

A small grille opens high up, man's voice, Yeah?

I keep my voice down, Open the door, mate, will you?

Members only, says the voice.

It's an emergency, moron. Just open the door.

You got an emergency you need to dial 999 love, says the voice, deadpan. This is a respectable adult establishment.

I'm about to kick the door when Lise pushes past me, speaks to the grille. Can you let us in mate? Only I'm five months pregnant and I don't feel very well.

I look at her. She's joking, right?

Oh and really sorry about my friend, she says, pulling a face at me.

Ahh right, says the voice, is this your first? Me and the missus we got three now, all little buggers God love 'em. Might be your blood pressure. How are your ankles?

I roll my eyes at Lise, jerk my thumb over my shoulder to where Glasses and her mates are waiting to skin us alive, Get on with it.

I just need a glass of water and somewhere to sit for a minute, phone a taxi, she says. Three? Really? That's great.

Just you, love, says the voice, Anyone else needs a membership card.

You're a total sweetheart, says Lise.

Marta nudges me. Up the road the wall of women starts moving towards us. I reach down, take my blade from my sock.

I hear the bolts draw across the back of the door and it swings open a crack. I grab the doorframe on both sides, swing my legs up, kick as hard as I can with both feet. It crashes back, knocks the poor sod behind it flying.

I push Lise in first. Half behind the door, half across the corridor, the Scouse version of the Incredible Hulk is lying, spark out. I scramble over, hold the door for the others. When everyone's through I try to shut the door but somehow he's got wedged. I can't move him, he's a dead weight. I hear the roar from the street and I know I won't be able to hold the door. Across the corridor a set of stairs goes down to a basement, music pumping. Downstairs, I tell the others, then scatter.

Down the stairs, past the ticket office, black-painted walls, silver mirrors, thick carpet. The place is gloomy, people sitting at tables or standing around a central platform, mostly men but not all of them by any means. If that's equality you're welcome to it.

Up on the platform half a dozen near-naked women, false tits bouncing, wrapped around poles pulling stunts that'd make your eyes water. Pinstripe punters glassy-eyed and panting. The place could be on fire and they wouldn't notice.

I throw myself underneath a table, start to crawl across the room from one table to another, heading for the other side of the room. Must be a fire exit, somewhere.

Six tables deep I get to the edge of the platform and take a right to crawl round it. I can hear the ruck back at the door even over the pump of the music, bouncers trying to stem the flow, got as much chance as a kid with a plastic bucket has of holding back the Mersey.

I crawl forward, find Lise crouched underneath the next table. She nods to the right, We can't get to it that way, I've tried, she says.

I turn to crawl back only to see a pair of Doc Martens right smack in front of me. I can only see up to the knees but I can guess who it is. Lise follows my eyes, so can she.

81

Shit shit shit Donna. What do we do now?

I peer up round the edge of the table. I'll have to jump her, I goes, then you run.

I glance back. Lise is unbuttoning her blouse.

What the fuck are you doing?

She slips her skirt down over her knees and her feet. The stage, she says, c'mon, get your gear off. They'll never look there.

Give her credit it's a pretty good idea, but there's no way I'm going up there in my boxers and monkey boots. I'll take her, you get up there, I say.

Lise is crouching now in her knickers, slips her heels on, a natural.

I crawl forward, undo the Docs in front of me and tie the laces together, leap up right in front of Glasses, give her a shove. She goes down with the table, takes half a dozen punters and a champagne bucket with her. You beauty.

Lise wriggles past me and up on to the stage.

I dart out round the stage towards the exit, no one minding it, bouncers running towards the place where Glasses went down. I push the door open and feel the fresh air rush in, glance back into the room and it's mayhem. I see Carla and Finn making their way over, no sign of Marta, Lise dancing her heart out in the nudd on the stage. To be honest she's not half bad. Get over here, I mouth at her.

She shakes her head, eyes wide, still dancing.

I'm not leaving you, I yell over the din.

Outside and we're running again, Lise trying to pull her top on, bra and skirt still in her hand, Mina dragging her along by the arm.

At the top of the street we turn left. I've lost my bearings, don't even know which way the van is, call a halt. We're going round in circles.

Christ I'm freezing, says Lise, hopping on one leg to get her foot in the skirt.

From the corner behind us I hear the sound of shouting and footsteps. Lots of footsteps.

I'm done running, goes Marta, these numpties are starting to piss me off. Let's just give them a pasting.

A solid line of women appear round the corner, Glasses up front. Twenty of them at least, and six of us.

Lise is starting to shake. Get behind us, I tell her, and when we reach them you run.

On my count, I goes, then charge them. Fan out round the edges at the last minute, come back in from behind.

A shout goes up behind us. I swing round, a dozen more women heading up towards us and we're back where we started – Plan B, then. I take a deep breath. Back to back, and no one bottle it or we're dead. We form a circle, link arms.

Another shout, Hold up.

At the front is the blonde from the bar, beside her a handsome dyke with a trilby, long dark-red hair.

The blonde jogs up to Carla, My cousin, she goes, jerking a thumb at the one in the trilby, we can help.

Carla looks at me, like, Well? My first thought is why should I trust them? My second is what other choice do we have?

Mina steps in between Carla and the blonde, curls her lip. We don't need you, she says.

I glance up the street at the poison dwarf and her hod-carriers. Shut up Mina, don't be an idiot.

Before I can say anything else the Trilby walks past me, straight towards Glasses. I'm braced for the kick-off, but they reach each other and stop, face to face. I can't hear what they're saying. OK girls be ready, I say.

Glasses is turning away, shrugs, says something to the rest I can't hear. Then they all turn and walk slowly away. I watch them disappear round the corner, can't quite believe it. Maybe it's just some clever trick to catch us off-guard. Sonn nudges me.

Stay ready, I say.

The dyke in the trilby walks back towards Carla, holds her hand out, Mel, she says. She nods towards the blonde. Our Whitney says you come to her rescue?

Carla looks at the hand like she's wondering whether to shake it or spit in it and I realise this could still go to shit in a nanosecond, you never can tell with Car. I step forward, hold out my hand.

Donna, the Brontes. And you're welcome, no problem. I nod my head to the corner, How'd you do that?

Mel laughs, tips her hat. Her eyes are bluer than blue.

Toxteth Tigers, I own Fiery Jill's and the club. Her eyes twinkle. Amongst other things, she says.

Truth be told Mel controlled half the women's scene in Toxteth, clubs, security, bars, the lot. Her and Carla had a thing for a while after that and Mina never quite forgave me. Still, I guess she's forgiven me now.

Mel takes off her jacket, sits down at the table, Jen stands by the wall. When everyone's got a seat or a view I tell them about Tony, what he said, and there's dead quiet. I look round the room. So that's it, he's not gonna help us, I say.

Finn looks at me, and I know she's thinking about Danny. It's not like she loves him or anything, but everyone knows he's baby-daddy to her little one, Shiloh. Hey, don't sweat it, I trust you, I say.

Fuck that, goes Sonn looking daggers at Finn. No offence.

To be honest, Sonn's had a downer on Finn ever since I can remember, something about her once being straight. Most times if Sonn makes a call I'm the first to stand by her, but I can't have her diss me, right in front of the crew. We wait around for dykes to be born and not made, that's slim pickings in anyone's book. You got no call for that, Sonn girl, I say.

Now Finn's looking at Sonn like she wants to leap over the table, pull her heart right out of her chest, makes me see red. I bang my fist down hard on the table, and everyone jumps; Rio shoots off the chair and right on to Sonn's knee. Then I hear myself shouting. That's right, let's not wait for those fuckers to do us, let's just do it all by ourselves, save them the bother, is that it?

And wherever Staffies get that hard-faced rep from I guess no one ever told Rio, because now he's whimpering. Sonn puts her hands over his ears. Don't shout, you'll be scaring him.

I rest my head on the table, feel the wood cool on my forehead, breathe in Mr Sheen. When I look up everyone's looking back, even Rio, waiting. I shake it off, no point losing it.

Look, I say, we got no room for this shit. If we do this we need to stick together, whatever, and anyone wants out they better say so now, no shame in it, you all know where the door is.

No one speaks, but no one leaves either.

Things go round the table and I let everyone have their say.

No surprises. Sonn's all for war right now and who gives a fuck who's on what side, a Cheetah's a Cheetah when all's said and done.

We're going to fight a war we need a proper strat, got to rally some troops or we'll get pissed on, says Mel.

Lise thinks we should let things settle, get in touch with Mike, let him know what's going on.

Finally it's my turn and they look at me.

We're not deciding anything today, I say, not until I know for definite what's going on. But we need to be ready.

I tell Mel and Jen to get their women together, the sound ones, see how much firepower we got. Jen says we can use the safe house in Warrington for the hardware, the one they use for a refuge, even their own boys don't know about it.

The way some people tell it, used to be we could call on Women's Aid when a woman needed protection, way back when they put women first. Now all that council funding comes at a price, and that's usually your kids. Before you know it they've got the police around asking questions, trying to make her grass to keep the roof over her head, making appointments with social workers, testing her piss. And if you've got any kind of paper trail, been in care or in prison, or you're on the radar, you might as well forget it. No understanding of what goes on for women round here, what the risks are, what she's got to give up just to leave. So now we do it ourselves.

Warrington's empty right now, Mel says. Any woman needs protection though and we'll have to double up.

You can't have kids around hardware, says Lise.

Anyway you don't want to go storing all the stuff in one place, I say.

I put Marta in charge of communications, tell her to get an extra scanner so she can hear what the police are up to, keep us all up to date.

I've got an Alinco, says Jen, pretty old. Gotta turn it right up to hear the transmissions but it works. Reckon I can get us a couple more handheld, got some army contacts in Crewe.

I'll do a new network, new codes, says Marta.

I shake my head.

Marta looks back at me, No?

Messages in person. No phones, no internet, no SatNav. No trace, I say.

Yay, back to basics, says Sonn.

Now the rest are staring. You what? says Marta.

I slap the table. Can't think why I haven't thought of it before. That's what always gets the lads in the end, isn't it? Think about it. The big trial at Bolton last year? The importation one at Preston last month?

Silence.

All those logs, surveillance, everything, I say. Police didn't have any independent witnesses, not a shred of old-fashioned forensics. In the end it was all down to GPS and that Mile End pillock with the SatNav.

You mean matching up locations with calls, using SatNav and mobile records to prove someone was somewhere or knew about something? says Mina.

Yeah, never mind the calls and texts, I say, and now Gartside thinks he's William A. Rawls.

87

Lise chips in. I heard they spent millions on those 3-D inter-satellite things last year.

Mel leans forward, smiles slow, And that's what they concentrate on...

I smile back and nod, Gartside thinks he's got it all sorted. Got a headquarters full of techno geeks now instead of real coppers.

Old-school, says Jen with a nod, I like it.

So how about we step outside all that nerdyboy-video-game bollocks, ditch the phones and the net? Be smart, I say.

I look round at the nods. We're agreed.

Now don't get me wrong, I'm not looking for a war. No one with any sense goes looking for one of those mothers. The problem with war is keeping control, all your cards turned face-up on the table before you know it, people taking pot-shots at each other when they've forgotten what the fuck they're fighting about in the first place, everything up in the air, no one even knowing where their own shit-pile will land. Then Gartside and his mob stroll right in, straight through the middle, no one paying any mind, and anyone left standing goes down for twenty years. Oh the coppers love a good war. So chances are if you're anyone you're gonna end up dead one way or another. Strikes me that kind of chaos is for boys or those who don't know any better.

But preparing for war, now that's different. You've always got to know how far you can push it if you have to, otherwise you've got nothing to take to the table, nothing to make you feel strong. Prepare for war and that's the best way to make sure you never have to fight one, I reckon.

I wrap it up, send everyone out with a job to do, keep them all happy.

When I get an idea or something needs sorting, best thing is to keep moving, not think about anything at all, let things take shape somewhere at the back of my head. If you try and see an idea before it's ready it melts away from you, like when you wake from a dream and there's only the shape of it left. And the harder you try and see it, the more it fades away. Like knitting fog on the M62.

I get out Carla's old gloves, pull the bag out of the corner, fix it up on the bracket. It's not long before I've got a rhythm going, then I step it up. Right left right. Left right left. Right left right left right left.

I'm sweating now, right left sidekick, right left sidekick, right left right left. I speed up, aim to stop the bag moving in between, right left right, left right left. Leftkick, left right left, rightkick. Right left, right left.

The breath burns in my chest and I feel the pain hot in my shoulders, all down my arms, nearly there.

I keep it going until I get to the special place, the one with no pain, just the sound of your breath, thoughts floating away. Once you get there it feels like you could go on forever, only clear space in your head, everything else moving all on its own, like a dance you've done a million times before. Before I know it I catch myself smiling. Pretty much like a half-decent line if I remember right, only cheaper.

I know I said you feel like you can go on for ever, but truth is, you can't. Ten minutes later I'm lying on my back on the floor, arms out wide, gloves still on, wondering if I'm ever going to breathe again.

I look at the ceiling, wait for the buzz in my ears to die down.

Then all the bits come together, ring up in my head like a slot machine, ker-fucking-ching, and the very one I've been hoping for comes tumbling out.

Someone in the Darts must have okayed it before Fats came for Carla, for the Cheetahs to have walked right into Heaven that night, no face-off, just Lloyd on the door. And Lloyd must have had orders from somewhere or they'd have never got past him with the hardware.

I see Danny's face come floating back to me. *Finn, she's not coming.* So he must have known something was going down. But if he was in on it, why warn me? Something's not right. And Mike would never let all that happen, not with the truce holding up like it was, not without giving me the nod.

Unless Mike didn't know. And if Mike didn't know, then the only other person that could have okayed it would be Tony. But only if Tony knew the arrests were going down that night, knew he wouldn't need Mike's permission for Heaven.

And that can only mean one thing. Both those dawn raids and Carla's death got Tony's pawprints all over them.

11

Geeta: r u ok

Geeta: wer r u

Geeta: tex me

Geeta: ok c u tomoz

12

By the time I get to Finn's I'm shaking. I park the bike up outside, bang hard on the door. She opens it, smiles, but I just push on past. Shiloh's in her highchair and she gurgles at me.

Friday night, I say. Just tell me.

Finn looks at me as if I've gone loop but I can't stop.

Just tell me, I says, and I can't help it, I reach for the blade.

She pushes Shiloh behind her and that brings me up fast.

I sit down, put the knife away, eyeball her. What happened to you Friday? Why weren't you there?

Her eyes fill up. I should have been, but Shiloh, she was sick. I'm sorry, God I'm so sorry.

She comes over, puts a hand on my shoulder, I shrug it off. What kind of sick?

She tells me Shiloh been over at Danny's that day, like every Friday, only this time he brought her back early, said she'd been sick twice, once all over his mam, so Finn couldn't risk it, didn't want to leave her.

I feel terrible, she says, I should have been there. Then she's brimming. I miss her, she says, eyes wild. Maybe if I'd been there, maybe if Loh hadn't been sick like that...

I cut her off, Did you ask Danny to tell me you weren't coming to Heaven?

She looks at me squiff and I can tell she doesn't know what I'm talking about.

Look, I would've text you, let you know I wasn't coming. I should've. Only I put Shiloh in my bed, see, stayed with her in case she was sick, fell asleep, next thing I know it's half-six in the morning, Lise banging on the door.

She looks puzzled. And Fridays Danny does the door at Metro-X, so he wouldn't be in Heaven, would he?

I believe her. I'm not sure what to make of Danny. But whatever he's up to, he's not telling Finn. He's Tony's right-hand man now I guess, so maybe Sonn was right. Maybe we need to be careful about what we tell Finn, just in case.

Yeah, forget it, I thought that, I say.

I get back to Carla's and there's no sign of Ror, as if I haven't got enough to think about.

I'm just thinking about going over to Marie's to drag her back here when the mobile goes and it's Mina, says she needs to tell me something. And even though I'm still mad with her, and she's the last one I want to see, something in me just can't pull away.

Yeah OK come over then.

She's on the doorstep, soaked through from the rain, so I hold open the door. Don't try it on though, I say.

Then her face folds like wet newspaper and she's holding on to the doorframe, just to keep herself up.

To be honest I don't know what possessed me. Maybe it was all that together whatever, or maybe I'm just pissy and shabby and weak. But there's something about her, the way she was with Carla, makes me have to get close. I don't have to spell it out, I guess.

There's something about the eye of a storm that I just can't resist, and pretty much it's always been like that. Carla was the only other one who got it, that beat, the one that makes going to the edge of things so good. I reckon that's one reason why nothing, not Mina, not Louise, not a hundred other women, could come in between us.

And I never really thought about it till now, how it might all pan out, that thing we had going, because it seemed like we had forever. Like we just were each other, you know, and so long as we were together then nothing could break.

After, I'm just lying there in the half-dark, Mina asleep on my arm, watching the street-light through the gap in the curtain trying to work out what just happened. Me searching, turning Mina inside out looking for Carla but no matter how deep I went how she just wasn't there.

Then I'm thinking maybe if all that stuff hadn't gone down with me and Mina I might have put my foot down with Carla over that Kim bitch. Then she might still be here. So when Mina turns her head, looks up at me with that look still in her eyes, I can't stand to see it. Get moving, I tell her. You'd better get home.

She looks at me, pathetic, like a dog that's been kicked but I'm too pissed off with myself to give a shit about what she thinks. And all that close stuff has just picked itself up and walked right away and the more she bleats the more something in me just wants to smack her around.

Get the fuck out of here and leave me alone, I say.

It's gone eleven when I get to Marie's.

She's out cold in the chair, TV blaring, half a bottle of vodka and empty tinnies all over the floor, and I can hear the sound of someone doing the pots in the kitchen.

Get the fuck out here Aurora.

Nothing happens so I go over, pull the kitchen door wide.

Then I see her, half Marie's pissy sheet stuffed in the sink, the other half trailing all down to the floor.

She turns and looks at me.

I can't get it all in, she says, and her eyes brim right up.

Then all the sharp ice-cold stuff that's been packed up under my ribs just melts away and we're standing there, the two of us, holding on to each other. Scriking our eyes out. Hey leave it, I say, let's just get you home.

On the way out I chuck a blanket over Marie, which is well more than she deserves, turn off the fire. Ror goes to pick up the cans. Leave it, I say, she can do it herself.

I drop the latch and shut the front door behind us.

Then I take the keys off her, put them through the letterbox. She can come and see you at ours, if she wants to.

On the way back, Ror slips her hand into mine. I thought you weren't coming, she says.

Back at the house I feed Sappho and I'm just about to send Ror for a wash when I get an idea. Wanna sleep in your mum's bed?

She flicks me a look, With you?

And I must be going soft, because whatever it was that I just saw in her face, that flicker, I just can't snuff it out.

Yeah, I suppose so, I say, if you don't fart or snore.

13

At first I don't know where I am, grey light coming in through the gap in the curtains same as always, the rain on the glass. I stretch out, hit something warm and for a second I think it's Louise.

I turn my head. Ror's curled up like a pup, fast asleep. Then everything comes racing back in a wunner, makes it tricky to breathe.

Downstairs I look into the living room, see the kitchen chairs set out in a row. Lise is in the kitchen with Sonn and Rio, just waiting. I make some coffee, put everyone an extra sugar in. No one speaks, so when the front door bell rings we all jump.

She's here now, says Lise.

I open the front door. Skinny lat in a greasy black suit, little knot in his tie. He nods at me, folds his hands in front of him like something off Oliver Twist. Needs an iron, that suit.

Behind him I can see the black car, windows down the sides so you can see right in, all shiny with chrome. I can make out the long wooden box inside but I don't want to look at it.

When they get her inside, the men put her down, balance the coffin across the chairs. Want me to open it, love?

Lise looks over at me but there's no way I'm letting that happen, four men in suits looking down at her when I don't even know what they've dressed her in. Leave her, I say.

OK love we're off then. Mind you can't put the fire on…

Then Ror's in the doorway, Rio squinting up beside her. I want my mummy, she says.

I look at Lise. Get her outta here, I says.

The room's baltic, rain lashing on the window, grey light creeping in through the gaps in the curtains. The screws are halfway out, ready, so I unscrew them all the way, take them out one by one, put them in the little painted cup Carla keeps on the mantel for pins.

I catch myself breathing funny, blowing out through my mouth slow, like Finn that day when we thought Shiloh was coming early and we had to jump all the red lights and then we got to the hospital and it was a false alarm.

I try to slide the lid but it won't budge. I grip it hard on both sides, lift it up, and it comes away all sudden.

I pull back, expecting some kind of smell to be honest, but there's just a faint whiff, somewhere between the hospital and opening a fridge, comes right up from the box. I stand the lid against the wall, heart thumping, take another deep breath. I never stuck around long enough to see somebody dead before, except me mam but that was smack and that kinda death got a look all its own, especially when you're only eleven. Looks violent somehow, everything that should be on the inside coming out of everywhere.

So I brace myself just in case.

When I look down, she's lying there in that hospital nightie, small. So still it makes your heart ache. They've brushed her a fringe, and she hates all that shit.

I reach my hand out to push it back and her skin's so cold and hard it makes me jump. Like touching your own fingers when they've gone numb on the bike, feels solid, somehow.

I look down at the tips of my fingers, and they're all powdery.

Take me to the water and wash me down.

Hey Lise, get your make-up bag and get in here, I shout.

Ten minutes later and we've wiped all the old woman stuff off her. Shit, we'll have to use something though, says Lise. Can't just leave her like that.

And she's right, because under all that foundation the skin's a weird shade of blue-grey, and then down under her neck it's all bright purple clouds. Looks like the worst kind of bruises, like someone kicked the shit outta her down at the morgue.

I'm just about to kick off when Lise puts her hand on my arm. It's just where all the blood's settled, she says.

How the fuck do you know that?

She shrugs. *CSI* innit, she goes.

In the kitchen, I tell Sonn to take Rio out for a walk, take Ror with her. It's raining, says Sonn, but I'm in no mood for fucking about.

Just do it, and don't come back for an hour.

I shut the door behind them. Then I lock it.

I fill the washing-up bowl, squirt the rose handwash into the water, put a dash of washing-up liquid in for bubbles, then I get an idea. I race upstairs, get the squidgy vanilla thing off the side of the bath, put a dollop in the washing-up bowl, turn the whole thing milky. Then the smell of Carla floats off the water, making my throat ache.

In the front room Lise got the blanket spread out on the floor, looks at me, You sure?

I don't say anything, get hold of Carla under the arms and then we lift. It's like she weighs a ton, even though she looks so tiny. Don't you fucking drop her Lise.

Down on the floor she looks a bit more like normal, without all that scratchy silk stuff trapping her in. People think it's there for comfort or decoration or some such, but really it's there just to hide things. Dunno why I never got that before.

Lise got her sleeves rolled up, ready. Then it's like I'm rooted to the spot and can't move, and I know this is the one thing I gotta do alone.

I send her upstairs for Carla's red top and her new G-Stars, tell her to leave them outside the door. Then just leave us alone till I shout you.

Now it's just me and Carla.

I put a chair under the door handle just to be sure, dip my hand into the bowl to check it's not cold. Then I kneel down beside her, start to undo the nightie.

Hey baby, I brung the water, I goes.

By noon everyone's heard, and there's people I've never even seen coming in for a look. Marie in the corner with a can of Special Brew, wailing to anyone who'll listen, me by the coffin, Sonn and Rio keeping guard by the door. I'll be honest it's not the way I'd do it was just up to me, letting

99

all and sundry peer over her like that, but there's something final about it and I can see how some folks could need that. Then some old guy called Mr Lowski, says he's from up the street, brings a quarter of whisky and some toffees for Ror. Better watch him, I tell Sonn.

Lise and Marta are making butties in the kitchen to soak up the booze so by the time Father Tom comes in with a bottle of malt, a big tin of Quality Street, there's hardly room to sit down. He takes off his leathers and sits down by Marie, lets her snivel all over him.

You'd never know Father Tom was a priest just from looking, and if they were all like that you might even think about going along for a sing-song once in a while. Fact he has to live all on his own and can't love anyone, ever, just seems like a waste.

Then he hands me the tin. Fairy cakes he says. I made them myself.

Well it's bad but Sonn catches my eye and I'm trying not to laugh out loud and the more I try, the worse it all gets.

By the time I get out to the back yard it's all bubbling up inside me like Red Bull when you go to pull the ring off. Then I'm laughing out loud and can't seem to stop.

I put one hand on the wall, try to get my breath, and there's a sound like the low-down hum of the ship canal in the fog. Then I realise it's me.

I try and breathe, get the hum to stop, but it just gets louder. Then I'm leaning my face on the cold wet of the brick and it's all fizzing out.

When things die down I sit on the step, look down at the flags, the weeds coming up through the cracks. Carla would've been down on her knees by now, pulling those fuckers out. Me, I wouldn't bother on account of how it's just a shitty back yard, damp running down the walls, and an old outside toilet where she keeps the bag of compost, keep it out of the rain. But Carla she was proper proud of her yard, even though that toilet never even worked. Who cares nah, I got two bathrooms, she said.

I look over at the pot with the clematis that just wouldn't grow no matter what she did. Clematis clitoris she said when we saw it in the garden centre, on account of all the petals were that fragile, and every shade of purple and pink you could think. To me that's just bad taste, but Carla never gave a toss about stuff like that, just laughed right at me, Hey prudie, she says.

She was proper mad when we got it home and all the petals fell off, reckoned they shouldn't be allowed to do that, B&Q, selling people stuff that only grows right somewhere else. False Pretences, she called it. It's too dark here, she said, things need sun.

Then I'm thinking about that time we took the bikes all the way to Newquay, just to see Fistral Beach, and how soon as we got there she stripped right off on the beach not even caring, spinning round and round like a loon, nut-brown and just this black triangle of hair, arms held up to the sun. How I told her Chrissakes at least put your boxers on, they'll be selling tickets next. How she didn't want to come home.

Things need sun.

So I never even hear Ror creep up on me. Watcha crying for, Deed?

I pull her down beside me. Hey Christmas Fairy, I'm not crying, I say.

Next thing, Lise is on the step, face like a smacked arse, says, Better get in here, because it's gonna kick off.

I go inside and Tony's squeezed in the hallway, doing a *Terminator 2*, eyes sliding all over. I tell you, if there ever was any sun this side of the Pennines, he's the kind of fucker be blocking it out.

Behind him I can see Tools and Danny. Sonn's got her arm across the door to the living room, keeping them all out.

Tony rolls his eyes, nods towards Sonja. Sniffs. Just wanna pay me respects.

I look over at Sonn, Let him in.

She looks at me as if I'm barking. You're kidding me, she says.

I hold my hands up, Hey. Force a smile. Don't mind her, mate, we're all just upset.

Tony curls his lip and Sonn looks like she's gonna stab him, right there and then, so I pull her arm from the doorjamb and walk her into the kitchen double-quick, tell her to back off. We don't let him in and he's gonna know something's up for sure. Don't make this complicated, I say.

He can go fuck himself, she says, what's complicated about that?

Sometimes with Sonn you just want to hug her, on account of she just can't get past it if someone pisses her off or disses one of her mates. Other times, it gets wearing. Like when things call for a bit of over-easy or you need to box clever and stuff. Don't get me wrong, I never just ignore it, because Sonn's got what you'd call judgement. It's just that, once she knows something, there's no gap between the knowing and the doing. And that's the smart little gap where the thinking comes in.

I'm in the kitchen when this woman walks in, dressed up like it'd take your breath away, holding a tray of samosa and a bowl of mint dip. She's got a silk blouse on over her Levis, pattern sewed round and round with tiny stitches, sky-blue. Shimmery green-scarf-thing wrapped around her head and down on to her shoulders, thin like a veil, makes her look like she's standing in a waterfall.

She pushes back the scarf with one hand. Her hair's all tied back and rolled over, but loose, so you can't help notice how thick it is, shiny, like coils of soft rope just waiting to be undone.

Then she tells me her name. Kaheesha.

I say it back, and it's like turning smooth stones over in my mouth.

Lise takes the tray of samosa, slams it down on the counter, mimes from the sink, Geet's mam, stop staring.

I pay her no mind, try and decide what colour the eyes are.

I'm Donna, I say. And you're beautiful.

Then, I swear it, she blushes, and just how cute is that?

I'm trying to ignore Lise, over by the sink, head whipping side to side like the umpire at Wimbledon, slashing a hand across her own throat like a knife, For-get-it.

But that's the trouble with Lise, no sense of adventure, like having your key-worker right up there on your shoulder, just waiting to put a stop to all the good stuff.

Ror's nowhere to be found, Lise having a fit looking for her everywhere. She can't have gone far, says Sonn, on account of Rio's gone missing as well.

By the time I find them, Ror shivering down on the floor in the outside toilet wedged in between the compost and the pan Rio snuggled up to her legs, it's gone dark. A wedge of light from the kitchen makes the wet flagstones look shiny.

Hey, I say, and I hold out my hand.

Ror shakes her head, Bugger off, I'm not moving.

Just then, the latch on the back gate clicks. I grab Ror by the hand, pull her up, shove her back towards the house.

Hey, you're hurting, she says, twisting away.

I get behind the gate just in time and it swings open. Some kid with a hoodie steps into the yard. I grab him from behind, get a headlock going, What the fuck do you want?

The gate swings open behind us, and there's the two pairs of eyes, Paddington-bear height, duffel coats drenched with the rain.

I rip back the hoodie and it's Kim, just about the last person I want to see right now. Or ever again, if I'm honest.

What the fuck you doing here?

Can I see her? It's a whisper.

I look at her and I know she's been crying but that's hardly my fault. Some women bring things on themselves and I reckon she's one of them. Forget it, I say, sling your hook.

I've let go now, and she's hanging on to the gatepost, kids staring up behind her.

I'm scared, she says.

Congratulations, I say, you're not as stupid as you look.

I try to stay tough but then I'm looking at her, eyes all messed, hoodie wet through, little bird fingers twisting at the toggle.

So now I'm just starting to think maybe she's on the level, and Christ who wouldn't be scared with Fatboy on one side and me on the other, her all alone in Ardwick with them two little kids. And maybe it's not all her fault, because, of all the mad things Carla ever did, this one takes the garibaldi.

Then she blows it. She loved me, she goes, all pathetic.

I don't know who she thinks she is, coming up telling me who Carla loved and who she didn't, especially when if it's anyone's fault what happened to Carla it's hers, and I tell her, no messing. Shove her back towards the gate.

She scrapes at me with tiny claws, desperate, Let me stay, I can help you, I know things.

I shove her out through the gate, Get yourself back to Fatboy, take what's coming, you're not wanted here.

Now she's bleating about what she's gonna tell him, how he's gonna kill her if she has to go back.

What do I care what you tell him? Tell him we kidnapped you, tell him what you like. Now get out of my sight.

I slam the gate, turn back to the house and see Lise on the step, giving me that look as if I just drowned a kitten with a registered disability.

Harsh, she says, shaking her head.

Then she looks at the ground. I guess Carla musta liked her.

Bollocks, I goes. Don't you fucking start.

14

I look up through the branches, bare, coal-black, water dripping everywhere, it's barely light, early-doors.

Southern Cemetery is grim at the best of times, half of Manchester boxed up and buried in the mud, lanes and lanes of us packed up tight, shoulder to shoulder. No room to move in this city even when you're dead.

It's always raining here. God only knows how high the water table is and if you weren't already dead when they put you in you'd probably drown. They can't dig the hole more than eight hours early, don't want it filling up with water before the funeral, puts everyone off. So those poor council bods got to work all through the night. And if it's raining already they might as well not bother, hole just fills up anyway.

I can hear the cars whishing past down the parkway in the rain, people setting off for Liverpool or Warrington or coming into town on the early shift. I close my eyes and it sounds shush like the sea.

I push the bike past the vault with the flashing Madonna that lights up at night. Big Shaun and Jason Dooley, little coloured photos of them sunk in the stone.

The Dooleys are massive, major shotters from Ardwick, five more brothers still kicking and plenty of room for them. Heard old Ma Dooley bought up the whole row in advance, just to make sure. Comes to something when you expect to bury your children but Ma Dooley wears it like a squaddie wears stripes.

The day they buried Shaun I was only a kid and there was hell on, the whole of East Manchester shut down, schools, shops, offies, the lot. The council made out it was for safety, but we all knew it wasn't, it was out of respect. You can't move in Ardwick without permission from the Dooleys, and you're not telling me the council is any different. Which is how come Big Shaun got all the security contracts after they went out to tender. There's something spooky about a Dooley being the one to lock up the town hall every night or patrol the magistrate's courts, in between murders.

Shaun was a proper psycho, feared of no one, but that was before he started sampling the merchandise. Ma Dooley likes to pretend it was a contract that got him, but in the end things just came at him sideways, stabbed in the gut by his own dealer over a tenner, right outside the King's Arms at Crown Point. The way I see it, sometimes life's got its own way of saying Fuck You.

Anyway, come the day of the funeral it was a proper show, all the Dooleys walking out in front in their rows, helicopter phwat-phwat overhead. Then the horses jet-black, all feathered and shiny, kids running alongside, pulling Shaun along like he's Princess Di. Everyone knows the Dooleys, doesn't matter who your peeps are, and that day we were all out there, hundreds of us, a proper day out.

Gone to the Angels, the stone says. I doubt it.

Through the trees and I see something yellow moving, catch sight of the digger and I know that must be where they're going to put her. I look back, just to get my bearings.

I push the bike under a tree and watch, two blokes in yellow jackets standing back talking. The one on the digger jumps down, goes over to his mates for a cig. The fat one looks up and and sees me. Alright love? You lost?

I go over, ask him if it's for today.

Yeah love, just these three today. He points over to where the holes are, offers me a Benson's. Then he lights it for me.

I take a drag, look over at the holes. Is there water in it?

He looks up at the sky through the trees, watches the drips, puts a hand on me shoulder, kind. There's always water in it love. Don't worry they can't feel it. Is it your mam?

A mate, I says, me mam's already gone.

Ahh love I'm sorry, he goes, for your loss.

I ride back to Carla's the back way, nothing on the roads. It's still early when I pull up outside but the lights are on in the front room.

In the kitchen and there's Lise and Sonn, Ror just staring down at the table.

I sit down. Lise is making toast, slaps some down on a plate, pushes it over to me.

I push it back.

She pulls her face, nods her head to where Ror's just looking at hers. Eat it.

I take a bite, try to swallow. Eat up Ror, I says.

At half-nine I take Ror into the front room, tell her it's time to say goodbye.

Carla looks pretty fine now in her new red top, Diesel buckle polished and shining, rosary curled up round her hands on her chest. Lise done a great job on her face but her mouth still looks weird, teeth just showing in the middle, nothing we could do about that.

Ror's crying now, holding on to the side of the box like she can't let her go.

I don't know what to say but I'll have to try.

Your mam's not in there, Ror, and, even though it looks like she is, she's already gone. Like when you get a mix-up from Shah's and you eat them and there's only the empty bag left, nothing in it, it's done with.

Gone to the Angels.

She's in Heaven with the Angels, I say.

I can't see it myself, Carla pitching up at the pearly gates, bumping into Big Shaun Dooley on the way in, there'd be war on for sure, but what the fuck am I supposed to say?

That's just her old paper bag in the box love, she don't need it no more.

Ror looks up at me, knuckles white on the box.

Can we keep the bag, Deed? Please?

No lovey, I tell her, not this time.

Mel turns up about half-nine with some of her crew, just as Father Tom pulls up out back, puts his head round the door.

Come to check everything's OK for later, he says.

He puts his helmet down on the kitchen table, takes off his gloves. He's got those little white flaps on instead of a collar.

Lise offers him some toast and he shakes his head. I'll have a brew though.

Then he asks me how it's going. Wouldn't like to think there'd be any trouble, he says, looking over at Ror.

I nod. Me neither.

He tells us what's going to happen, what he'll say, how things will go down. Then he looks over at Ror. Do you want me to say something for you love, for your mam?

Ror thinks for a bit, looks at him, steady. Do you know Heaven?

Father Tom nods and smiles, like she's just asked him if he knows Old Trafford.

I think me mam's there already. Can you get her a message?

He nods again, serious, I expect so.

Ror creeps round the table, whispers something in his ear and he smiles back at her, puts his hand on her head. Oh, I think we can do better than that, don't you worry, he says.

After Father Tom leaves, Mel drops me down at the lock-up to pick up the Ducati.

I give it a quick polish, wheel it out to the alley, turn the engine over. For a minute things go still as I listen to the engine, chest tight like a drum. I see Carla up ahead, low on the handlebars, taking the turns, feel the moors falling away behind us, then she's gone.

I love you.

And if she was here now I'd batter her senseless, just for saying it like that and then going away. Idiot, I says out loud, eyes filling up. What the fuck were you thinking?

Best get any scriking over with now, I suppose, keep my

wits on for later. On the way out I grab a vest. No point in taking any chances.

By half-ten there's a dozen of us hanging outside the house by the bikes waiting for the hearse, when a brand new red Ford Focus pulls up. A man gets out, young, smart-looking in a dark blue suit, looks a bit like Amir Khan, proper handsome. He walks straight up to me, sticks out his hand. Sanjay, he says, smiling, Geeta's dad.

Behind him, Kaheesha climbs out of the car, dark blue silk jacket and matching skirt, cream leather kitten heels that aren't gonna last five minutes in Southern Cemetery, make her ankles look tiny. She's got a big bunch of flowers in her arms, all kinds of pink, and Carla would've loved those. Sanjay puts his arm round her waist, then she smiles up at me and the whole world goes slack, takes me by surprise.

We'll take Aurora for you, she says. In the car.

I tell them there's Marie as well so Sonn will take them in the van.

We'll take them both, she says. Plenty of room.

I look back at the Focus, see the three little heads in the back, dressed up smart as paint, shake my head. Nah, she's drunk, making a show of herself, you don't want to be bothering with that.

Kaheesha just smiles, Where is she?

In the front room, I say, you can't miss her. Just follow the noise.

Two minutes later and Marie's slumped against the doorway, Sanjay with one arm round her waist, pretty much carrying her, Kaheesha right behind them her arm round Ror's shoulders.

Geeta jumps out of the car, runs over to Ror, takes her hand. We'll see you there then, says Kaheesha to me, over her shoulder.

I watch them go, like a proper family.

Lise looks at me, eyebrows right up. So he's nice then?

I want to slap her. I suppose so, I say.

By the time we carry Carla out all the neighbours are out on the pavement nebbing for England, both sides of the street. We slide her into the back of the hearse, put the flowers on top and I'm glad Ror isn't around to see it all. Stick together, I tell everyone, we'll take them round the parkway, in at the West Gate, out on the East.

And I'm glad I checked it out this morning, put my mind at rest. We'll be fine on the way there, no doubt about it, but afterwards that's a different thing. Never hurts to know where your exits are.

Half an hour later we're out-riding the hearse down the carriageway, ten miles an hour, Carla in the middle, me up front on her pride and joy. Seems like we're picking up riders and cars on every corner. I spot the girls from XS Bar on the Didsbury turnoff, the bar staff from Manto, that bent accountant from Chorlton in her branny red Porsche.

Patsy from V-Bar pulls alongside on her Harley, gives me a nod.

Last time I saw Patsy was the night V-Bar reopened after the fire, must be a year ago, me and Carla and the girls heading out together to check it out. They had a great MC back then, mean Salford slaphead called Tricks on the doors. Tricks is supposed to be a woman but none of us believes it for a minute – brick shithouse with a crew cut comes to mind. Male or female, every Salford player is a rock-hard fucker, loyal to a fault, and back then they ran all the doors in the gay village bar none.

Anyhow, that night at V-Bar we were out to have fun not find trouble, and maybe that's why we let our guard down. Carla was on the guest list on account of a one-nighter with Patsy, the new owner, so she was straight in, no bother. When it got to me and the girls Tricks stepped out in front of me, put her hand on my chest, Uh-uh, sorry.

I knew I was going to feel the outline of that hand on my chest for a while if I didn't sort it. Disrespectful, goes Lise.

I pulled the hand from my chest. You need to keep your hands to yourself love. Or is it mate? And then the gauntlet was down.

Even Carla's charm didn't work on Tricks, though she wobbled a bit and who wouldn't? So in the end Carla had to go and get Pats to let us in.

We're waiting outside for Patsy when the Sale footy girls join the queue.

Now football girls are a breed of their own, real mad fuckers. Drink like fishes, kick off over nowt, love a good scrap and a sing-song. Most of them are a real nuisance. Give me rugby girls any day. Anyhow they seemed to think it was funny, us all waiting outside.

Once we're past Tricks, we head for the bar. I can hear the footy girls cooking up a riot to the left.

Ignore them, says Car, they're not worth it.

I look over and one of them is on a table already, pint balanced on her head, stripping off her shirt to a slow handclap. Jesus Car, I just hate them.

Then they spot us. The handclap becomes a cheer, then a boo, then they're yelling and chanting and pointing our way.

She's a twat she's a twat she's a twa-at,
she's a twat she's a twat she's a TWAT...

There's only so much a girl can take. I push Carla to one side and launch myself, grab the leg of the girl on the table. She comes crashing down, pint of Stella, table of drinks, the lot, and I'm just about to follow through when my feet leave the floor. Tricks has got me by the scruff and I'm dangling, useless, but I've no problem changing channels to give that bitch a kicking instead. I twist round, catch Tricks on the side of the jaw, then give her a kick to the groin.

I've seen it on films where they punch someone hard, expect them to go down but they don't. Never actually happened to me in real life, until now.

Tricks gets me in a headlock, punching at my face, starts to drag me to the exit. Then I hear a crack above my head. Not the crack of a gun but that sick kind of sound, like a rounders bat on bone.

All of a sudden Tricks lets go and I fall forward, turn to see Carla clinging on to her back, smacking her round the head with a full bottle of Becks, cap still on. Now you'd think that's got to hurt. To be honest it just bounced off but it was enough to stun her a bit, let me go.

Now it's full-on and our girls wade in behind us, glasses and bottles smashing, chairs flying through the air, the lot. Lise standing on the sidelines, swinging her arms and snapping her head like a conductor at a concert. I should mention that Lise got a pass when it comes to fighting and everyone knows it, so nobody picks on her if they can help it. She's useless when it comes to anything with her hands, can't change a plug or hotwire a car, and if someone tries to punch her she wraps herself up in a little ball on the floor and shouts for help. Which means me.

Well by this time Salford get wind and wade in about thirty strong, three deep, the front doors of V-Bar a funnel for all the door-staff on Canal Street. Football girls don't look so cheerful now and it's worth a good pasting just to see the look on their faces.

Jump the bar, there's a back way, says Carla, dragging Lise by the arm. Still conducting.

I nudge Sonn, Let's get out of here.

Are you fucking kidding me? says Sonn. And miss this? She launches herself at a slaphead.

By the time the rest of us get out back, Patsy holding the door open, we've got the giggles. Ah, fuck it, says Carla, that was fun.

Out in the alley we split up and then split, all except me and Carla.

She looks up Canal Street. So which one you fancy then? she says. What about the S&M club we got barred from last year? We could turn over a few more tables?

I look at her. Don't be mad, they'll never let us in.

Well, it's not like there's anyone on the doors right now, she says with a smile looking back at V-Bar, sound of glass smashing on cobbles.

Hey, let's do it, I say.

The hearse pulls up at the lights. I scan the pavements and the road in front, force of habit. Have to remind myself to calm down. I see Carla, that day she got so pissed off with the lights on Hyde Road she paid Sparky to fix them, skip red. Went from amber to green and back again for a whole month before the council clocked it. Seemed we laughed all the time back then. Then I'm wondering who's gonna have my back now, who's gonna make me laugh.

I look round at the girls, bikes so close together when they turn into the corner like one long smooth wave, makes my eyes smart.

After the Chapel we carry Carla through the cemetery, Father Tom at the front.

Someone's put a plastic cover over the other two holes, and now there's just hers, yawning out like a cold wet mouth, pile of earth at one side. My heart feels like it's stuck in my throat. I look over the edge, try to gauge how deep the water is, then try not to think about it.

People don't think about kids when they get themselves buried, otherwise they'd never put them through it. Well worse than standing in the Crem with your key worker, watching the red curtains pull over, gentle music and stuff. Can't think how I'd have stood it if I had to watch them put me mam in the ground, everyone watching.

Father Tom says some stuff, long gown flapping, wind cutting his voice out at the important bits. Then he looks right at Ror and he winks.

We're gonna sing a song now, for Carla, he says.

What the fuck is he up to? This wasn't on the itinerary so it better be good. Ror's smiling right back at him, looks like she knows what's coming.

Then Father Tom turns his face up to the rain, sings loud as he can, and all the time he's smiling at Ror and she starts singing along... *you are my sunshine*, the tune that Carla used to sing her when she couldn't sleep, or when she hurt herself, just to make her smile.

Everyone's looking at him now like he's gone loop but he just carries on. Ror's beaming at him now and she claps, then everyone catches on and claps and then we're all smiling, and I want to go right up to Father Tom and hug him for making a fool of himself and not caring just to make Ror smile, but I don't know what the rules are on hugging a priest, so I don't.

It all gets easier from then, even the bit where he goes ashes to ashes, and throws the bits of earth on.

After it's done, I wait and make sure everyone gets away, Ror and Marie in the car with Geeta. I walk over to the bike, get ready to head out.

There's nothing much on my mind. To be honest I'm thinking would it have been so bad to keep the belt buckle, just for something to remember her by, and now I wish I had. Then I'm remembering Mina's face as we threw the earth on, how she looked to me for something, how I just blanked her.

In the back of my mind Carla smiles, shakes her head at me. *Harsh.*

Jesus, Car, give me a break, I can't look after everyone all the time, I say.

I catch something moving, just out of range, duck back, just as Kim comes out of the trees. She walks over to where Carla's just a pile of fresh earth now, gets down on her knees in the mud. I can't move, can't go anywhere or make a sound: who knows whether Fatboy's with her?

After a while she gets up slowly, turns and sees me, jumps a mile. I signal her to be quiet.

It's OK, she says, no one's with me.

That's all I needed to know. I turn and fire up the bike, get ready to shoot off out of there, then all of a sudden she's right beside me, face teary, mascara everywhere.

I've gone back, she goes. Like you said.

She's got two new black eyes, so obviously.

I can see that, I goes, and I care because?

I need to tell you something, she says. It's important.

I've had enough for one shitty day so I shake her off, rev up the bike. She grasps on to my leathers at the elbow and I nearly lose my balance, makes me see red. I push her in the chest, not hard but she goes over, makes a little cry as she falls, pathetic. Then I'm out past the Madonna, hit the parkway at eighty, don't give a crap who sees me, I'm too far gone.

That's the thing about having a temper then losing it: it's not clever. Makes you do stuff you'd never do if you stayed cool. Losing your temper almost never pans out good and mostly I try to hold on to mine for that reason, but now I'm so angry I'm not even looking for the tail. Might as well put a blindfold on, both hands tied behind my back, stand in the middle of the Ordsall Estate and tell everyone I fucked their mother.

I don't even see the car pull out behind me as I swing into the Close, just feel the whump of something hitting me, full force in the back, knocks me clean off the bike. I hear the sound of metal on tarmac, sparks flying out in my face, and somehow I see the bike skidding sideways away from me as I come to a stop and my lid hits the kerb.

I must have blacked out for a minute and when I come round I try to move but I can't. Can't even breathe. Somewhere faraway I hear tyres squeal as a car turns on the road up ahead of me, comes racing back, brakes and skids to a stop. I hear a car door slam and I wait for the bullet, wonder if I'll see Carla, what'll happen to Ror.

Then all of a sudden I hear someone shouting, the tikka-tikka blast of a Skorpion behind me, hear everyone scatter, car doors slam and the tyres screech away. My chest breathes in on its own and the pain makes me feel faint.

Mel's face looms over me. Jesus Donna, are you hit?

I can't lift my head but I manage a smile. Got a vest on, I tell her. Fucking hurts though. And where the fuck did you come from?

Came back to check on you, hon, she says, saw the whole thing. Can you sit up?

She pulls me up until I'm sitting on the kerb, pain white-hot in my shoulder. I think I'm going to be sick.

Who was it? I ask. As if I didn't know.

Audi, she says, snide plates. Didn't see the shooters. Can you walk?

I'm not sure so I lie back on the pavement to get my breath. How's the bike?

Turns out there's not much damage to the bike. I've lost some skin in one or two places, nothing that won't grow back, but it hurts like hell to breathe. Mel shakes her head, prods my chest. Coulda broken a rib or two there, she says, And you're bleeding.

She puts her hand on my shoulder and when she brings it away it's all bloody. Better check it out, she says.

I try to sit up, head swimming. Oh right, smart-arse, go to A&E and say what?

Then I must have passed out.

There's a ton weight pressing down on me. For a second I think they've buried me alive and I'm panicking, until I open my eyes, see light coming in through the van windows, hear the hum of the engine. We jolt over something and the pain's so bad it makes me cry out. I can make out Mel, leaning over me, someone else in the background. I try to tell them I can't breathe but nothing comes out. Then it all gets dark again. Now, see, this is the point where if there really was something out there you'd expect me to see it, bright lights and tunnels and shit. But I swear there was nothing.

Not Carla, not me Dad, not nothing. Just black.

They must be carrying me because everything's weightless and I feel like I'm floating, voices coming and going. Then they must have put me down again because the pain shoots through me, up through my chest and my shoulder, white hot, and then hands touching me, pulling at my shirt.

I grab at the hands, try to lift my head but I can't, try to focus.

There's a face looking down at me, and even though it's all blurry I can tell it's not someone I know, sends me savage. Touch me again I'm gonna kill you, I say.

People laughing way out in the distance.

You'll have to cut the shirt off, someone says.

It must be a while before I wake up because now it's dark, shafts of street-light coming in through a curtain. Then Mel's right there, leans over me.

Where am I? I say.

Droylsden. Try not to move, she says.

Then there's the face again, only this time it's not so blurry, little pointy-girl face, ring in one eyebrow. She leans over me, touches something and I nearly go through the roof. This is going to hurt a bit, she says.

This here's Sherry, says Mel, she's a nurse.

It's only later I find out she's a midwife. Best they could do at the time I suppose, no point whining.

Behind Sherry and Mel there's three other women. Jen's one of them and she's holding a towel. They all look at me.

What?

It's a bullet, says Sherry, Your shoulder. Must have been a ricochet though because it's stopped at the bone.

Now I can't believe it. You mean they hit me, those useless bastards?

It'll get infected, she says, if we don't get it out.

Sherry holds out some kind of pipe, shoves the end of it into my hand. The pipe's attached to a tall cylinder by a hose.

What the fuck is this?

Gas and air, she says. Just suck on it. Trust me, it helps. She waves a syringe. Pethidine for afters, she says, I can give you a shot.

Fuck that, I says, give me some K, knock me out so I can't feel it.

Sherry shakes her head, Can't gauge the dosage with ketamine. Too much and you're not coming back, slows the heart rate right down.

Chrissake you're a nurse I tell her, teeth gritted against the pain. I thought K was an anaesthetic?

Yeah, says pointy-face, for horses.

I look over at Mel. Get rid of her, I says, through gritted teeth. Then find a vet.

They smile at each other and I know I'm outnumbered.

Oh fuck, just get on with it then. I roll over and grab on to the pillow.

Jen leans over me, holds my shoulders down, both sides. I was right about the Grace Jones thing: that woman is strong.

Seems like the pain goes on forever, Sherry prodding and poking, and every time she moves those tweezer things about, I nearly pass out. And, just when I can't stand it any more, I've found it, she says. It's right there by the bone.

Dig it out then, I tell her, face right into the pillow.

I must've passed out again, because next thing I know she's got the tweezers down near my face, waving something at me. Looks like a massive ballbearing but squashed at the top. Put it in my jacket, top pocket, I say. Then I feel the needle go into my hip and things slow down and get far away, and I must have slept for a while.

When I come round there's nobody else in the room. The ceiling is all shadow-shapes, and I'm trying to work out what they are. Then I see the kiddies' lamp turned on by the bed, tiny blue fairies with wings stretching their arms out to each other, on the shade. Weird how something so small can cast such a big shadow when you put a light behind it. Outside there's just the sound of the rain.

I know I can't just lie here, I need a plan or I'm on my way to hell in a handcart, no doubt about it. I think about who I can trust, come up with the answer I always come up with. Just us.

I touch the pad on my shoulder. Still hurts but duller somehow, or maybe that's just the pethidine. I flex my hands, move the arm about. It hurts to lift it up, but I reckon I can still ride.

I sit up, feel like someone's punched me in the chest. Seems like where I took the hit on the vest hurts way more than where the bullet went in. I reach for my shirt from the floor, get one arm in and go dizzy, have to stop.

Then I'm trying to get my other arm in when I realise there's only half a shirt and one sleeve. Bastards.

Who cut my fucking Fred Perry? I yell. D'you know what they cost?

Jen's face appears in the door. Awake then, sweetness?

Don't push it, I say. And get me a shirt.

15

Half an hour later and I'm heading down through Gorton towards town, off my head on pethidine, trying to steer straight with one hand. Avoiding the corners.

The A557 heads out east from town, right through Ardwick, Belle View, Gorton, then it's the A57(M), Denton, Ashton, Stalybridge, Hyde, and right out to the Pennines and High Peak. At the end of the dual carriageway you can turn right for Hattersley, though I don't really advise it. Ricky Hatton's a Hattersley boy but that's about the best of it. Turn left and you're down past Mottram Cut and out to Glossop Woodhead Pass or the Snake. Keep going, weather permitting, and you might get to Sheffield. Me and Carla loved that road.

Gorton's the kind of place makes a person feel lucky to come from Moss Side. Or from anywhere really, seeing how Gorton's a grade-A shithole. Five-lane carriageway, abandoned shops, grim little terraces standing on the sidelines, weeping in the rain.

Every so often there's a patch of scrub and rubble in between the houses, where they knocked something down and forgot to put anything back. No grass anywhere, not even any gardens. This is where Myra Hindley grew up with her nan, and that's no surprise to anyone, not when you think about it.

Round here people remember places by the murders, and we got way more than our share of those. East Manchester reads like a Brady and Hindley travel guide and Harold Shipman put that other shithole Hyde on the map single-handed. Seems as if everyone knows someone who knew someone who knew one of those bastards and Keith Bennett's mam Winnie, must be seventy-odd now, still follows that road to the moors every week, like she has for forty years, searching. Pinning thin bunches of flowers to fence posts in the wind.

Every couple of years there's a dig for Keith, and thousands turn out. Carla bought us both a new spade for the last one. Out there digging all night, only a Twix between us, till the fog came down so thick no one could see a hand in front of their face any more. Gave me a proper eerie feeling, I can tell you. No one found anything, they never do, and last time old Winnie was on *Granada Reports* You had to wonder how someone could carry all that pain and still be standing.

Gorton, Droylsden, Ashton, Stalybridge, Hattersley, Hyde, our places are dark. We're loyal and fierce but if you come from round here there's a stain, a sort of shame that clings on to you that you just can't wash out, can make you go savage. You have to know us to get it. We're Mancs when all's said and done so we hang on to stuff, even stuff that no one in their right mind should want, just because we get so much taken away. And that's how come someone down south can make a picture of Myra made up of babbas' hands, hang it up in the Tate, call it Art. As if it was just a thing that happened way back. As if poor Winnie Johnson didn't even exist. Put that up in the Whitworth and he'd have been hanging up right alongside it before you could say Jack Shit.

I pull up at the traffic lights, Belle View, past the multiplex where Carla used to bring Ror when there was something worth watching. Then I'm remembering that time we all went to see *Avatar*, how me and Ror hid the 3-D glasses in our coats, took them home even though we weren't supposed to, did our impression of *Men in Black* in the front room just to make Carla laugh.

I get to the traffic lights at Ardwick and turn off at the Apollo. I've taken some stick for living in no-man's land, but I reckon it's safer. Most people think I live at Carla's and that suits me fine. This way, I'm harder to find, always got some place to go when the heat's on. The block is full of kids having kids, then alkies, a few students, people coming and going all the time, nothing settled. No one gives a shit who I am, and that's the way I like it.

I leave the bike round the corner behind the garages, walk to the block, take the stairs. Could kick myself now for bringing the Ducati, practically glows in the dark. Trust Carla to get a bike everyone wants to look at. Might as well get a tattoo on my forehead, Shoot Here.

The flat's in darkness, lock still in one piece. Just a matter of time though, I guess.

I let myself in, quiet, use the torch. Gives you the willies creeping round your own place with a torch instead of putting the light on, but I can't risk it.

In the bedroom I grab the small rucksack, get out Dad's watch from the drawer, put it in the side pocket. I change my mind, pull it out again, put it on my wrist for safe keeping. Not that it's worth money or anything, just an old Timex with one hand missing, hasn't worked for years, but it's all I've got left.

I was twelve when Dad was locked up, though it wasn't the first time, obviously. I went into care that time though, being how Mam was dead. After a month or two a social worker took me to see him in Walton. You be brave now, Dad went. Mind your manners, I'll be out before you know it. Then he gave me a hug. Be my good girl, he said.

After that I got to see him once every three months, more or less. And that was only because I kicked up a fuss. He died in Walton, near the end of his three-stretch, stabbed through the heart, me just short of sixteen. Never found out who did it but one day I will and then they'll get what's coming for certain.

The day I left care, my key worker gave me a plastic bag. Inside was the watch and his baccy, a picture of me, two pounds twenty in cash, nothing else. Not one for things, me dad. Used to laugh and tap the side of his head with two fingers. This is where you keep the things that matter love, and no one can take that away.

I sit down on the bed, his watch still in my hand, and all of a sudden it feels like it did after he died. Only me all alone under the huge dark sky, no one else in the world.

Then I hear his voice just like it used to be. Why you got to swim upstream every time love?

And I used to laugh at him, back then. Keeps me fit, Da, I'd say.

Truth is, it was just in me, and I never really got what he was trying to tell me. I look down at the old Timex, get a grip, shove it back in the bag.

Maybe when this is all over I'll find a gulf stream Dad, but don't hold your breath.

Back at Carla's, everything's still in full swing for the wake, people spilling out on to the pavement, too drunk to notice much. In the front room it's packed out, all singing, drunk as skunks.

I creep past to the kitchen, open the door. Lise, Sonn and Marta round the table, bottle of Southern Comfort in the middle, full glass beside it for Carla.

Everyone looks at me and I can't just say nothing, cuts on me face and the leathers all ripped. How's it going? I go, bright.

Lise looks up at me, face tight, white as a sheet, Where the fuck have you been? We was worried.

I try to shrug but it hurts like hell. Come off the bike, I says, I'll be fine.

I go upstairs, slow, into the bedroom, shrug off the jacket then the vest, go over to the mirror, twist round. In the middle of my back there's a bruise the size of a hub-cap, centre of it coming dark blue already. I touch the ribs, try to count them, realise I don't know how many there's supposed to be. Then I'm thinking I bet Ror would know. Makes me smile.

I peel the pad off the back of my shoulder. Where the bullet went in there's a raggy hole, black round the edges, all swollen up.

The door opens, and it's Lise. She looks at the hole. Fucking good job Ror's not here, she says. And don't give me that shit about the bike, I've been worried sick.

I guess if I had a wife that's what she'd sound like. Kinda cool.

After I've told her everything, she helps me pack.

What about Ror?

She'll be fine with you and Sonn, I says, they've got no beef with you, it's me they're after. I need to get out of here, or nobody's safe.

She wants to know where I'm going. I say I don't know, tell her to keep everything going, the lock-up, the business, everything. Act as if everything's normal, I say.

She tells me Ror's at Geeta's tonight.

Good idea. Let her stay there if she wants to, I say, till I'm back.

I go into the back bedroom, lift the floorboard, take out the nine millimetre and a box of cartridges. I go to the top of the spare wardrobe where Carla keeps the money, pull down the box, take out a couple of wads. Then I remember how Carla was saving for Ror's Holy Communion, put one of them back.

When I've got everything I need, I give Lise a hug, let myself out the back door into the yard.

Sonn appears at the back door with Rio. I could drive you.

I shake my head. Look after them, I say.

At the lock-up everything's quiet. There's no windows in the workshop so the lights won't show from outside but I'm too jumpy to turn on the light. I prop the torch up against the bench, wheel Carla's bike into the back, start to change the plates on the Moto Guzzi. Then I get a better idea.

I wheel the Ducati back into the workshop, strip it down right to the frame, spray the last red bits and the shiny silver spokes with matt black Hammerite, change the plates. Spray an old lid for good measure. I find the drill, fix an old travelling rack on the back. Then I rub everything down with some oil, scrape up the earth between the flags, wipe it all over the bike. Looks filthy now, mean. Like nothing Carla would ever want to ride. Sorry babe, I say.

Then, just as I'm finishing up, I hear a noise outside in the alley, sounds like footsteps, then an empty can going over.

I grab the torch, kill the light. Something falls against the doors, makes them rattle.

I hold my breath, start to creep towards the bench. Then there's a woman's giggle, a half-arsed protest, murmur of a male voice in the background. No chance, she's saying, but she doesn't sound as if she means it even to me. At least I hope not, because I haven't got time to sort out any domestics tonight. The doors rattle again, hard. Then there's laughing and footsteps and it goes quiet again.

16

By the time I get to Fatboy's it's eight, nearly light. I'm feeling well queasy. Pethidine must be wearing off.

I park the bike by some bushes, walk, reckon no one's gonna expect me to turn up bang in the middle of a Cheetah estate so I'm pretty safe. I wait on the corner, just out of sight, behind the hedge.

It's not long till I hear the door bang shut. You can tell the sound of a steel door shutting if it's fitted proper, sounds like a fridge, only louder.

Kim's walking towards me now, pushing the little one in a buggy, Dora the Explorer hanging on to her hand. Over her shoulder, a pink plastic lunchbox.

I wait till they pass me, then slip out and follow them.

The school's only a couple of streets away and I wait as she disappears into the yard. Five minutes later and she comes out with the buggy, bends down to wipe the babba's face with a hanky.

I walk over, come up behind her. You got something to tell me?

She jumps a mile, steps in front of the buggy, and I see her eyes flash down to my hands.

I turn them out, open, palms up. Relax, I'm not gonna hurt you.

She looks at me long, then nods up towards the park.

Bench by the swings in ten minutes, she says.

I kick the needles away, sit down on the bench, look out over the asphalt, reckon this might be the stupidest thing I've ever done. The way I see it I'm as good as dead already if something doesn't change, so there's not that much to lose. And there was something in her eyes yesterday, looking up at me from the mud, made me want to slap her and trust her, all at the same time.

The clouds are dark grey and purple, scudding across the sky, making shafts of light over the high-rise across the park making everything luminous. The wind's bitter, picking up the litter and tossing it down. Chills you right to the bone.

Maybe she's not coming. Which isn't the worst scenario I could think of. Far from it.

I zip up my jacket against the wind, watch the clouds.

Then from the corner of my eye I see her, small, pushing the buggy, wind whipping her hair up round her face.

It's only when she sits down next to me, looks me in the face, that I can give it a name, the thing in her eyes that makes me want to get cruel. It's like looking in a mirror. Everything I ever lost looking right back.

Her eyes are shadows, glazed over, dark circles underneath. The bruising's come out on one eye, purple and blue, and there's a swelling on the right side of her forehead. Her hands are on her lap, wrists thin, bony like a bird.

Straight off, I do exactly what I told myself I wouldn't do.

So, how long were you seeing her?

Two tears, fat, well up and slide down over the bruises and I have to fight not to reach over and dig my nails into her hand, give her something to cry about. She must've felt it, because she turns her head away, reaches for the buggy, makes to stand up.

I put my hand out, catch her wrist and the skin's smooth under my fingers. Alright, I'm listening. Don't flake out on me.

She sits back down, starts to talk, quiet, and I guess I could've written the script myself, if I'd thought about it at all. Saw each other in secret, for a month or two, loved each other. Gonna run away together, someplace warm naturally. That's how come we couldn't tell anyone, she says.

I hear myself snort, turn it into a cough. Carla was a lot of crazy things but you couldn't ever call her a coward and no way Kim would have been a secret if Carla had really been in love. That was always Carla's problem, see. She didn't care about the risks even when she spotted them, which wasn't often. Just made her want to do something more.

I think about telling Kim how much shit I've had to clear up just because Carla can't keep her mouth shut and her boxers on but something stops me.

There's no way she'd have kept something that big a secret, not from me.

OK, I admit it, Carla was full of dreams and shit and sometimes we used to talk about how good it would be to get right away, how we'd have a swimming pool and a barbie and maybe she'd take a course in hairdressing or run a boat for the tourists. How we'd pick off the hot ones, trade them in every fortnight. But that was just what she did, made pretty stories up out of nothing, no harm in it.

I love you.

And no way would she be leaving me, everything she'd ever known, not on account of a two-bit shag.

I'm sure that's what she told you, I say.

I let her keep talking, get stuff off her chest, and letting her ramble on gives me half a chance to work out where she's coming from.

She tells me about the night she went home, how Fats locked the kids in the bedroom, gave her a proper pasting. Then how he kicked her upstairs, tried to throttle her on the landing for good measure. She unzips her jacket, pulls down the scarf, shows me the marks round her neck. Christ, it looks like he was trying to hang her.

I must've looked shocked. Don't worry, he won't kill me, she says.

Then she gives this tight little smile. Not unless I leave him. That's why it had to be a secret.

By the time she gets round to telling me what I've come to hear, the sky's one big dark cloud and it's started to spit. Kim takes a raincover out of the back of the buggy, covers the babba. Tiny face peeping out, fat cheeks raw with the cold. I hadn't really noticed before, but she's got her mam's eyes. Kim gives her a dummy and her eyes start to slide up under the lids, then, even before her mam's sat down, she's spark out.

They're gonna waste you, she says.

No shit Sherlock. I can handle the Cheetahs, I say.

She shakes her head. Tony and Daz, they're in it together.

Had a meeting with Fats, she says, early-doors yesterday, in the house.

Everything slides into place, like a bolt in a breech. That's how come Fats could shoot Carla down in a safe Darts club, how come Lloyd didn't stop him on the way in. Tony wasn't just in on it. He gave the order.

I see Danny's face float in front of me. *Finn, she's not coming.*

A cold hand squeezes at my guts and I feel sick. Was Danny there? I say.

No.

I dig my nails into my palms. What's in it for Daz?

Tony's promised him half your patch in return for him wiping you out.

Piece of fucking shit. Did they mention Mike?

Mike's finished, she says.

I take a deep breath. So who was in the Audi? Who shot me?

They just said it'd be done on the way back from the funeral. I tried to tell you.

That's why you came looking? To warn me?

I watch her, one long strand of hair whipped over her face in the wind. She brushes it away. Could be she's on the level. Which makes me feel a right twat for treating her like a slag.

On the other hand, could be it's a set-up. I check the exits. Why are you telling me all this?

Because she loved you too, she says.

I love you.

I see Carla's sweet face and my heart does a twizz.

Said you were the best friend she had, like sisters.

This time the pain goes right in, like a knife between the ribs. Yeah, like sisters, I say.

We're silent for a bit. I ask her what she's gonna do now but she just shrugs. I know I should walk away but I feel like I owe her something.

There's places, I say. I can give you a number.

She looks down at the pushchair, gives this sad little smile, shakes her head. There's nowhere, she says.

I watch her walk away across the asphalt, shoulders hunched against the wind, wisps of long hair flying out around her head.

And even at the corner, she doesn't look back.

17

By the time I get to Warrington the rain's turning to sleet, steams up the visor, making it hard to see. The traffic's backed up from IKEA, all the way to the sliproad. I weave in and out of the cars.

Ten minutes on the ring road and I'm in Collingwood Close, wide, tree-lined.

The house is one of those old Victorian semis. Could be nice, if it wasn't falling down. Most of the houses round here were bedsits for years, until all the doctors and lawyers started buying them up cheap, turning them back into whole houses.

I push the bike up the front path, over the piles of dead leaves, round to the side of the house. The side gate's rotten, I push it and it creaks open, strains at the hinges.

Through the gate and into the garden. There's a high hedge all round, overgrown, keeps things private.

At the bottom of the garden there's a plastic swing and a slide, bright yellow streaked black from the rain.

I kick against something, nearly trip. Fuck's sake. Fisher-Price dumper truck, one wheel missing.

I park the bike up by the back door, use my key. Inside the kitchen it's even colder than outside. I go over to the boiler, switch on the heating, nothing happens. Fantastic. I flick on the light-switch and at least there's electricity.

In the sink there's one mouldy plate, a couple of dirty cups, a baby cup. Looks like no one's been in here for months.

In the back living room it's bare except for a mattress, but the grate is full of ash. Someone must have had a fire in here, some time.

I put the rucksack down, look round.

The curtains at the window are filthy but they're lined, must have been up since year dot. I go over to the window, look out over the garden. The frames are wooden and loose and I can feel the cold coming in, even through the glass, but they got window locks so they'll do.

I look out over the back and to each side, but all I can see are the roofs, no one overlooking, the gardens are that big. Not that they'd care about looking in. That's the great thing about posh places, no one gives a shit what's going on next door. You can do stuff you'd never get away with in Moss Side or Gorton, everyone knowing everyone's business. Round here you could bury your missus under the patio and no one would care unless you put the earth out on the pavement.

Still, I draw the curtains nearly shut, just in case.

In the living room there's an old electric fire, three old sofas lined up against the walls, a box of toys. Looks like a waiting room, carpet shabby, covered with stains.

Upstairs smells like old nappies. In the big front bedroom there's three mattresses, stripped, lying side by side. One double, two single. Big stains in the middle of both the singles. Probably where the smell comes from. I go back on to the landing, pull the door shut tight behind me. I check out the other four bedrooms and climb up the twisty stairs to the attic. Just mattresses, empty wardrobes, piles of blankets, an old chest of drawers painted red.

I decide on the downstairs back living room. Less chance of being seen, if anyone comes looking, and nearest to the exit.

Not that I'm expecting anyone. The Warrington girls have run this house pretty tight since 2003, ever since Jimmy Doyle threw their Kylie downstairs holding the baby, only three months at the time. Kylie went down like a sack of spuds, and the babba hit her head on a step on the way down, fractured an arm. Social Services took the baby away from her when it came out of hospital, even though she gave a statement about Jimmy, stood up against him in court and everything. Even though she knew he'd kill her for it if he ever found her. Social worker said she should've left him ages back. As if it was all her fault. As if she had somewhere to go. Even though most of the refuges been closed since the nineties when the funding dried up. Thing is, the ones that still operate, there's nothing secret about them any more, work hand in hand with the police and Social Services and Probation. No place there for a woman whose life is, well, complicated.

After that, we needed to find somewhere for women to go that was secret, and that's how come we ended up with this. Some of Mel's rugby contacts out in Cheshire, all bugger-me and jolly-hockey-sticks, lawyers, surveyors, all with money to burn and the guilt to go with it, found us this house.

That's the thing about the lesbian network, it's like a web no one else gets access to, cuts right across the things that make us different, brings you into contact with people you wouldn't spit on otherwise. I don't fool myself that only works one way, either.

We don't ask how they got the house, who it belongs to, and they pay the council tax, keep the electric on, don't ask us who stays here or for how long. Suits everyone, pretty much.

Back downstairs I get out some blankets, put the nine millimetre under the pillow, lie down on the mattress for a think. My arm's playing up so I hold it in front of me, practise squeezing the fingers together.

Next thing you know, I'm asleep.

I hear the sounds of the lock before I'm really awake. The whispers.

I'm up like a whippet, grab my jacket and shoes, race up the stairs two at a time in my socks. Fuck, the bike's outside. How the fuck did they find me?

I crouch at the bottom of the attic stairs, hear voices, can't tell if it's men or women from here. No point hanging around to find out.

I creep into the bedroom, slip the sash. The old wood creaks like the front door of the Munsters. The window frame sticks halfway.

I slide under and out through the window, sit on the ledge, grab the drainpipe and give it a tug. There's no other way down. It holds.

I say a quick prayer and put my weight on the arm that's holding the drainpipe. Swing out and grab on with my free hand so now I'm facing the wall. I find a hold for my right foot where the grout has come out between the bricks, no hold for the left.

I look down. In between my feet I can see down to the ground, grass all soggy and thank God for the rain. Question is whether to let go and jump now and risk breaking a leg or try to climb down the pipe, risk it collapsing and making a racket.

The pipe creaks so I let go and jump.

I hit the ground with both feet and let myself roll, stand up. Nothing broken. Just a sharp pain in my thigh, I must have landed on something.

I look back at the ground. Hannah Montana stares up at me in her army camouflage, arms pointed upwards. I've been stabbed by a fucking doll.

As I get to the bike and push, the kitchen door opens beside me. I squat down but it's too late. I reach for the gate. A woman's voice.

It's the famous disappearing woman. Still creeping in and out of women's windows in the night, then?

It's Louise. Better than Mad Daz or Tony. But Louise? Fuck Fuck Fuck.

Lou, hi, I'm sorry, I haven't time, I say.

No change there then, she says. Don't worry I'm not here for you. Just brought a woman and her kids in from Sale.

I've got to go Lou really.

Course you have, she says. Don't mind me, I don't care what you do.

18

Right, fish and chips tonight, goes Geet's Mam, and I know she's probably doing it for me just by the way everyone looks at her.

Don't bother, I'll have curry like yous lot, I says, I can do curry, I'm not a total retard.

Geet's Dad smiles, makes me feel like I am one. We always have fish and chips on a Wednesday, he says.

To be honest I've changed me mind about Geet's Dad, ever since he carried Nan to the car yesterday, lent her his hanky when her face was all snot.

It's hard at Geet's, even if they are nice. They're always on you somehow, let's all do this, let's do that, hey let's all play this now. I can't be bothered with it. Geet gets no time to herself and you have to wonder how she copes.

I'm at Geet's because everyone's left me. Well, Mam couldn't help it but everyone else just disappeared. Donna can't help it either, Lise says, being how she's Busy, Sorting and Stuff, but I think you can nearly always help things unless you're dead. I wonder what Nan's doing. Nan thinks I should stay with her but Donna said no way, she just wants me for a skivvy. Can't see how she works that one out, when here we have to do stuff like set the table and Nan never makes me do anything like that.

Later, I'm copying Geet, putting out the knives and the forks, little spoons across the top, when she reaches over, laughing, swaps the knives and forks round. Dillock, are you stupid? she says. Kaheesha comes up from behind her, takes her hand away, gives her a look as if she's going to give her a telling, only she doesn't. It's like that at Geet's, people not saying stuff but just looking, so you have to try and guess what the rules are all the time, no one saying what they mean. Puts you on edge.

So I ask. Are they wrong? Geet's Mam shakes her head. It doesn't matter, some people are left-handed, she says. Geeta, leave them.

Ror's not left-handed, says Geet, because she scores with her right.

I look at Kaheesha. Just tell me, are they wrong?

Not wrong, honey, she says. Mostly people have them the other way, that's all.

Wrong then.

I push her hand away, turn the knives and forks round until they're all facing the same as Geet's. I push Geet out of the way on the way to the stairs.

Keep your fucking table then, I don't care.

I climb on to Geet's bed. She's got this great duvet, fat, little pink and white flowers all over. If I lie down quick, it huffs out all around me, then sort of whispers back down slow. Feathers, Geet says.

I lie back and stare at the ceiling, lift me head a bit, bang it back on the pillow a few times but it's no good, the thing is still there. I take a deep breath, bang me head back as hard as I can, up and down, up and down, keep on going until me head starts to gets all spaced, goes empty. I go faster and faster till I'm dizzy then I let out me breath all at once and feel everything go loose. The room feels like it's still going and there's a whole lot of nothing, just the space in me head. I close me eyes tight, watch the lights in me head whirl around, all sparkly and spinning. Well nice.

I must have fallen asleep because next thing I feel a hand on me forehead. I open me eyes and the room's nearly dark, just a soft shape leaning over me.

Mam?

No love it's me.

It's Geet's Mam, tells me I must've fallen asleep. Her hand's still on me head, warm. I turn away, on to me side, shake it off, squeeze me eyes shut and wait for her to go. I feel her stand up and then she makes a sound, soft like a sigh. It'll get better love, you'll see, she says. Tea's nearly ready.

When she's gone I climb out, go over to me own bed, pull the blankets up over me. I lie there for ages, and when Geet comes up, turns the light on, I don't even let on.

It's gone seven, Geet's Dad's not home, and the table's been set up for ages. Everyone's starving by now, but we're not supposed to eat if anyone's missing, which means we're not supposed to eat if Geet's Dad's not home being how he's the only one who ever gets to go anywhere and if he's ever stabbed or run over we'll probably starve. So I'm relieved when the front porch door slams. He comes into the living room, big box in his arms and a huge plastic bag, M&S on the front, puts it down in front of me. That's yours now, he says.

Inside the box there's a brand new duvet, big, white, fluffy. I take it out of the box and it puffs out like a cloud. Inside the bag there's a duvet set and a sheet, bright blue with teeny white flowers on, well nicer than Geet's. Can I take it home with me, I says, when I go? Yes sweetheart, he says, of course you can.

Next day, he takes us to school in the car. Seatbelts on please. Geet kicks me under the seat, hisses at me. I'll never get to go on the bus now, it's your fault, she says.

At school, Geet's Dad takes me to the Head's office. Hello O-Rora, goes Mr Grimley. He stands up behind the big shiny desk, doesn't even look at me even though he's speaking. I want you to know we're all very sorry about your mum.

I don't know what I'm supposed to say, so I don't say anything at all.

He starts going on.

On the bookshelf there's an ornament, a little pot girl in an orange headscarf. She's kneeling down with a basket on one arm, feeding tiny baby chicks, don't know how I never noticed it before. In the background I can hear Mr Grimley's voice, dim, and then Geet's Dad's, like I'm listening through the wall. I try looking at them, but it doesn't make any difference, I can't hear the words. I go back to the girl. She looks lonely.

After a while Mr Grimley stops talking and we're walking out into the corridor. Please contact me if there's any problem, says Geet's Dad, putting out his hand.

Into the classroom and everyone turns to look at me, stops what they're doing, like when Donna and Mam used to talk about Things I'm Not Supposed To Know About and I walk in on them. The Wiz comes over, puts her hand on me shoulder, nails painted all pink and shiny like little shells. She's got a long blue cardy on with a belt and a flowery skirt and I can see the hairs on her legs through her tights. Mam used to shave hers in the bath and now I know why. Looks disgusting.

She'll be fine now, says The Wiz.

Geet's Dad says something back but I don't really hear it, then he's gone. Come on dear, you can sit next to Geeta, says The Wiz, and she squeezes me shoulder. I want to shake off the hand but it's too much bother, so I just stand there.

Doesn't matter where you put me, I'm not stopping, I say.

In the yard at dinner, Mrs West is on duty, and I can see The Wiz nebbing from the staff room window, nosy cow. I feel tired, find a bit of tarmac without any snow, sit down against the wall. Geet comes over, leans against the wall, holds out the ball. You can be goalie, if you want to, she says.

I don't want to, so she walks off again, puts Marvin in goal.

After a bit Mrs West comes over, Westie's Nan when she's not a dinner lady.

You alright lovey? Do you want to go inside for a bit? You'll catch your death, sat down there. God, I'm sorry love, she says, that's not what I meant. C'mon inside for a bit.

I shake my head. I've not got the energy to get up. I'm alright here Mrs West, thanks.

When the bell goes everyone lines up. I walk along the wall, no one looking. At the gate I slip through and keep walking.

19

When I get to Nan's the door's on the latch and once I'm in I put the snib on just in case. Nan's still flat out in the bed, snoring, doesn't even hear me come in. At least she's not Wasted Away. I take off me shoes, sit down on the bed, watch her muttering, mouth all wet where she's dribbled.

It's me, Nana.

She's too far gone to hear me so I lift the covers, climb in beside her. She jerks her head, opens one eye. Nnhhh?

She puts a hand up, wipes the spit off, puts her arm out to pull me in beside her. C'mon in love, she says.

There's banging in me head. I wake up sweating, push the covers back, realise I've still got me coat on.

Now the banging's not in me head, it's at the front door.

I lie there and listen for a bit.

I can hear Geet's Dad shouting, through the letterbox. Aurora, are you in there? After a while it stops, I hear the car start up, and then I must have fallen asleep again.

By the time it's dark, I've got things nearly back to normal, pots in the cupboard, ashtrays washed, cans in the bin. I give everything the once-over with the u-bank. The Complan is still on the table where I left it, not even touched since last time, nothing else in the fridge.

I go to the drawer where Nan keeps her purse, count out the money. There's enough for a loaf and a tin of beans, some milk. I get Nan's keys from the drawer.

Just as I'm going to open the door someone knocks on it, busy, rappa tap tap.

I creep down against the wall and wait. It's not someone I know, not with a knock like that. Sounds like our rent man but Nan gets her rent paid straight to the council from her disability so it can't be that.

Then there's voices outside, sounds like two women. A little white card comes through the letterbox, flutters to the floor. I hear footsteps, then a car start, and it's quiet again. I pick up the card. *Christine Walker, Social Worker.*

There's a mobile number written in biro on the back.

I put the card in me pocket, go back into the bedroom, give Nan a shake. Nan listen. I'm going out to the shop, don't answer the door, I'll be back in a jiff.

Nan nods without opening her eyes, goes back to sleep.

If I went over to Shah's Nizam would likely give me tick but I daren't risk it. I go out the back way over the fence and into the ginnel, walk round the back way to the Co-op.

Inside the Co-op it's warm and sparkly, chocolate Santas piled up near the till. I put the basket down on the conveyer, look round. On the next till there's a lady in a big coat with a furry collar and a belt, could be a model or something, trolley piled up with tins of biscuits, Quality Street, all sorts. Behind her there's a little girl, holding a Santa, goes to wander off and the woman doesn't even notice. As she walks past I put me hand out to stop her, just in case she gets lost, and she drops the Santa.

Before I know it the woman with the coat has hold of me, shakes me hard.

Hey! What do you think you're doing?

Before I can say anything, she's pulling the girl away by the arm, snatches the Santa up, puts it on the trolley, and now everyone's looking. I want to explain but I can't make the words come out, so I leave all the stuff right there on the conveyer, make a run for the door.

Outside it's freezing, sleet like tiny needles on me face and me knees. The Thing comes right up inside me, and if I ever see that lady again I'm gonna have to hurt her, bad. I hope her babba gets pinched and taken away to live in a shed like that one on the news. That'll just serve her right.

At least I've still got the money. I go into the 7/11 on the corner of Ship Street, get everything there.

On the way back to Nan's I see old Mrs Watson on the other side of the road, keep me head down, walk faster.

When I get to the corner I look down the street towards Nan's, then I see them, the cars. Ugly little Micra that Donna says no one in their right mind would have, and a green and white one. The Dib.

Standing outside Nan's front door there's two women, one with a briefcase, and three police, two men, one woman. I can see the policewoman banging on the door.

I turn across the road, one eye on Nan's, head for the ginnel on the other side. No one even sees me. I'm just hoping Nan remembers not to answer the door. Round the corner, up the alley and I peep back round, watching. Now I'm praying, Don't answer the door, Nan, please.

Nan must've heard me, because after a while they all get in their cars and go off so I leg it across the street and up to the front door.

I'm so cold me hands have gone numb and I drop the keys. I blow on them, but they feel heavy like they don't belong to me, won't do what I tell them. Probably what it feels like when you're dead, can't make anything move even when you tell it to.

Then I wonder whether when you die you're still in there, but locked up inside, not feeling your own hands, not knowing what to do to get out, and me heart starts to hammer.

Then I remember what Donna said, about Mam being gone to Heaven and that, but leaving her old body behind, and that makes me feel better.

I get the key in the lock and turn it.

Inside, it's dark. I put the bag in the kitchen, go into the bedroom and Nan's still there, fast asleep. I daren't turn the lights on just in case the Micra women come back, so I get in beside Nan, snuggle up. Nan turns over, Nnggg, and I creep into the warm bit.

When I wake up again there's only the street-lights coming in through the curtains, fingers of the alarm clock glowing green in the dark. Nan's right on her back snoring and I watch the covers going up and down with her chest.

I slip out of bed, go into the kitchen. The houses out the back all have their lights on, so it's not really even dark once your eyes get used to it.

I boil the kettle, get out the milk, turn on the gas for the beans. Nothing.

Back in the bedroom I put the mugs down, give Nan a shake. Wake up, Nan, I've done you a brew.

Nnggg? She sits up, gives me a sly smile. Was I slavering, hen?

I laugh back at her. Yeah. The gas has gone, Nan, where d'you keep the tokens?

She reaches under the edge of the mattress, pulls two out, gives them to me, nods. Robbin' bastards'll never look there, she says.

Nan's never been robbed in her life far as I know, but she talks about it all the time. I go over to the meter, put the tokens in. No one's gonna rob you, Nan.

Just a matter of time love, she says. Nip out and get me a can, will you?

I daren't go out so I tell her about the Micra women, the card through the door, the police.

When I'm finished she doesn't say anything, just nods. There's that Tia Maria your Mam got me, in the cupboard, fetch me that then, she says.

I get the bottle down, but it's empty.

Nan puts her jeans on over her tracksuit bottoms, pulls on her shoes, no socks. The veins show up blue under papery skin. Sit tight now. Lock the door behind me, she says.

When Nan gets back she hands me a Twix and a can of Coke, gets a halfer of voddy and six tinnies out of the bag.

We'll have a picnic in bed, she says. Get those beans on.

After I've eaten the beans and half the Twix and Nan's on to her second can, she gets cheerful.

Go into the wardrobe, she says, bring me the green shoe-box at the bottom.

I take the box back to the bed and get in.

I've got pictures in here, she says, of your Mam.

The box is stuffed full of junk. Old photos, bits of ribbon and plastic, some papers. Nan's got her hands in it, touching stuff, turning things over. She unfolds a paper with writing on.

This here's your Uncle, she says.

Now I know she's lost the plot because I haven't got an Uncle, not a real one. Not even a pretend one. Anyone tells you to call them Uncle you tell me about it, Mam used to say.

I mustn't look sure because Nan raises her eyebrows as if she knows something I don't, hands me the paper and I look at it.

It's typed, like a proper notice of something.

27th January 1979. Baby Robertson. Stillbirth. Male foetus. Full-term vaginal delivery. 7.8 lbs. Then some words I don't understand.

I look at Nan. Male what?

I was a babba meself, she says. Hadn't a clue what was going on.

I still don't get it. What does full-term mean?

It means he was alright inside me, she says, Then he just came out dead. No reason.

You had a baby before Mam and it just came out dead?

She nods.

What did it look like?

Don't know, I never saw him, says Nan.

What, not even at the funeral?

She shakes her head slowly. They just took him away, no funeral, no nothing. Not even a name.

She smooths out the paper.

Now I know the pop's gone to her head, just like Donna always said it would, because Rosie Shadbolt had a baby brother Cam who came out dead last year on account of coming too soon, but there's pictures of him in the living room. Even Rosie got to see him, and Mam and Donna went to the funeral. And Rosie and her Mam have a cake every year now, on his birthday, like he's a proper person.

I shake me head. No funeral? Don't be daft. Where's he buried then?

I don't know, she says.

He must be somewhere, Nan? Think.

She looks at the paper. They didn't keep tabs love, back then. I tried to find him after but they just said he would have been put in with someone else, underneath like, without telling anyone. So there's no way of knowing.

Why though, Nan? Did he come too soon through the drink?

Nan looks straight at me, and if I didn't know she'd already had two tinnies and a chaser I'd swear she'd gone stone cold sober. You listen here, she says, I never touched a drink back then.

Then she strokes the paper, folds it back up, pops open another can. Too many questions missy.

After that we sit on the bed for ages and she shows me paper pictures, most of them blurry and creased, but you can make out Nan with her hair all done nice, holding Mam when she was a baby and smiling. Oh, says Nan, she was always a bonny one.

There's one of a tall man with trousers all wide at the bottom and a kind of sleeveless knitted top, leaning on a weird-looking car. That's your Granda, she says. Car-mad, he was.

At the bottom of the box there's a little tiny see-through plastic bracelet.

What's that for?

Turn it over, she says, and you'll see.

I turn it over and there's writing inside. Baby Robertson, St Mary's Hospital.

It was your Mam's, that, when she was born. I saved it, she says. Then she picks up the bracelet, starts to cry. Pass me over that halfy, she says.

I root around in the carrier bag, find the half-bottle of voddy, pass it over. Then she's going through all the pictures again, humming, *Daaah da dah dah pahrumpah pum pum*, over and over, under her breath.

I sneak the picture of Mam in the white dress at her Holy Communion, put it under me pillow face-up, snuggle down so there's only the pillow between us, cheek to cheek. Then Nan looks up, looks round the room, nods. We'll have to get everything sorted, she says, kind of vacant.

She must mean the mess.

Don't fret Nana, go to sleep. I'll do the tidying tomorrow, I say.

20

By the time I get over to Warrington it's half-eleven. Jilly's is packed and I have to fight my way to the bar.

Mel and Jen are already there with a message from Lise. Aurora's gone missing, says Mel.

I feel my stomach hit the deck. Have they tried her nan's?

They haven't. Relief washes over me. It's OK, she'll be there, then, I say. Tell Lise to kick the door in if they have to. I'm gonna swing for Marie.

I check out the bar. Nothing out of place. Deena behind the taps serving, girls from Crewe at the back table, rowdy, laughing. Harj wrestling with some babe on her knee. She gives me a nod and I nod back, keep one eye on the door.

We go over to the back, to the leather settees raised up on the plinth, three girls drinking champagne, giggling, one with a dark bob, cute, in a white leather mini.

We turf them off. They pick up the bottle, move away.

I sit down. Jen and Mel opposite, across the coffee table. The Crewe girls pull up their stools.

I only let my guard down for a second and someone pulls at me from behind, puts a hand over my eyes. I grab the hair, pull down, hard. Someone comes flying over my shoulder, hits the coffee table smack in the middle, crashes on to the floor. Then I've got my knee on her throat, glass everywhere.

In the corner of my eye the Crewe girls are on their feet, ready to party.

It's Bambi so I let go.

Jee-sus Donna, she says, picking herself up, brushing the glass off her vest. I've missed you too hon.

Now me and Bambi got history, but not the sort you talk about and that's all I'm saying. All you need to know is she can be trusted, no matter what, and there's insurance on that.

I've got some bother, I says, by way of apology.

She sits down beside me, looks around, looks back at me, brows raised.

No, they're all cool, I tell her.

When everyone's sitting down again we get back on it, and I bring things back round to the boys.

It's not just Fats and Mad Daz any more, I tell them, Tony must be in on it, has been since the get-go. Want to get rid of us permanent, divide our patch up between them.

So first we need to roll him, I say, but it's got to look legit. A proper deal, something he'd kill for. Get him out somewhere to do the pick-up, and then we'll be waiting. But it won't work if he thinks it's coming from me. And don't think he won't check it out, I tell them. He's a paranoid twat at the best of times.

I'll get Izzie and the girls up in Morecambe to set it up, says Jen. Got a direct line to the south, they bring everything over at Jerez, then via Paris to San Sebastian where we pick it up. Float it up to Bindle Cove in the north, back down the M6. Route's sound, never been rumbled yet, Tony will know that.

Sounds too easy, says Sonn.

It's got to sound like a big shipment, I say, make it worth his while.

Mel pipes up about the new stun-guns. Pick them up in Bangkok market, a ton each, no questions asked, she says.

Gonna put the life sentence out of business for armed robbery, Jen says. Well smart.

Or Skorpions, says Mel, worth their weight in gold, cheaper to run than a Mac and only one or two getting through since the Brummies shut down the link; everyone's desperate. She shrugs. Even if the stun gun catches on for armed robbery, we're still gonna have to smoke someone now and again, aren't we?

Can't argue with that.

Leave it to Izzie, says Mel. She can think up a package that'll bear up if he checks.

Still leaves Fats and Daz, says Mel.

When you've got two armies coming at you from both sides, you got to think things through careful. No point doing more work than you have to, taking something head-on when you could slip round the side. You have to think about what they've got in common, and, more to the point, what they haven't.

I got an idea, I say, but it's a long shot. The Darts and the Cheetahs both want us gone, I say, but they won't trust each other completely, that's for sure.

So we turn them against each other, says Sonn.

Then they'll be too busy with each other to work out what we're doing? says Mel.

I drain the rest of my Coke. What do you think Tony would do if he thought Mad Daz had double-crossed him?

Everyone laughs.

Then we can let Tony take care of the Cheetahs, says Mel.

And vice versa, says Sonn.

Now you're talking, I say, if we're still alive by then.

Another couple of hours and we've got a plan.

You've all got your jobs, let me know when it's sorted, I says. Now get me a drink.

Jen comes back with a jug of margaritas and a couple of stray women in tow.

Suzy wants to meet you. She says it Sooozeee like a kiss. Then she smiles, as if she's offering me something sweet.

Suzy comes over. Painted red mouth, a perfect bow, Jessie J. on acid. Any other time I might have played along, but I haven't the heart for it tonight. I guess the stress must just be getting to me. I manage to say hello, just so's I don't offend anyone, but they can tell my mind's not on it. After a while Suzy shrugs, whispers something to Jen, wanders off.

Another round of drinks. The sweet salt of the margarita makes me think of Carla, how she said one day we'd drive down through Mexico in the back of a pick-up drinking tequila gold, watching the dust billow up from the wheels, sun low like a blood-orange over the dunes. God knows what film she saw that in.

Mel holds out a Benson's, You staying over?

I get a grip. Hell yes, let's drink to the plan. And I reach for the jug.

By three a.m. we're on the third jug of margaritas and Deena has got the tequila shots lined up on the bar. Suzy turns up right next to me, and somehow she looks a lot better than she did before, or maybe she's just got closer. Whatever.

I watch her lips move, red bow flexing in and out, smile even though I can't hear a word over the music. I hold up the shot, nod over at Mel, *Here's to oblivion.*

Mel looks a bit worried so I grin. *Theirs, chickadee, not ours.*

I wake up at nine, head banging shoulder throbbing mouth like the bottom of a ferret's cage, Suzy doing a reasonable impression of a death-rattle down my ear. I hear someone banging around downstairs in a kitchen.

I pull my good arm out from underneath, roll over to the edge of the bed, and wait for the dizziness to pass, stand up. I sit down again quick, think I've pulled a muscle in my leg.

Carla grins. *Less acrobatics, more loving,* she says.

I go over to the window, pull back the nets, look out. The glass mists up with my breath, ghostly. I wipe it away with my fist.

From the window I can see across the yards and down the ginnel, into the terraces backed up on the next street. Across the ginnel there's a house with boards on the windows, steel mesh on the door where the council have secured it. Someone's taken a spray can to the bottom boards. A big heart, Trafalgar red, *Fuck Love* written right across it.

Across the back yards, grey snow clings on to the roof of a shed, in between the barbed wire and glass shards on the tops of the walls.

Then something catches my eye at a bedroom window three down, little soldier in Batman underpants, hardly even school age, standing right up on the windowsill, watching me. One slip and he'll be through that window, down into the yard. I wonder where his mam is, whether he's got one. He gives me the finger.

Behind me, I hear Suzy turn over.

I drop the net down, reach out for my clothes. Time to get going.

21

I kick the bike into action, head back out on the A57.

My arm feels strange, pins and needles in my hand, and this travelling around is going to get me noticed soon, I reckon. It won't be long before someone spots me over at Jilly's or round Warrington way, reports it back to Tony or Daz.

People don't look for things right under their nose, Dad used to say. The closer you are to something the less you can see it, and the first place you come to is the last place you'd look, and by the time I get to Mina's I reckon I've got it.

I let myself into the yard from the alley. Mina's in the kitchen when I get there, and I whistle low, just to let her know it's me, it's OK. She opens the back door and lets me in, locks the door up behind me.

She gives me a hug and her hair smells warm and light, lemony. Takes me by surprise once I'm in there, how safe I feel.

Hey, you're sweating, she says.

I push her away, more rough than I mean to, sit down at the table.

I tell her most of it, apart from the Suzy thing, which was nothing and even if it was something it's none of her business. Don't want to risk hurting her either, on account of how pain has a way of clouding people's judgement.

I'm going to move into the lock-up, in the cellar, I say. That way I'll be close, can keep an eye on everything.

Good idea, she says. They'll never expect it.

I tell her I'll leave the Ducati here, in the back shed, bury it under some old boxes she kept from the move. Then she'll spread it about that I've taken off on Carla's new bike. Just the thought of those shitheads running round chasing their own tails looking for a brand new red Ducati with CAR 1 on the reg makes me smile.

After a while I tell Mina about Kim, don't really know why, make her swear to keep it secret. She nods, and, even though I can see the pain dull in her eyes, I feel sorry for her, she says.

I'm feeling weird now, sweaty and cold all at once, must be getting the bastard flu.

Mina tells me to take my jacket off, gets me a clean sweatshirt, asks me if I want a can.

Got whisky? Painkillers?

I put the kettle on. Mina goes upstairs, brings down a blister-pack of codeine, pushes two out on to my hand. Put the rest in your pocket, she says, I can always get more. She brings a half-bottle of Grouse out from under the sink.

I fill the mug halfway with whisky, top it up with hot water, put three sugars in to take away the taste, take the codeine. I need to lie down for a bit, I say.

Upstairs and the pain is a dull throbbing now, but the sweats are still coming. In the bathroom I look in the mirror, see my face pasty and grey. I lift my arms to take my T-shirt off and go dizzy, the room spinning. Shouldn't have taken codeine and whisky together on an empty stomach, I guess. Either that or the flu's got a proper hold.

I grab the sink, twist round so I can see. In the reflection the skin around the bandage on my shoulder is red, tight and shiny, looks swollen.

I press on the bandage and the pain's hard and hot, makes me want to spew. I try to remember where I'm supposed to be going next, who I'm seeing, but everything's gone dark at the edges somehow, sticky, as if I can't get my breath.

Next thing someone's pushing at my feet and I hear Mina's voice. I realise it's the bathroom door pushing against me and I'm jammed face-down between the toilet pan and the sink, feet against the door. The pain I thought was in my shoulder has moved up to my head only ten times worse.

I bend my knees, pull my feet away from the door then Mina's leaning over me, Christ, Donna, what have you done?

I grab hold of the sink, pull myself standing. One side of my head feels like someone's done me with a machete.

Shit, I dunno, I say.

Mina pushes my hair back. You must have hit your head on the way down, girl, that's gonna be a shiner.

I look into the mirror and already my left eye is barely open, huge egg coming up over the eyebrow. I press my cheekbone gently and feel a stab of pain.

I shake my head. Fainted. Then knocked myself out on the bog. What a twat.

I hear this noise, halfway between a cat that's been stepped on and a snort.

I look at Mina and her eyes are bright, shoulders shaking. I put one hand up, hold my face. Fuck, don't make me laugh, it hurts, I says.

Then we're off, me clinging on to my face and the sink for support, her with her legs crossed, fist jammed in between her legs, giggling like a couple of kids at a fart competition. All we need are the matches.

Afterwards things calm down, she helps me and we sit down on the bed. Help me get the sweatshirt on, I says. I can't stay here.

I feel tired all of a sudden, lie back on the bed feet still on the floor. She lies back beside me, takes hold of my hand and we stare at the ceiling. You alright? she says.

Half an hour later she's back with the van, parks it in the ginnel, helps me up into the back. The codeine must be working, and apart from my face I feel almost normal.

Thank the Goddess for tinted windows, she says.

Fuck that, I say. I tinted them myself. What's the Goddess got to do with it?

Then we're off laughing again and she's shaking so hard she has to put the blankets down, and if anyone came round that corner now we'd be dead meat.

Once we're in the lock-up, Mina opens the van doors, helps me out, starts to unload the boxes. I go over and open the hatch, swing the ladder out with my good hand. We use the pulley, lower the boxes down.

Inside the shelter it's cold and still. I unpack the camping stove, put it on the ammunition box, roll out the sleeping bag on to the stone shelf.

You can't sleep on that, goes Mina, you'll do yourself a mischief, it's too hard.

She's right.

Come over here then, I say, take my mind off it.

22

I wake up early, listen to Nan snoring for a bit. I get up, get dressed, take the pots to the kitchen, get Nan's purse from the drawer. Empty except for a piece of ribbon and two bus tickets.

I go back through and sit on the bed.

Wake up Nan.

Nan opens her eyes, all bleary. Alright love? What's up? What's the time?

It's nine o'clock, time to get up.

Christ Almighty that's the middle of the friggin' night, she says.

Go and get your money Nan, we need shopping.

Shopping? She pushes herself up on her elbow. I can see the sticky bits in between her eyelashes. Shouldn't you be at school?

I'm not going to school no more, I'm in hiding, I tell her.

In hiding? What's that when it's got its keks on? snorts Nan.

Get up Nan, I say, I'll run you a bath.

I go into the bathroom, turn the taps on, look round for some bubble bath but there isn't any. I go into the kitchen, get the washing-up liquid, apple and raspberry leaf, sniff it.

Smells nice. I squirt a load into the bath, watch the bubbles foam up like magic. I go through to the living room, put the fire on. Then Nan shouts from the bathroom, Where d'ya find the bubble bath then? Lovely!

Back in the bedroom I pick up the clothes from around the floor, get Nan a clean pair of jeans and a sweatshirt out of the pile by the wardrobe where Mam folded them all nice, ready to wear. Nan hasn't been near them in a week judging by the whiff of her this morning. I put the clean clothes out on the bed, check the sheet. Dry.

I sniff me own sleeve in case. I've only got one lot of clothes here and if I don't want to smell like Nan I'll have to wash them. I take everything off, put on one of her clean T-shirts, then a cardy on top, comes right down to me knees.

I pile all the dirty clothes in the washer, look around for the soap powder. I check the cupboards but there's not much of anything really, except The Complan. I get the washing-up liquid, squirt some into the tray, turn it on.

Back in the living room, I tuck me feet under the hem of the T to warm up, make a list for Nan.

Mister Muscle
Bleach
Washing powder (get the cheapest)
Meter tokens
Bread
Milk
Tea
Eggs
Sausages

I think about it for a bit, then write Chocolate Biscuits, but last in case the money runs out. Then I scrub it off again, seeing how it's selfish when only one of us likes them.

When Nan's gone to the shops, I tidy the kitchen, wipe the tops down, do all the stuff Mam would have done. Through the back window I can see into the yard. Mrs Watson's stripy cat jumps down from the wall to the windowsill, light as a feather, looks in through the window straight at me. Her eyes are browny-yellow and soft, make me think of Sappho.

The washer smells nice. I look over and me heart nearly stops.

The window on the front is pure white with foam, no clothes to be seen, long trail of foam coming out of the little place where the tray fits in, dropping down in big glops to the floor. I take the tea-towel over, wipe it away, but it just keeps on coming.

I pull the plug out, stand back, look at it. Nothing for it, I'll have to do them in the sink. I open the front and water and foam pours out, all over me feet, all over the floor. I can't believe there's so much of it when I only put a tiny squeeze in. There should be warnings for that.

I drag the clothes over to the sink, wet running down me arms, squishing through me toes, run through for a towel to soak up the water from the carpet. By the time I've finished, I'm soaked.

I'm still mopping up when I hear Nan's key in the door, so I go through to the living room to tell her about the washer before she walks in and sees it. She's standing in the doorway with her carrier bags. Beside her the two Micra women and a man in a police uniform, radio crackling.

Oh Nan, I goes, what have you done?

Sorry hen, they was waitin' on me, she says.

The Micra women are looking straight at me and I don't know what I look like, standing there in Nan's T and her old cardy, dripping wet, feet all bare.

I think we'd better sit down, says The Fat One, and she looks over at Nan. What about a cup of tea, Mrs Robertson, while we sort this all out?

Nan goes into the kitchen to make the tea and I close me eyes, wait for her to shout when she sees the washer and the wet clothes piled up in the sink and the water all over, but she doesn't make a sound. I can hear her fill the kettle.

The Micra women look at me. The Old One's got grey hair cut short and at first I think she must be well older than Nan, but the skin on her face is smooth and pink, looks soft, so maybe she's not. She's got a square leather bag like a briefcase, puts it down by her feet. Lace-up shoes, shiny, neat. The other one's young like Mam but a real chubber, nervy, eyes everywhere at once. Got a nasty look about her somehow.

The Fat One gets up, follows Nan into the kitchen. Now I'm done for.

I look at The Old One and smile. She looks at me, smiles back. You're wet, love. Do you want to get dressed?

I can hardly tell her I haven't got any clothes because I've gone to wash them and messed it all up, can I? I'm alright thanks, I say.

The Old One says her name is Christine. I nod, but you can't get me that easy. That's the oldest trick in the book, Donna says, acting friendly, telling someone your name so they'll tell you theirs without thinking about it. I press me lips hard together, so nothing slips out. She asks me a couple more things but I don't answer and in the end she goes quiet, looks around the room, writes some things in a notebook.

Nan comes back in with Fatso, who wants to see the bedroom.

Nan looks at her, What for?

Then it all comes out. I've not been to school and Nan's encouraging me, The Christine One says. She looks straight at me. Look, she's not even dressed. What did you have for breakfast? she asks me.

I think about the best breakfast I've ever had. It was that time I went to Blackpool with Nan and Mam and Harry who doesn't live at Nan's any more. Stayed overnight in someone's house and the lady who owned it had little hairs in her chin and there were fat pink towels but Nan made us use the one she brought so we didn't spoil nothing.

Sausage eggs and bacon, tea and toast, I says. I don't say the orange juice in case it sounds like too much.

There's no food in, only alcohol, says Fatso, smug, I've looked in the cupboards.

My heart's pounding. Show them what you got today Nan, I says, the sausages and that. Then Nan can't look at me and I get this feeling in me belly like a stone.

I go into the kitchen. The carrier bag from this morning is on the table. In the bag there's a new six-pack of Stella, half a bottle of vodka, twenty Bensons and a Twix. Not even any milk.

I'm afraid you can't stay here, Aurora, says The Christine One. You need to get your things together now, and we'll take you where you'll be safe.

I'm safe here, I says. Nan must've lost the list. Did you lose the list, Nan? It's OK, just tell them.

Nan just looks at them, starts to cry. Don't take my baby, I won't let you.

I go over and stand in front of Nan. I'm going nowhere, she needs me, I say.

Christine nods at The Police One and he stands up, gets a paper out of his top pocket and reads off it. Something about an order, Police Protection. He looks over at Nan. I'm afraid Aurora will have to come with us. It'll be better for her if there's no fuss.

Now I reckon it's time to stop playing dumb, start talking.

No thanks, I'll stay here with Nan. Look, I can even go to school if you want. Nan can look after me no problem. Can't you Nan?

Nan's doing those big heaving sobs, but she nods.

I don't want to go back to Geeta's, I say, I don't like it there. I like it here.

Everything starts moving mega-fast after that. The Christine One gets the blanket off Nan's chair, wraps it round like a coat, tells me to put some shoes on. Nan starts screaming, goes to lamp Fatso, then The Police One gets her down on the floor. That's it for me, and I jump on his back.

I can feel hands all over me. I kick out, catch someone's leg.

Next thing, Fatso gets hold of me, drags me off and we're out on the pavement, me still kicking for England.

Behind me I can hear Nan screaming and see Mrs Watson looking out from her front door across the road. I try to shout, Don't worry Nan, I'll phone you from Geeta's, but it comes out like a croak and I don't know whether she heard me or not. Then they put me in the back of the police car with Fatso, drive me away.

In the car, Fatso puts her hand on me arm, starts to say something. I put me mouth on her hand and bite down as hard as I can. She screams out but I hang on. She goes to punch me away, catches me on the side of the head and I let go. Hurts but it's worth it. I can see the red tooth-marks in two long curvy lines on the back of her hand. It'll bruise, that.

We get to the big offices on Sardinia Street, underground into the car park, and Christine pulls in beside us in the Micra. I grab on to the seatbelt, refuse to get out.

OK, tell Geet's Dad to come and get me, I says.

Fatso's got a proper evil glint in her eyes now, still rubbing her hand. She stands back, lets The Police One prise me fingers off the belt, yank me out the door. You won't be going back to Geeta's, she says, smug.

Upstairs Christine puts me in a chair beside a desk. Do you want some water, love?

My head's still throbbing where Fatso punched it. I suck me teeth at her.

She smiles, takes me by surprise. That's clever. Where did you learn to do that?

It won't be long till Geet's Dad comes to get me, and then you'll be sorry, I says.

Fatso comes back in and sits down and they look at each other then look at me.

Listen to me, Aurora, says The Christine One, We're going to have to find you another place to stay. You can't go back to stay with Geeta.

I feel like I'm going to be sick, heart thumping in me chest. I didn't mean it, I say, double-quick. When I said I don't like it. It's OK there, honest.

I'm sorry love but we think you'll run away again if you stay there. We can't risk it.

Run away? Since when was going to your Nan's running away? Going to your Nan's when nobody wants you and she's the only one that misses Mam as much as you do isn't running away. But now I know I was right first time, I should have kept shtum.

You can all fuck off then, I says.

I sit there for hours while they phone round, saying all sorts of stuff to people I don't even know. No, OK then, no problem. Yes, it needs to be out of the area. No. Well thanks anyway.

After a while a woman comes in with a sandwich, ham and pickle, a packet of crisps, Smoky Bacon, a can of Lilt. I can't eat in case it's poisoned.

I come over all tired. I go over and lie down in the corner by the toy box, pull Nan's blanket over me, close me eyes. Then I remember me feet and how they're all dirty underneath on account of having no shoes on. I tuck them up under Nan's rug in case they think I'm a minger.

I close me eyes, think about Mam, how soft her face is when she goes to kiss me goodnight. I try to see it, her face, but I can't see the whole thing, only tiny bits at a time, and the more I try, the more I just can't. Then I get the smell of her as if she's right there, and it makes me eyes prick.

I wake up numb, stiff all down one arm where I've lain on it. Christine is leaning over me, moves back when I open me eyes. I sit up.

She points to a pile of scuzzy clothes on the chair. What size are you? she says, looking at me feet.

She tells me to put the clothes on, goes out of the room, comes back in and picks up her handbag, goes out again.

I wonder where they get the clothes. They smell old, like the smell in the Macmillan shop on the High Street, the one that Mam used to go in just in case there was any good stuff. Dead people's stuff, Donna says.

Maybe they brought some other kid in here and she died of the shock and now I'll be wearing her clothes. Maybe she ate the poisoned sandwich and died from that.

The trackies come right down over me ankles so I have to bunch them up. I pick up the T-shirt, all bobbly, disgusting. I can't be putting on some dead kid's T-shirt so I leave it folded up on the chair, put on the sweatshirt being how it probably hasn't touched the dead kid's skin. I put the socks on last, thick and blue, scratchy.

Then I sit back down on the chair, and wait.

Christine comes back in, holding a pair of black trainers, Gola, gross. I'll have to put them on and just pray nobody sees me.

We'll get you some clothes of your own when you're settled, she says, hands me a scabby puffa.

In the Micra I have to go in the back like a kid beside Fatso, even though there's no one in the front seat. We drive down the parkway and on to the motorway, take the M61. A sign says Stockport. There's a bus goes from the Arndale that says Stockport. Just when I'm thinking about jumping out, a lorry passes on the inside lane, spraying water up everywhere. I'd better wait a bit.

It's nearly dark now and we're heading up towards the

Sale road, The Christine One driving. Donna took me all the way to Sale once, watch that posh mate of hers play rugby in the freezing cold, ice on the mud. Afterwards we went in the changing rooms, looking for her, and I saw everyone's bits and bobs.

I sneak a look at the door, check the button under the window. Full-out. What kind of person doesn't even put the child locks on?

Beside me Fatso's got her phone out, texting, not paying any attention. She's lucky she's still got a phone, being how they took mine right off me, which is stealing. She doesn't notice me undo me seatbelt. Loser.

I see the traffic lights up ahead, green, start praying. Go on, go on, go on.

The lights go to red and me heart starts thumping. Seems it takes ages for us to reach the truck in front, slow down, come to a stop.

I can hardly breathe. There's cars right up against us everywhere, just waiting to run you down if you jump out. I take a deep breath. Faint heart never won fair lady, Donna says, and once I asked her what it meant. It means don't ever be a yellow-belly, she said, giving me a cuff and smiling over at Mam, it's Deeply Unattractive.

I take a deep breath, pull on the handle, kick the door and I'm out, dodging through the cars across the lanes, out on the other side. Then I run.

Donna woulda been proud.

23

We sneak over the railway sidings until we're behind the Darts lock-up, squat down.

Izzie puts plugs in the earphones, hands me one plug, bangs in the numbers.

Someone picks up.

Hey, says Izzie, into the phone, it's me again.

Tony answers. Yeah hi, so what you got?

Izzie winks at me. Two dozen boxes of fireworks, she says. Twenty sparklers, two rockets you can have. Throw in thirty bangers as well, she says, if you want them. All sound.

Silence.

There's a noise in the background, like a door shutting. Hang on a bit, says Tony. Then I can hear another voice, sounds like Danny but I can't be sure.

Hey, it's your call, says Izzie. Got someone else interested round your way if you've changed your mind.

Tony's voice is icebox. Like who? Bingo.

You know how it is, Izzie says, can't really say. But this someone reckons there's gonna be a massive bonty round your way soon, sounds like there might be some trouble.

And I'm not the only one he's been to. Don't sweat it though, I told him mine were spoken for.

A grand says he's got a name.

Izzie sucks her teeth. No names. Let's just say you know each other. Two grand says I know where he lives. Now do you want this stuff, or not?

You could hear a pin drop.

Yeah, two grand for the address, he says, it's a deal.

Sweet, says Izzie. I'll let you know where and when in a couple of days. Cash on delivery. Price stays the same. Happy Bonfire Night.

The address, says Tony.

Oh yeah, says Izz. And then she gives him Daz's address.

After she rings off, we look at each other and she grins. Either we're gonna be very rich, or very dead, she says.

Me, I love a gamble, keeps everything interesting.

You've gotta be in it to win it, I say.

24

Just so everyone knows, I'm not scared.

By the time I get to the precinct it's late and there's no one around. Across the grass I can see the lights of the underpass. The doorways to the blocks are lit up, lights on in the windows. Outside there's just the street-lights shining down on the grass, making fuzzy pools through the sleet.

My foot feels like there's a blister coming on one heel where the trainers are rubbing, too big. I sit down in a doorway to have a look. There's a big patch of blood on the heel of the sock, a bit more seeping through on the baby toe. No point whingeing, so I put them back on.

I daren't go to Nan's or Geeta's, being how they'll be looking all over for me, try to catch me again. I go over to the underpass, see who's around.

There's no sign of Tools or Space, just some people I don't know, hanging loose on the corner beside a car, hoods up. I put me head down, walk past.

The one on a push-bike nods at me, Alright?

I put me head down. Piss-wet through and nowhere to go, do I look alright?

I don't say that, I'm not stupid, I just keep walking.

Another one shouts me, Hey kidder, where you off to? Fancy a ride?

I reckon now's about the time to run, so I do.

I take a short cut, slip on the grass bank on the way down. Underneath in the underpass there's the clap and splash of footsteps chasing, all echoey, then I realise they're mine.

At the other end of the underpass I slow down, lean on the wall to get me breath, see a squad car slow down outside on the road. I duck down behind the concrete bollard, wait for it to cruise past.

Just then I hear a push-bike behind me and some younger swerves right in front of me, nearly comes off. I stand up, get ready to run again, just in case.

He pushes back his hoody so now I can see the colours on his scarf. Darts, but you can never be sure from a scarf, Donna says.

His eyes are dark and still. You Carla's girl? Everyone's looking for you.

I'm so relieved I nearly show myself up and cry. Yeah, do you know where Donna is?

I'll take you, he says.

Now he's pushing the bike, walking beside me back up through the tunnel towards the precinct. I ask him, Where is she?

He looks up the underpass to his mates by the car, gives them a wave. Don't worry about anything, we'll take you there, he says.

My heel's proper smarting now. I have to jog to keep up, which makes the trainer rub even worse. I ask if he's got any plasters but I don't think he hears me.

At the car, I get in the back between the others.

The Bike One stays outside, leans in through the window, says, Got any plasters? He raises his eyebrows, nods over at me. She's bleeding, her foot.

Everyone laughs, and there's something about it makes me throat tight and me heart start to thump. Then the central locking clicks on.

I've changed me mind, I says, reaching for the door handle, I can walk.

The one next to me puts his arm across me like a seat belt, grabs me wrist.

Walk? You don't want to be doing that this time of night, love, he says. It's not safe.

I can hardly breathe, head pushed down between me knees, hand on me neck, holding me down. On the floor of the car there's an empty crisp packet, cheese and onion and a plastic sandwich wrapper, smell knocking me sick.

I try to count the corners but it's no good I keep losing count, and every time the car goes round another one I think I'm gonna throw up.

Ages later, we stop and they let me lift up me head, but before I can get a proper look round, someone puts a cloth thing over me head. Sweaty, feels like a T-shirt that needs a wash.

Then they're dragging me out of the car and I scrape me knee on the door. Whenever we get to Donna I'm gonna tell her how they scraped me, and she'll go mental. Then they'll be sorry.

Out of the car and then I'm tripping over because I can't see anything, feels like a kerb. One's got his arm tight round me neck, holding me against him, hand over the cloth across me mouth, stinks of Lynx.

Then one of me trainers comes off.

Leave it, a voice says.

Don't be stupid, says someone else.

Now it's smooth under me feet, like a path. I hear a door open in front, and then it's warm so we must be in. They push me up some stairs and then I think I'm on a landing because it feels like carpet.

Someone pushes me forward, hard, then lets me go, fast, and I nearly trip. I hear a door slam shut behind me and the scrape of a bolt going in, hear footsteps going back down the stairs. Then it's quiet.

I stand there for a bit, waiting.

Maybe it's a surprise, like on birthdays, and everyone'll be standing there when I take the cloth off, balloons and cake and everything. And if they are, I'll probably not grass The Lynx One up about the scraping thing.

I can hear voices downstairs.

I reach up for the cloth-thing, pull it off me face, look round. The room's nearly dark, just a smidge of light coming in between the curtains and some under the door.

I go back to the door and, try it, but it's locked, I can feel the bolts jiggling on the other side. I turn on the light switch and nothing happens.

I go over to the curtains, pull them open a bit. The moon's round and bright, scraps of shadow passing over it, must be clouds. The sky is inky and black, little stars scattered everywhere, winking.

There's some kind of mesh on the inside of the window, little holes in the wire, tiny triangles. I press me finger on one of the triangles and it comes away dented. Outside the snow in the back yard is melty and grey. Behind the yard is a rec. Across it I can see the back yards of the houses on the other side, far away, street-lights shining in pools on the snow.

Could be anywhere.

After a while I can see a bit better, moon coming in through the window. In the room there's a mattress on the floor. It's got sheets on and a Peter Pan duvet cover. Wendy laughing, flying, John in his top hat.

Beside the bed on the carpet, there's a colouring book and some crayons, kids' stuff. I go and touch the radiator. It's on, and even though there's nothing much in the room it feels like a proper house, just without all the furniture.

I need the toilet, so I bang on the door. No one comes.

I sit down on the mattress, take the trainer off. The other sock's wet where it's been in the snow, so I take that off too. I lie down on the mattress and pull Wendy up over me. It's not cold but I still can't stop shivering. Got into me bones, or whatever Nan says.

Whoever the toys belong to will probably be back soon, and they'll tell me what's going on I suppose. I try to think of Wendy flying away over the sky, holding on to John's hand, turning left at the star and straight on to Neverland, to cheer myself up. How she left everyone behind for Peter, even her Mam. Then I'm remembering how even when he shot her down with the arrow she still loved him. Mental.

Then it comes to me all at once. The Co-op. Me wishing the baby would be locked up in a shed just to get back at her Mam. Now I know why I'm here and it's all me own fault.

25

I wake up, sweaty. The sheet's wet where I've done it again.

I hear the door open a crack and someone creeps in, light from the hall behind them so I can't see them properly. I hold me breath. You're not supposed to sneak into a person's bedroom, The Wiz says, and anyone who does that is just Up To No Good. My heart's thumping so loud now it's like a drum going off.

I squeeze me eyes tight and in me head there's the Little Drummer Boy singing, *Daaah da dah dah, pahrumpah pum pum…*

You alright love? A woman's voice, floaty.

I feel a hand on me and I hold the sheets tighter, wiggle away.

Dah dah dah dadada, pahrumpah pum pum…

She puts something down beside the bed.

I'm Shantelle, she says. Be a good girl and you won't be here long, no one's gonna hurt you. She puts something down. If you want a wee, love, you'll have to use that.

After she's gone, I open me eyes. There's a can of Fanta beside the bed. In the corner is a red plastic washing-up bowl. She must be kidding.

I pick up the colouring book, open it. It's a baby's book really, and whoever lives here must be way younger than me. I wonder what the baby was in here for, whether they did something really bad, for a baby, and where they've gone now. How long they had to stay.

I look at Dumbo, remember the film me and Mam watched last Christmas, On Demand, him crying for his Mam and me getting all teary, even though back then I didn't know what it felt like for your Mam to be dead. Now I'm grown up I know that sad doesn't have to be crying, it can just be a big black hole in you and maybe crying would be better. I get it now, Dumbo.

I expect I'll have to stay here till I've been properly wronged, but I don't know how long that'll take, to be honest. I think of all the bad things I've done but there's too many and the first ones fall out of me head just when I push the last ones in and I have to start again. Then I realise, I don't even know what counts as a bad thing any more. How am I supposed to know, when they won't even let me go to Confession yet, and all the bad stuff built up for ten years is fit to burst?

I start off with an easy one, like lying to Mam about the tenner and Mr Lowski. I don't know whether to count it as bad though for telling lies, or good for not dropping Space right in it and maybe another good for Mam not having to worry. But then she went and worried about Mr Lowski anyway, so that bit might still count as a bad. Which leaves one good and two bad. By the end of it all, there's just one thing I done I can think of that's never had any good in it and it's wishing a babba would be locked in a shed. Father Tom says you Reap What You Sow unless you've been to Confession. Mam says it's probably rubbish, some things just come back and bite you on the bum, no way of knowing which ones, just luck, but best to go to Confession in case. Lise calls it Karma and you have to burn a joss stick. Donna says that's all the same mumbo-jumbo, just means you get what you deserve. Which must be how come I'm here.

Confession doesn't count unless you've been done. Now I'm wishing I had me Holy Communion Card, the one Father Tom writes in when I go to Communion class on a Sunday. Maybe if I had the card it wouldn't matter so much that I haven't been Done yet.

Still, Baby Jesus probably knows I'm here because Father Tom says Baby Jesus Can Always See You, however well you hide, so asking him for help has got to be worth a shot.

I take out a crayon. At the back of the colouring book there's a nearly-blank sheet, just a few little words at the bottom. I tear out the page.

Dear Baby Jesus,
I am sorry for wishing the babba got took to a shed.
Please let me go home.
Love Aurora Grace.

Grace is my Special Name, the one I'm getting from Father Tom on the Special Day, the one Baby Jesus probably knows me by already. It's a stupid name but it's way better than Magdalena, which is what some people get.

I fold up the paper, put it under the mattress. If Baby Jesus can see everything, seeing through some scuzzy old mattress should be no problem.

I hear footsteps down the stairs. The sound of metal scraping. Then the sound of a front door slamming and something heavy and metal scraping again. Then there's feet coming back up towards me. I race back to the bed, put me back against the wall.

The door opens. The woman comes towards me.

She walks weird, like she's got some kind of limp. I crouch down, back against the wall.

She stops. It's OK, she says. It's me, love, Shantelle. I'm not going to hurt you. Are you hungry?

I shake me head.

Do you want to come downstairs and watch some telly?

I nod.

She smiles at me, and I can see that she's pretty even if she has got a limp.

She walks to the door, turns round, ruffs me head. Come on then, she says.

I follow her down the stairs. The front door's bolted top and bottom, massive thick wedges of steel across the middle.

I follow her into the lounge. She checks the curtains, makes sure they're shut, points to the settee, Sit down there.

The TV's on but there's no sound.

She hands me the Sky remote. Can you work it?

I nod.

Go on then. Put whatever you like on.

She smiles and her eyes are nice. I've got *Crimewatch* on Sky Plus, if you fancy, she says.

I don't really fancy it tonight, being how me and Mam and Donna always watched it, how Mam used to shriek at the telly whenever some paedo or rapist came on. See that face, Ror, she'd say, pointing at some mugshot, now that's a Bastard. You watch out for the likes of him now.

Well she was wrong. If Lynx Boy had even a bit of a squint or gammy leg, or had greasy hair over his ears and bad teeth, I'd have recognised him as a Bastard straight off. Then I wouldn't be here now, I'd have run a mile.

She takes the remote off me, flicks through the channels. We could watch the re-runs of *Skins*? Have you seen that?

I have as it happens. Haven't you got anything with a decent story in it, I say.

In the end I choose *Law and Order USA*.

If he comes back you'll need to scoot upstairs fast, she says, or I'm in trouble.

I nod.

Later there's the sound of a car outside and Shantelle jumps up to the window. I head for the stairs.

No time, she says, pulling the settee out from the wall. Get behind here. Stay quiet. He's never in long.

I get between the settee and the wall, hear her go towards the door. Before she gets there I hear the key turn in the lock, the door open.

I recognise the voice straight away. Get us all a brew love, says Daz. Three sugars for Tony, that right mate?

I'm not stopping, says The Tony One, but I could go a biscuit.

Through the gap I see Shantelle go past towards the kitchen.

One sugar for Fats, Daz calls out. Sit down lads.

Someone heavy sits down on the settee so I nearly can't breathe. I squash the side of me face against the wall, bits of woodchip digging into me cheek, try not to panic.

The sound of the kettle.

You all set then? says Tony.

Sounds good to me mate, says Daz.

Better we should go in it together, split the cost and the delivery. Just you and Fats though. Don't want to go mob-handed, unsettle the natives when there's no need. I'll bring Danny.

Just me and Fats, says Daz, no sweat.

Sorry it's short notice. Can you come up with the cash?

No worries, says Daz, I can do the money.

There's a pause. I hear Shantelle come back in with the tea.

Go OK with the kid? says Tony.

I hold me breath. Dolly Dingers they mean me. My heart thumps in me ears and me chest hurts.

Shantelle sits down on the arm of the sofa, tucks her feet back across the gap in front of me. I look at her shoes. One sole is much thicker than the other, different shape like a boot. Must have a gammy.

Yeah no problem, says Daz. Safely tucked away up in Preston with Tiny's missus and his kids like you said, sound as a pound.

I feel sick.

Tell him to hold on to her, says The Tony One, we'll flush that bitch out in no time. You heard owt?

Nah. Got the lads on it though, says Daz. We'll find her.

All of a sudden the settee moves and I can breathe and there's room to move me head.

OK then I'm off, see you later, says Tony. Ta Shantelle for the biscuits. I'll take a couple with me, he says, ta-ra then.

I'm going to check the car out, make sure it's right for Sunday, says Daz. C'mon Fats.

I listen to the front door open and shut. Shantelle's face appears in the gap between the sofa and the wall. She looks scared.

Right missus, get up them stairs before he comes back.

What did they mean? I ask her. Flush who out?

Nothing for you to worry about. Go on up now, chop chop.

26

The first thing I see when I open my eyes is Sonn, sitting on the ammo box, silent, watching me. Lise is beside her. I push myself up on one elbow and the pain in my shoulder makes me wince, my head thick from a dream. I swing both legs over, start to pull on my boots, Fuck's sake, what's a girl got to do to get any sleep around here?

Lise looks away. Rio starts to slink into the corner, tail between his legs, a sure sign something's up.

What?

They've got Ror, says Sonn.

My guts do a twizz. Who have?

The Social. Won't let her go back to Geeta's. Won't even let them see her, Kaheesha says.

Rio's curled up, face to the wall, and he whimpers.

Shut that fucking dog up, Sonn. Where've they put her?

We've put the word out. Someone's gonna turn up something, says Sonn.

At least she'll be safe, says Lise.

Lise is the only one out of us who hasn't been in care, ever, and care's like a shit joke, you have to have been there to get it.

Me and Sonn just look at her. Safe? I say. In care? And what planet would that be on, Dorothy?

Find out where she is and go and see her, I tell them. Tell her to keep shtum, tell her we'll get her home.

How we gonna do that?

Everything tightens up in my chest, feels like it's going to explode. I throw my boot at the wall. What the fuck were you thinking, Lise? I told you to get her from Marie's.

Lise fills up like she's going to cry and that sends me right over the edge, being how I was only clinging on by my fingernails anyway. Get out of my sight before I twat you, I say.

When she's gone, I sit down. I shake my head, try to clear it. Decide I'm not taking any more of that stuff no matter how bad the pain gets.

Ease off her, says Sonn.

Keep an eye on her then, I say. And watch her with the merchandise for God's sake. Lise on a ski-trip, that's all we need.

Sonn reaches into her pocket, jangles a key in front of me, smiles. Locked it all up, she says.

Go and put the word out – everyone we know. I want to know where Ror is, I tell her.

Then she tells me how Jess, that bouncer in the Bluebird, owes her a favour. Her mam works day shift in rezzie over Miles Platting way.

She'll know someone who knows something, says Sonn.

I'm not so sure.

We need more people in the system, I say. Higher up, not just wiping arses in rezzie. It's not like you can just pay someone for information any more, not safe enough, needs to be tight. You want someone to shovel shit for you these days, you can't afford for them to bring their own spade.

We'd need the money to train them, she says.

Maybe if Jess comes through this time we could think about it but right now I can't think of anyone I hate enough to send on a social work course, so I drop it.

Don't tell me what we need, I say. Get out there and do something about it. I want Ror found, before anyone else finds her.

I start to pull on a vest.

You can't go out there, says Sonn. They'll be waiting.

I lift up the lid of the ammo box, grab a magazine of bullets and load the Glock, shove a spare magazine in my pocket.

Doesn't matter how much I blame Lise or Sonn, I know it's down to me this time. I should've been there, should've thought about it, made proper arrangements for Ror. But I didn't, did I? Just like no one did it for me, or for Carla. Things going right down the line on repeat whether we mean them to or not.

I head for the door. Out my fucking way Sonn, I say.

27

The first time I saw Carla she was in a headlock, face pressed sideways against the floor, fuckwit care worker with his knee in her back. Whoa-whoa! Lie still, lie still.

She tried to spit but the way he had her against that shitty brown carpet the spit couldn't go nowhere, just dribbled down the side of her mouth so she had to lie right in it. Didn't stop her trying though, and right then I knew I was going to like her.

Sounds harsh, but we were used to it back then. Once they'd got a grip they locked you in a room with no blankets, just a mattress on the floor, left you there till they felt calm, which could be never, or at least no time soon. The time to look out was at the end of a double weekend shift and we all knew it; used to take bets on who would get it this time. Don't ask me what they thought they were achieving.

Anyhow, there she is face-down on the carpet, eyes flashing, kicking and spitting, wriggling like a ferret to get free. Herpes-Head-the-Ball was cursing and trying to keep a hold, shouting over his shoulder for some help from the office, rest of us sitting right there on the stairs watching the show. Even then, there was something about her, that made me want to get near, kick that fat bastard right on his back, help her up. I can still see her throwing her head back, trying to nut him, long curls of her hair bouncing so thick and dark I couldn't take my eyes off it.

By now I'm sitting on the bottom stair, ten or more kids behind me ringside chanting, Kick him, kick him, kick him. Her trying, him dancing about to make her miss.

Then he half stood up behind her, jerked her up by the neck to her feet, head bent right back, choking the living day out of her.

All of a sudden she wasn't spitting any more, more like spluttering, and I saw her eyes roll up wide, lips peeling back, legs right off the ground and kicking the air.

So I jumped on his back.

Then I'm holding on round his neck with one arm, fingers reaching up for his eyes, punching in at his ear from behind with my free hand, hard as I could, legs wrapped round his waist so I didn't fall. I reckon it was only the shock made him let go, probably the only thing that saved him losing an eye, or worse. Carla fell forward on to her knees and he threw himself backwards, me still hanging on. I never even saw the wall coming till I was knocked nearly senseless, sliding down to the floor, wondering what the fuck just happened, ton weight on my chest. I tried to breathe in but nothing happened. Just then I felt a hand grab my shoulder, pull me upright just as I sucked in the best breath ever.

C'mon, she said, let's just go.

We're sodden by the time we got to the canal. Under the bridge and I crouch down beside her, both laughing, steam coming off our breath, snorting like wild horses into the cold dark night.

She bunks down, turns to look at me.

It was her eyes got me first, warm treacle toffee shot right through with gold in the lights. Like the stone Dad brought me back from a trip. Tiger's eye, he said, turning it over in his fingers. You ever seen anything more beautiful?

And, until the day I met Carla, I hadn't.

I must have been staring, thinking about the tiger's eye and Dad, getting all caught up in it, because she smiled at me then and her top lip went way up, showed all her teeth at the front, lazy like a snarl, but sexy as. One tooth at the side a tiny bit crooked, always went on about getting it straightened if she'd had the money, but to my mind it just made the rest look more perfect. You know the way those things can be.

I can see that face now, creamy skin splashed with black freckles so cute you'd try to count them. Something flashing across the darkening space in between us, pulling me home.

Hey let's go to Blackpool, see the lights then, she says.

I look at her, Don't be mad. How we gonna get there?

Then that smile. I swear, in all the time we were together, *how* meant nothing to Carla.

You'll think of something, she said.

And that's the way it's been ever since, I suppose. Her wanting stuff, or wanting rid of stuff, me working out how to do it. Me getting it done. Only this one might be too much, Car, even for me.

There's no way I know of getting a kid out of care once they're in. Once people in their offices got their minds made up, no use fighting. Hit out and they'll just tie you up in your own punches, use your own weight against you and the harder you come at them, the harder you'll fall. The Social got their own story for things, and once it's planned out everything you say gets caught right up in it, feeds in, until it's set round you like concrete, no room to manoeuvre. Can make you want to top yourself, that, Dad used to say.

I wind up on the step outside Geeta's. Sometimes I fucking hate myself, I'm so transparent. That's not one of mine, it's what Carla always used to call me, when she saw me crank up the gears for a cruise. Said she always knew when I was on to someone. There was me, thinking I was being all complicated and meaningful and shit. Transparent?

Means see-through, she said.

Whatever.

Kaheesha answers the door. I see her shape through the stained glass and my heart starts to pound. What the fuck will I say? Then she opens the door, sees me and her face flushes pink. I was right, it's just a matter of time.

She leads me down the hall past a table with curly legs and a mirror above it, a chair beside the table that looks too low for anyone to sit on. On one side of the mirror there's a line-up of photos in dark wooden frames.

Everything's wood. Not the cheap stuff, but smooth and dark and shiny, makes you want to run your fingers along it.

I follow her down the corridor, past two other doors that are shut. The wooden floors are polished, catch the light through the stained glass of the door.

At the bottom of the hall she pushes open another door and then everything's light. Across a huge room where the end wall should be there's just glass, right from one side of the room to the other; I can see across a patio to the lawn and some trees at the bottom of the garden, smart orange and blue climbing frame in the corner. Out in the middle of the lawn there's a statue, three half-dressed women holding up a concrete bowl for the birds. Makes me think of Tony and his disappearing baby-mama propping up the underpass. Fancy having something like that in your garden.

She opens the fridge, big as a shed, gets the milk out. Puts two mugs down on the breakfast bar. Coffee?

I pull a stool up, sit down. She scoops up some papers from the worktop, shuffles them together, puts them on one side. Just work, she says. I nod and look around.

The room is one massive L-shape, kitchen at one end, sofa and chairs and bookshelves at the other, huge table with candles by the window looking out over the garden. You could get the Sale women's rugby team round that table.

I've told them we'll have her here with us, she says, her back to me, reaching into a cupboard. For ever if necessary. I'm sure they'll come round.

I nod. She's not used to things being hopeless, I can tell.

I watch her sift coffee out of a bag and into a cafetière without using a spoon. She holds the glass jug up to the light checking the measure. Her eyes catch the light from the window.

Are they green?

She's pouring the water from the kettle now, into the jug. Sorry?

Your eyes. I mean, it's unusual, isn't it?

I'm stumbling around like an idiot. Can't believe what just came out of my mouth. Totally losing my touch.

She laughs, not loud but a short kind of humph. For somebody with brown skin, you mean?

I watch her carefully and shrug, I suppose so.

Actually, it's not that unusual where my family come from. My grandparents came from the north of Pakistan, borders of Afghanistan. But don't fret, you're not the first person to ask.

Is that where Sanjay comes from? I keep my voice level as I say his name.

She smiles. We're both English, both born here. San's family is Indian, comes from Karachi originally. We met at uni in London, moved up here for San's job.

I like the way she says uni, not university or college. How long have you been married? I say.

We're not married. She smiles at me. Anything else you want to know?

I'm not sure I heard right. You're not married?

It's complicated, different religions. Anyway, we don't need to be married.

I've never heard anyone talk like that and I'm not sure how to handle it. I feel out of my depth. If he loved her he'd have married her wouldn't he? Chrissakes, *I'd* fucking marry her and that's got to be a first.

You could have got married in a registry office like everyone else, I say, watching her face.

She laughs properly now, out loud.

It doesn't mean anything if you don't believe in it, does it? she says. I mean, I can see the point if you believe in God, if you want a Christian marriage, or a Muslim or Hindu or Sikh one. Or a registry office if you just want to be owned. But what's the point otherwise? It doesn't make people love each other more.

I never really thought about it like that, never wondered what the point was, or whether there was one. Then I realise there might be someone knows more than me. Then I'm thinking what the fuck, I'd deffo want to own her, and if she's not really married I might be in with a chance.

You don't believe in God?

Let's just say I'm not convinced about the merits of organised religion.

I just love the sound of that, whatever it means. Come to think of it I love the sound of it all. I think about leaning across the breakfast bar and kissing her smack on the mouth, bottle it, stir my coffee instead. I need your help to get Ror back, I say.

The phone rings and makes us both jump. She answers it, turning away from me into the receiver, probably Sanjay.

It's Social Services. She turns to me, pale. Ror's run off, she's gone missing.

I reach over, try to get the phone off her but she pushes me back, signals me to stay quiet, puts the phone on speaker and rests it on the breakfast bar between us.

A man's voice says Ror jumped out of the car at the lights on the way to the children's home, could've been killed. No, no, she's not hurt, not as far as they know. The police are on it, they think she'll come here, will Kaheesha ring them if she does?

Yes, of course I will, she says.

When they hang up, she puts her face in her hands, elbows leaning on the worktop. I fight the urge to lean over, take her hands away, cover her face with my own. Cover her.

They're bloody useless, she says through her fingers. What kind of Social Services Department can't even keep hold of a ten-year-old?

She looks up. *In loco parentis* my arse.

I stare at her.

Means in place of a parent. It's what a local authority is supposed to do when a child's in their care, she says. Act like a parent.

I've heard it all now. I've known some shit parents in my time but all of them better than being in care. Oh, Carla would've loved that one. And I must have looked shocked because then we're both laughing and she's got this way of putting her hand up to her mouth when she laughs, like she's shy of her own pleasure, makes my stomach flip over.

She stops laughing first, looks at me, face still flushed.

Seriously though, Donna, where would she go? Back home? To Marie's? Here?

It's the first time she's said my name and I can't look her in the eye. I shake my head. Don't worry, she's not stupid, she'll be looking for me.

Then one of my phones rings, makes me jump.

It's Sonn. Leave me alone, I tell her, businesslike, for God's sake, I could be anywhere.

I know where you are, says Sonn, and I hear the smile in her voice. Stop thinking with your fanny and get back over here where you're needed.

I look at Kaheesha, but I don't think she heard.

Thanks for that, I say into the phone.

Then I cut her off, put the phone in my pocket. She's right of course, could be a patrol car outside any second.

I stand up, I've got to go, I say, I'll see myself out.

Let me know what I can do, she says.

28

I've had the darkness with me ever since I can remember, and most likely it's from me mam's side, though I can't know that for sure. Sometimes I feel it under me, like balancing on a tightrope and underneath it's just a cold dark space, a bottomless pit. One slip and I'll fall right in, disappear. Other times it's what keeps me awake at night listening, thoughts creeping about the edges like shadows, when everyone else is sleeping and the only sound is the yowl of a cat or the sound of a car shishing past in the rain. It's what makes me have to go and sit under the bridge on my own, down by the canal, when anyone else in their right mind is pissing it up on Canal Street, and me, I just want to leave them all to it. Not normal, that, Carla used to say.

So one time I asked her, What's normal?

She looked at me funny and shrugged.

Not having to ask what's normal, she said.

When I get to Dusty's it's packed, black and red with white leather sofas and a PVC bar, Sixties or something, some historical thing.

It's pretty quiet because it's still early. I'm just getting settled with a Red Stripe and a tequila shot when someone sidles up, digs me in the side with one bony elbow. Alright Donna?

Maeve. Skinny as a lat, not six stone wet through. You'd think you could snap her in half with two fingers but she's fit as a butcher's and three times as fast. Out on the wing she's a proper whippet and she throws a punch with the best. Last summer she did the Great North Run and me and Carla and a whole gang of us drove over to Hexham, two cars and a van, just to see her come in. Ribs like running boards, flat as a boy except where the bony bits stuck out, not an attractive look to be honest.

There you go then, Carla said, pulling her smug face. Living proof running's no good for you.

The only kind of exercise Carla had time for was dancing, or sex. And she could be a real bitch when she wanted.

It's too late to pretend I'm not here. How's it going Maeve, I say, not too interested if I'm honest.

Turns out there's some college student she met at the track, over by the exit looking for some action. I look over where she's pointing, just to be polite. Against the wall there's a cute little thing with a blonde wave that curls all round her face. Babydoll hair, babydoll dress, babydoll smile, Jimmy Choos. Christ, I feel tired just looking at her.

I know about the shoes because Lise is always on about them, cutting pictures out of *Heat*, shoving them under my nose, reminding me when her birthday is. Maybe I'll get her some next year. Anyhow, Babydoll's pretending to look in her bag but you can tell she's watching. And she's definitely straight. I catch Shauna's eye behind the bar, motion for another shot, better make it a large one.

Leave it out Maeve, I say, I don't want the mither. I'm in mourning.

Maeve looks at me like I've grown horns, and that gets right on my tits. Not tonight ta, I say.

The thing about some straight women is they irritate the shit out of me. Always thinking we'll fancy them, just because we're dykes and they happen to be female, no matter what. I don't know whether to be flattered or insulted. If we shagged around half as hard as they seem to think we do we'd be withered to nowt. To my mind that's fucked up. Still, I guess it can't be much fun being straight these days, like looking for a diamond with your teeth in a bucket of shit.

I don't mind the ones who were straight because they didn't realise there was anything else, and then one day they meet it, the else, and it blows their heads right off their shoulders and they never look back. I can cope with those. No, I mean the collegey ones just thinking about their sec-shoo-alitee, telling you how they just never had the chance, well apart from they kissed a girl once at school and they liked it. Oh yeah and wow, now there's You. Those are the ones to walk away from, quick-time. Problem is, telling the difference, and while you're trying to work it all out they're all over you, no matter how hard you try to fight them off. I swear, no one takes liberties like a straight woman out looking for kicks. So after a while you give in, because by now you can't think straight and hey fuck it you're only human. Then just when there's no turning back she's up and off, scalded cat style, and you won't see her for dust. It's not you... I just don't think I can do this... No? Really? You could have mentioned it. Makes you feel used up somehow, dirty. Next night she'll be telling her mates on a girly night in, or worse laying it on some yah-boy just for a bone. Yah, well, I nearly did once, you know, it was so cooool. Sister take it from me, only baby dykes and fully paid-up nutjobs think that kind of shit is a challenge. So that's numero uno in the survival guide for smart dykes – no straights.

Then Kaheesha's face floats in front of me, makes me mean. Just get lost Maeve, I say.

I knock back the shot, watch the lights send slow shapes up the floor and the walls, cocktail girls shimmying about in their lurex minis. I think about beating Tony's face to a pulp, blood everywhere, makes me feel better.

By now Dusty's is humming, women climbing over each other to get to the bar, I can hardly hear myself think. Mel's right up behind me before I clock her, all six foot of her, eyes dancing like cornflowers in the sun.

Pay attention geeal, she goes, with a grin. I coulda been anyone.

I slap her on the shoulder. I need you, I say.

I'm back at the lock-up around eleven. I'm about to crawl on to the shelf and pull the blanket over me when I hear the crash from upstairs, the doors going in. This time I hear the voices and there's no mistaking them.

I leap up, pull the ladder away from the trapdoor and run through to the shelter. Pull the steel door shut behind me and lock it. How could they know?

I grab some ammo from the box and make for the trap door to the canal, lock it behind me.

Out through the crawl space and into the tunnel, arched brick high above me like a cavern, Blue John mines. There's a narrow shelf, two bricks wide, along the wall beside me, leads to a narrow towpath. I inch along sideways, below me the water, almost black, no knowing how deep it is. When I hit the path I start to run, my footsteps echoing in my ears.

I reach the steel maintenence ladder and race up it, turn the handle. The door is locked from the outside. Fuck, fuck, fuck it. Down the ladder and along two hundred yards and there's another ladder alongside a manhole.

I wedge myself at the top of the ladder, pull the iron clip and the manhole comes loose. I push with all my strength. It weighs a ton but then it scrapes loose and I can push it over to the side a few inches. I get both hands through the gap, push some more. Then I'm out.

I push the manhole back, lock it in place.

I hear a noise and look up. Some old wino with a can of Foster's swaying in the wind.

He waves the can at me. You alright love?

I wave a hand, put my head down, try to walk away slowly, stop my chest from heaving.

Then I get to the corner and run.

29

The Sacred Heart's dead quiet, not much warmer inside than out but at least it's dry. Down the aisle there's a dim dusty glow from the lanterns overhead.

In the corner of my eye a woman wearing a blanket like a cloak waves her arms about, talks to a stained glass window in some kind of sign language. Jesus looking down on her, all those little kids on his knee. All round the walls there are bundled-up shapes half-sitting, some lying down.

Father Tom's up by the altar, parka zipped up over his leathers, beanie pulled down over his ears against the cold, fiddling around with the tea urn. I pick my way up the aisle, trip over a bag of rags, hear a groan.

Father Tom looks up and smiles, Alright Donna?

He leans across to a metal tray, lifts off the lid, Pakora help yourself love, should still be warm.

He bends back down to the urn. Bloody thing won't turn. You try, can you?

The tap's stiff, but it turns. A cloud of steam hisses out so I turn it off again, gently.

Father Tom wipes his hands on his jeans, shakes his head. You've got the touch, he says, and grins. Want a cuppa?

Something is going on behind me. I look over my shoulder and the shapeless bundles of rags are a silent queue now, stink making me gag.

After everyone's got a tea and some food it's quiet again. Father Tom busies himself with the urn. Carla says that's what he's always like, you can tell him anything pretty much and he'll never be shocked, but he'll never ask you straight out. Makes you feel everything's in your own time somehow, no pressure. He sits down on the bottom step of the pulpit, pats the step beside him. I sit down beside him with my tea.

Someone might need to stay here, I say, my eyes on the woman with the cloak, arms outstretched, spinning round and round in the aisle.

He blows on his tea, nods. It's a church, he says. Door's never locked.

Thanks. I'll tell her.

He smiles and points. There's blankets and coats in the corner.

Across the dark the double doors bang shut and I jump, but it's only another wino.

Father Tom squints at me. Maybe someone would be safer in the vestry he says. We get all sorts in here.

He beckons and I follow him to the back of the church. I can't tell you why though, I say.

He throws me a blanket, rolls his eyes and smiles. Let's just thank the Lord for small mercies, he says.

Inside, the room is small with wood panelling, smells of new carpet and old wood, kind of musty. A huge wooden desk stands in the centre, chair behind it, bookshelves all round. In one corner there's a built-in cupboard and a tiny sink; in the far corner there's another door with a key. Father

Tom takes the big square cushions from the chair, lays them on the carpet behind the desk side by side. Takes the blanket from me and drops it on top.

He points at a door. Leads through to the hall on the way to the kitchen. You can get out that way if you need to. Down the corridor and turn left through the hall.

When he's gone I open the cupboard. Pamphlets in boxes, a raincoat and umbrella, a black gown on a hanger, an old pair of bike boots covered in mud. In a black tin there are two white collar bands, starched and stiff. There's a kettle on the shelf with instant coffee and four cups, little sachets of sugar, an empty milk jug.

I roll up the raincoat for a pillow, turn the light off, pitch black. I feel my way across the room, lie down on the cushions and pull the blanket over me.

There's a hand on my leg. I sit bolt upright on the cushions, nearly knock someone flying. Jeeesus!

Not this time, says Father Tom, only me.

I can just make out his outline though he's only a few inches away. Sorry Father.

He turns on the light. I've had a visit, he says.

I'm on my feet faster than shit off a hot shovel, heart thudding. Who was it?

Three men, mid-twenties, maybe thirty, all white. I'd say the one who did the talking sounded local. Asked if I'd seen you.

My heart skips up a beat. What did you say?

That I saw you yesterday which was true. Don't worry, they don't know you're here – they didn't ask that. Just thought you should know.

I grab my stuff. Thanks, Father, I'd better be off.

They won't be back tonight. Come and have a cup of tea. Things can always be worse.

I look at him but he's not even joking.

We sit on the chancel steps and wait for the urn to boil. There's no one about now, just sleeping bundles of rags under the stained glass window and down the side walls. Even the dancing woman must be asleep.

Don't you get fucked off with all this? I wave my hand in the direction of the bundles on the floor. First off it stinks. How do you stand it?

He pulls a small blue and green pot out of his jacket holds it up for me.

Vicks, he says. Little dab under the nostrils works wonders, can't smell a thing. Tip from Manny Berman down Gorton. You know, the big undertakers?

The cold sterile smell from the coffin waves over me and my stomach turns over.

He hands me the tea.

We sit in silence for a bit and then I take a deep breath, I need to get going.

He looks towards the door. What's the weather like out there?

Dark, I say. Pretty stormy to be honest.

He takes a hip flask from an inside pocket, tips it towards my cup. Not the kind of night to be out without some protection then?

He pours a clear liquid into my tea and then his. It curdles the milk but goes down warm, makes my eyes water and I try not to gag. What the hell *is* that stuff?

Holy water.

I look into the cup, Give over, it's not?

He makes some kind of sign over my cup and grins. It is now.

Since when did you lot get a sense of humour? I say.

Oh, I don't know, since they started calling Manchester a city of culture?

He raises his cup to me. To Moss Side Moonshine or Longsight Liquor or whatever else they're calling it these days, he says, and we bump plastic cups.

We're quiet for a moment. How's Aurora? he says.

I wonder if he's heard anything. Fine, I say. We manage.

I count the pews down the centre aisle, sip at the tea. The flowers in the vase on the altar are dead and brown.

How about you?

I look at the door. What about me?

It's hard to lose someone you love, he says.

Have you ever loved someone? I say.

He smiles. Of course.

I don't mean like your mum or like God, I say, I mean s*omebody*, you know.

He nods again, not even offended. Of course.

I thought priests weren't allowed?

Priests aren't allowed to marry. You can't stop a human being from loving, Donna, it's what makes us who we are. He smiles a bit, shrugs. The church will catch up.

Down the aisle a bundle moves against the darkness, cries out. He looks sad and I feel bad now.

I never got to tell her, I say, by way of explanation.

Maybe there's a way you can show her?

Yeah, there is, I think to myself. I'm gonna do them, Tony and Fats and Daz and the lot of them. If it takes me forever. Do them all. What way? I say out loud. When she's dead?

You'll find a way, he says, and when you find it you'll know.

I shake my head. Then it's like he's reading my thoughts.

Some people can live a whole lifetime, Donna, and never really love. It's a gift. Don't let it turn into hate.

I grab my jacket, stand up. Now you sound like a priest again, I go, all preachy.

Come and talk with me, Donna, any time, he says.

I raise a hand in benediction. Bless you Father.

He shakes his head at me and smiles. Cheeky bugger.

30

I'm a Fucking Insurance Policy, whatever that means.

They're always at it, these two, rowing, fighting. Billy Chan out of F4 says that's what it's like when you've got two parents, getting in each other's way all the time, must be a nightmare.

Don't get me wrong, Mam can throw one all by herself, and sometimes it's a proper eppy right out of the blue, but it never lasts. These two go at it all the time. But like Billy says, you can learn a lot of stuff that way.

I put me ear to the door.

Shantelle sounds mewey, like she's crying. I can't do it any more. You said she was going to Preston, stay with Tiny's kids. One night, you said.

She's staying here. I don't trust him, not with everything up in the air like it is. Just call it my way of keeping us safe.

It's not right though Daz, she's only a kid.

He laughs, mean. *It's not right though Daz...* What's up with you? Thought you wanted a kid. You bleat on about it enough.

You mean bastard, she says.

Then the sound of the bolts drawing back.

Shut it now Shan, you're doing me head in. Give me your keys.

Don't lock me in, Daz. I hate that.

I have to because you can't be trusted, can you?

I hear the bolts drawing back, the clang of the door shutting hard. Then the sound of the keys scraping, the clunk of the locks. Shantelle sobbing.

After a while she comes up the stairs and unlocks the bedroom door, smiles, watery.

Downstairs she draws the curtains, puts the telly on, ruffs me hair just like Mam used to do. Toast then sweetpea? she says, on her way to the kitchen.

I look at the windows, the bars to keep people out. Or in, I suppose.

After she comes back, hands me the toast, I ask her, Does he always lock you in?

She looks over at the window. Course not.

Don't worry, I says, I don't fancy Preston anyway. If I can't go to Nan's I'll just stay here with you.

I only say it to try and cheer her up but it backfires and she starts scriking.

Then she hugs me tight so I can hardly breathe and I can feel the wet from her face on me cheek. Maybe it's you-know-what. Mam and Lise used to get theirs all at the same time, everyone shouting then crying all over the place till it drove me and Donna mad. I hope mine never start. Or maybe it's just him making her cry for no reason, and that decides me. One day, when I'm big, I'm coming back to smash his lights out.

She wipes her eyes on her sleeve, turns to Sky 1.

Eat your toast now, she says.

31

Over the moors the cloud hangs heavy, straggled. Dirty sheep's wool caught on barbed wire, rain coming down on my visor, din in my ears.

Up ahead is the slip-road so I look in the rear-view mirror. Blue Fiat Uno, red Mazda MX5.

I turn off on to the A57, cruise up to the lights, stop.

The Mazda pulls up behind me.

I take the roundabout easy, make sure they can keep up.

All the way round and I take the slip back down on to the motorway back on myself, watch the Mazda take a wide sweep left towards Glossop town centre.

No sign of the Fiat.

Back down the motorway again I take the next slip, do a yu-ey, ignore the signpost for Hattersley, go on down towards Glossop and past the Cut. At the junction I skirt through the queues and turn off.

A few minutes later, up ahead, through the rain, I can see the moors, stretching in front of me, and I open her up.

The turn-off is so overgrown I nearly miss it, have to double back and slow right down. The track is ridged and bumpy, grass growing down the middle, a ditch on each side thick with brambles and hawthorn. Half a mile or so on and the hedge becomes scraggy, the track forks. I pull up, lean the bike on the hedge, cut off a few branches with the Bowie, get back on again.

Up to the left is the old cottage, so I take the right downhill, turn the engine off and freewheel. Halfway down the hillside the track just peters out, the old dry-stone wall mossy and blackened by years of rain. A metal cow-gate hangs on one hinge.

Behind the gate and beside the wall the ground is muddy and clagged where the cows come for shelter. Someone has thrown a few stones from the wall into the mud to make stepping stones, hopscotch.

I look back up the hill to the left. The roof of the cottage is only just visible from here, Sonn was right. Another dry stone wall runs at right angles all the way up from the metal gate to the small copse that blocks the view of the cottage.

I lay the bike down by the wall just before the gate, at the end of the track, stash the lid under the handlebars, pull some branches from the hedge. Then I pull the dark green plastic sheet out and cover her over, lay the branches across her. More than a couple of steps back and there's no way you would see her. I take the keys from my pocket, put them under a fallen stone by the wall.

I vault over the wall, crouch low on the near side, wait.

The dark sneaks in, turning everything navy blue, luminous. Way down the hill there are lights, coming on one by one, flicker bright against the night.

Back over my shoulder and the hill rises up black; then the silhouette of the roof of the cottage beyond the copse, unearthly and still. I try to wriggle my toes but they're frozen inside my boots.

I crouch, rock forward and back on the balls of my feet to get the blood flowing again, try not to think of Carla, down in the earth. I used to laugh at her and Lise, all spirit-this and goddess-that. I'm wishing to fuck I believed in something now.

Something moves at the edge of my vision and I turn my head, look up at the copse. The light flashes again, then a low whistle, the signal that everyone else is in place.

Credit where it's due and all that, it was Sonn's idea to scatter and make our own way there. Makes getting away safer, she said. And if you only know where your own bike is, you can't lead them to anyone else, whether you mean to or not.

I cup my hands to my mouth, whistle back.

It takes sixty seconds to duck round and run up the side of the wall to the copse, make for the trees. It's dark between the trees so I crouch down, start to make my way through the scrub.

Then someone grabs my ankle and I nearly call out, stop myself just in time. Sonn. Fuck's sake, I hiss. You trying to give me a heart attack or what?

I look round. Lise is half in the shadow, Mel crouching beside her. We crawl through to where we can see right to the cottage, flatten out under the trees.

Where's the back-up, I ask.

Sonn takes up the torch, flashes once at the dark, then draws an S in the air.

I knock the torch out of her hand, What the fuck are you doing?

Look, she says.

All over the hills there's lights flashing, going off like silent paparazzi bulbs. Each one a zigzag, then an imprint blue in the air that hangs on for a second, just long enough to read.

Flash: J. Flash A, flash M, flash P, flash S, flash G, flash, flash. Until there's lights and letters appearing everywhere in the dark. Dozens of them.

Then it's dark again.

All over that hillside, says Sonn. I can just make out her grin. Next hill too. In case we need them. Watch this.

She flashes the torch twice, then draws a G in the air. A tiny light, far away on the opposite hill, flashes back three times.

Glasgow Easterhouse, she says, smug. Just in case we need serious artillery. Just got to show them the sign and they'll be over. She grins.

I've got to hand it to her, fair do's. No one fucks with the Easterhouse dykes and God knows what she's promised them in return. Still, I suppose we can work all that out later. If there is a later.

What's the matter? she says, super-bright. I told you I'd sort back-up.

Nearly twelve-thirty and it's the kind of cold you get in November, smell of frost and dead leaves, and charred wood and smoke; creeps into your bones.

Carla always said November's the smell of death, of things that grow in the earth dying, and, even if we don't think so, somewhere in our deep-down selves we know it, and that's why it makes us afraid.

Don't be a drama queen, I said.

217

Go on then, she said. Tell me why you never have a creepy story set in the sunshine? Tell me why more people get depressed in winter? See? You can't.

No use trying to argue with her when she was on one.

Jen comes out of nowhere, throws herself down beside me, passes me the binoculars. Through the glass discs I can see the side of the cottage, the front of it side-on, and the bit of scrub at the front.

We don't have to wait long until we hear the sound of a motor. A white transit, no lights, Salford Van Hire on the side, pulls up on the scrub.

Mel makes a strangled sound and I look at her, see she's laughing. Salford Van Hire? Not a brain-cell between them. We all have a giggle at that and it loosens us up.

I see Tony and Danny climb down from the van, look around, hold my breath as I watch them go inside.

A light comes on in the cottage, shines out through the open front door on to the scrub.

Then another motor, quieter than a van. An old Audi pulls up by the van and Daz and Fats get out. They go to the back, unlock the doors, drag out a couple of holdalls. Yo, the money, whispers Lise.

Fuck me, says Mel, makes us all jump. It's the car, Donna. The one that took you down after the funeral.

Are you sure?

But even as I say it I know in my heart it is. And then I know what it means and there'll be no going back.

I twist round and look at Lise, her hand shaking where she's holding the Glock. Mel clocks it as well, raises an eyebrow at me and she's right. Lise will be a liability in there, and if things hot up, who knows what'll happen?

I rest my hand on her wrist, stop it shaking. I need you to stay back here and cover us, I tell her.

Lise shakes her head at me, pleading, and I haven't the heart. Chances are none of us will get out of this in one piece so we might as well stick together. At least then she won't die alone in some scabby old field.

I give her hand a quick squeeze and let go. OK, I says. But you stay at the back.

Upside the cottage, Mel hangs back as lookout the way we planned it. Two whistles, you do the tyres, I remind her.

I crouch by the front step, peep round.

There's enough light so I can see right in down the tiny hallway, see the door at the end half-open, hear the voices rise and fall.

I'm going for the stairs, I says. Wait for the signal.

My heart's hammering but I make it down the hallway, treading the boards at the side, hoping to fuck they won't squeak.

At the bottom of the stairs I look back, give Mel the thumbs-up. Her face disappears.

Halfway up the stairs and one of them creaks, sounds loud as a gunshot to me. I hold my breath, flatten myself down against the stairs, out of sight.

The voices have stopped.

I hear the sound of a door opening wide into the hall. The click of a safety being released. Then there's only the sound of the sheep, coming from the open front door, and the rush of the blood in my ears.

There's sweat running down my spine now and I push my face down against the stairs, pull my right elbow back slowly until the gun's right by my head, ready to blow some bastard's face off if they look over the rail.

Footsteps fall heavy and dull on the floorboards.

Then I hear the front door jerked open wide, hear Danny's voice, No one here.

I hear the front door close, the slide of a bolt. His footsteps back through and into the living room.

After a minute I peer up across the banister, see the living room door into the hall's been left half-open. Fuck. I've got to get across to the front door, take the bolt off. Otherwise I'm in here on my own.

OK Carla, I whisper, let's see what your goddess can do.

I can hear voices rising now in the living room, make my way past and back to the front door. The bolt slides easy and silent.

After that I make it up the stairs and into what must be a back bedroom.

Just like Sonn said, there's nothing here except an old chair. The boards are bare and loose and the voices beneath me rise and fall. I lie full length, put my ear to the floor.

When I look back now it feels like everything happened so quick, but back then, nose pressed to the floor, every minute felt like a year. I can still hear the rise and fall of the voices, then the moment everything turns.

Where the fuck are they then? They should be here by now, says Daz.

Tony's voice is calm, dangerous. Why? Who are you expecting?

In the silence I can feel Daz's mind ticking over, whirling with the possibilities. None of them good. Up to now he's probably been relaxed, downed a beer or two, waiting patiently for the hardware that's gonna make him and Tony a fortune.

The fucking hardware, bro, says Daz. Stop messing about... His voice tails off, unsure.

I hear the click of a safety catch, hear Tony's voice. Who's messing about?

Daz is panicking now and I can't blame him. What? C'mon mate.

I imagine him looking from Danny to Tony and back again. Things taking shape in his mind. Unimaginable things.

Fatboy's pleading. You've got it wrong, Tony. Then a shot makes us all jump.

Sonn pokes me in the back. Don't you just love it when a plan comes together?

He's a hard fucker, Mad Daz. They kept at him for two hours, him denying everything, still tied to that chair. In the end he was begging them to finish it. I'm not going to bore you with the ins and outs. Let's just say it wasn't pleasant, even for me, and I hate the sorry fucker.

By this time Lise is lying beside me, Sonn by the bedroom window on lookout. No need to keep quiet any more. What with Daz screaming and Tony shouting, Danny putting his two pennyworth in the mix, they wouldn't have heard a grenade go off unless you shoved it up their arse.

We're all lying on the floor now, all except Mel.

Sonn takes out a penknife. Don't worry, they'll never look up, she says, prising up the floorboard.

I look down, see the top of Danny's head, half of Tony, then someone's feet and legs stretched out on the floor, must be Fats. Either he's taking a nap or someone's wasted him and my money's on a bullet. There is a God.

Now Daz is talking as if he has a mouthful of something and he can hardly get the words out.

Shantelle, he says.

Tony laughing. Don't you worry about Shantelle, he goes. At least she won't have to pay the rent when you're gone.

Daz moans. Danny says nothing.

I see Tony look at his watch. The lads will be there about now I reckon, they're just torching your house.

Daz is making sounds like a dog being kicked, a kind of howl.

Tony laughs. No don't thank me mate, no charge.

Shantelle's in there with the kid, moans Daz. Oh God babe, I'm sorry.

There's a silence. What kid? says Tony.

I hear Daz spit, see the blood hit the floor. Looks like teeth too.

Carla's kid, he says.

My guts turn over, feels like someone's sitting on my chest.

Daz is still talking. I try to focus.

Didn't take her to Preston. Kept her at mines, just in case, with Shantelle. Locked them both in there this morning. Then he makes a hollow sort of noise which ends in a sob. A woman and a kid, Tony, he sneers. You sick murdering bastard. You'll do thirty years for that.

I'm on my feet and down the stairs three at a time.

On the way down I hear Danny shout out and there's a scuffle and scrape, followed by the thud of something heavy hitting the ground. A gun goes off. And then another.

I kick the door open and it crashes back against the wall.

Tony's sitting on the sofa against the far wall, pale, nursing a bullet wound in his side by the look of it, still staring at Danny in disbelief.

I don't even think about it, I walk over to him, take his own gun, shoot him once, through the forehead, watch the splatter, thick grey and blood red on the wall behind. There's a smell like raw pork and the warm metal smell of blood and my guts want to heave.

I look round the room.

Danny hasn't moved but that's no surprise, on account of the Skorpion Mel got trained on him from the door. He's on his feet, stock-still, hand with the Smith and Wesson hanging down by his side. I reach out to take it off him and he just gives it up.

I put it up near my face. The barrel's still hot.

I nod towards Tony, can't help but smile. Fuck me Danny-boy, I says, did you shoot him? Danny nods.

I walk over to where Fats is lying, turn him over with my foot. He looks dead but you can never be sure. I point Danny's gun down at his head. This one's for Kim, I say. And I pull the trigger.

Daz is in the middle of the room strapped to the chair, blood and skin and vomit everywhere but still breathing. Looks almost glad to see me, poor bastard. I put Danny's gun to Daz's ear.

That true? You took Ror?

He nods once, like he knows what's coming but doesn't care any more. I pull the trigger gently, send him to hell on a nine millimetre.

Sonn walks up to Danny, puts the Black & Decker to his head. You piece of shit.

Leave it, I say. He's mine.

I reach into Danny's pocket, find the keys, throw them to her. You and Mel. Take his car and the van, I say, torch them.

Sonn looks at Danny, disappointed. Nods.

Come to think of it, do it in Salford, I say. That should keep them all busy for a while.

I reach down beside Tony, take the holdall of money, hand it over to Lise.

You know what to do, I say, and she nods.

She motions to Danny. What about him?

I tell Danny to stand against the wall, pat him down, pull out his mobile. Hand it to Sonn with his gun.

Wrap these and put them somewhere safe, I says to her, and fuck's sake keep your gloves on till it's done. Go with her Mel. I'll finish this.

When they've gone and it's just me and Danny I tell him to stand against the wall.

He looks me straight in the eyes and I can see him straighten up, get ready.

I nod over towards Tony's body, Tell me why.

Didn't know about Ror, he says. I don't do kids, he shrugs, everyone's got their limits. Then he takes a deep breath. Just get on with it, he says.

I empty his clip, tuck his gun in my belt. Not going to kill you, Danny-boy. I look round the room. Going to need someone still standing, take the rap for all this. I tap my belt and grin. Got enough ballistico here to send you down for the rest of your natural, you decide to get chatty.

I head for the door. Could do worse than have Danny heading up the Darts, now I've got him by the balls. The devil you know and all that.

And I'd take my time leaving if I were you, I tell him. *I* don't need to kill you but I can't speak for my back-up. Got some out-of-control sisters freezing their tits off out there on that hillside, spent all night stamping their feet to keep warm. That kind of thing can make a girl mean.

32

I get one-twenty out of her on the M57 and if the traffic's OK on the bypass I'll do it in seven minutes.

I'm riding on autopilot, can't think straight but I tell myself I've got to. Thinking about Ror, how that bastard must've took her, how scared she must have been. Wondering how I'm going to get into the estate and the house without a Cheetah escort, how I'll get her out, how we'll both get away. Then I'll drop her off with Lise and be away before dawn.

I've not gone three miles when there's this sick feeling crawling in my stomach and I'm seeing Tony's face half-gone, blood and brains on the wall. I pull over. In my mind I see Carla's face, her lying on the dance-floor, the smell of burnt flesh and metal, blood warm, turning thick on my hands. And then Ror, face pure white, looking up at me from inside the toilet in the backyard at Carla's, holding on to Rio like he's the only thing she'll ever have. Then I'm retching my guts out, sweat cold on my face.

When there's nothing left to come up the strength drains out of me and I lean on a wall so I don't fall. No one knows but I never shot anyone before, never had to.

They're for mugs they are, shooters, Dad always said. You need a gun love, it means you've lost someone's respect, no way back from it.

I wipe my mouth on my sleeve. Well it's different times now Dad, twenty years on. No respect left on the street any which way you look at it. If there ever really was any. Just little boys with their games, making up the rules as they go along. Trying to pretend it's not chaos. You'd think they'd have learned. Trouble is people round our way only ever look back through the bottom of a pint pot, and that's you included. And one of these days, someone's got to call time.

So I make up my mind there and then, me and Ror gonna go clear.

I know Tony was bullshitting about the fire, but I keep her full throttle anyway, take a corner so fast I lose the denim and the skin on one knee. It's only when I round the last corner that I see the fire engines, police cars and the yellow tape through the smoke. A cold hand squeezes my heart until I can't breathe.

I spin to a stop against the crowd, nearly take some old dear's legs off, fight my way to the front. I see people clock me, most of them Cheetah. I feel the heat of the flames and the smoke thick and black, choking, no air.

I push through the tape with my chest.

Someone puts a hand on my shoulder and I shake it off. In front of me a man in a yellow jacket has his back to me, holding the line. I grab on to his arm as he turns, yell, There's a kid in there, for fuck's sake!

Then everything slows. Past his shoulder I see the patrol car, three uniforms, looking right in my direction and one points towards me. A sea of blue and yellow moves towards me and I hear a shout go up. If I don't ride away now, I might never get the chance.

I swing round, see a way through the crowd to my bike against the wall, maybe ten yards, feel the blood flood through my calves for the sprint. Then I hear the crackle of the fire behind me, see Carla's face against the white of the hospital pillow, blood in her hair and her lips are just moving. *Aurora*, she says.

I let go the arm, duck underneath it, make the sprint for the house. From the corner of my eye I see three uniforms running in from the left, then they're on me. I dodge between two of them, and under and out, could have left Jason Robinson standing. The third catches me by the arm, spins me round, off balance and a voice comes from somewhere, Hey, you can't go in there love, it's too late.

I twist away, get my free hand to my back, pull the Glock from my waistband, point it straight at his face. Get the fuck back.

The minute they see the shooter the three of them step back, then I'm walking backwards, never taking my eyes off them, weighing up how many seconds it can be to the house, how long it will take the firearms unit to arrive.

I can get to her, I know I can.

I feel the heat on my back, the roar of the flames in my ears. Spin round, start to run for the house.

I don't even see him come in from the side until the pavement comes up somehow, smacks me full in the face. Then they're all on my back.

A boot steps on my wrist, kicks the Glock away. I watch it skid across the tarmac out of reach. I try to lift my head but there's a knee on my neck and one between my shoulderblades, and all I can see is bastard concrete and a trillion zillion stars.

33

How they got me in the van I'll never know. I was kicking and screaming like ten-men, calling them all the murderers and cunts under the sun, proper lost it.

At the station they take everything off me, throw me in an interview room, no brief, no nothing. I go no comment. Obviously. I know they'll get me for pulling the Glock and resisting arrest, fair do's, but I don't know what else they know. Everyone knows the fastest way to get stitched up is to start talking, before you know what-all they got on you. Most of the time they're just fishing around, got a cell door with your name on it, just have to make it fit.

They drag me into the custody suite by my feet, charge me with threats to kill and some bollocks with a deadly weapon. I reckon that's just for starters, but it lets me know they haven't got anything else, not yet.

Then they throw me into a cell.

Then I'm thinking about Ror, punching at the wall till my hands bleed, trying not to see her face in the fire.

It's a couple of hours later when the catch on the cell door rattles and the flap slides back, lets in the light from the corridor. The door opens and a female plain-clothes copper walks in, butch as you like. I've been expecting this so I'm up at the back of the bunk in a jiff, ready for anything.

I know what I'm in for, though, pretty much, me pulling a gun on her mates like I did. Wouldn't expect any less, I'm just surprised she's on her own. She shuts the door behind her, sound echoing down the corridor.

You don't know me, she says, her back to the door.

I size her up. She's taller than me, a bit older but solid, blonde streaks pulled back in a tail. Smart black diving watch. I watch the muscles of her arm tense under her shirt. Still, I reckon I can handle it. I watch her eyes, wait for her move.

She looks back to the door for a second, then sits down.

She smiles. Chill out sweet-cheeks, I've got a message. You're going to like it, she says.

She tells me Ror turned up at the pig-pen on Hyde Road before the fire even got started, so she's safe. They don't know how she got there or anything, because Ror's gone no comment too, little fucking star.

She won't tell me who sent the message or how she got it, not that it matters, and if I ever get out of here I'll find her on Canal Street and there's half a kilo with her name on it. Ask anyone, I always pay my debts.

34

It's the smell of the place that hits you first: stale piss, sweat and cabbage, the sharp smell of fear. You notice it the minute they shove you through the first door. HMP Styal, a real home from home. If you're a sewer rat.

We go through the metal detector, three female screws, one of them straight, two of them not, both watching my every move like they're starving and I'm breakfast. There's something strange about a woman who works in a prison, dyke or no dyke, attracts the wrong sort from the start.

Someone did an experiment once, Lise says. Put random students in a big basement, locked half up in the cells, put the others in charge with a big bunch of keys. Had to call it off after a week, before somebody died. Lise says it was because the guard ones just got to love it whoever they were before; thought up more and more punishments, beating up on the prisoners for no reason, starving them until they did stuff no one should make anyone do. The pretend prisoners came out of it alright in the head though – mainly because they stuck together I guess, looked out for each other – but you couldn't do anything with the guards after that, they were cannon-fodder. And that was after a week. Some of these fuckers have been here twenty years.

So now's the time to draw the line in the sand.

The one with the beer belly walks towards me, grips my arm, marches me into the back for the strip-search, kicks me hard on the ankle as we go through the door. Then tells me to take all my clothes off. See, that's what I'm talking about. What kind of woman wears chrome studs on a watchstrap anyway?

I strip off double quick, just to deny her the pleasure of saying, yeah, and those. I stand in front of her and her eyes are all over me, turns my stomach. Take a good look love, I says, it's the best you'll ever see without paying for it.

She walks behind me, holds me by the arm, punches me full-on in the right kidney and the pain makes me go light-headed. I turn round, bollock-naked, smile, pretend I never felt a thing. Temper, temper, I say.

I manage to walk to the cell without limping, screw on each side and killing where she punched me, but to be honest I feel good. Throw down the gauntlet or throw in the towel, one or the other, but never stand around waiting for something to happen, Dad used to say. Start that caper Donna, your life's not your own.

Women line the hall for a look and I stare them out. First-timers don't always know how things work, walking on to a wing with their head down, thinking it'll keep them out of trouble. Big mistake. There's only one thing that keeps a girl out of trouble in this place, and that's looking like a shit-load of trouble yourself.

I have to say though, I'm impressed. There's always a higher quality of woman on a wing than in a guard-house and this place is no exception. The tall dark one with the pixie face, leaning on her door, looks up as I go past. I give her a wink, clock the cell number, Laters.

Down the corridor the screw pushes open the door and nods me in, sarky. I guess your sort won't mind sharing?

That's original. You must be the one with the City and Guilds.

I look over at the far bunk. Weird skinny little thing with a face like Gollum, eyes like big saucers and wisps of hair standing up on her head, looks right back.

And credit me with a bit of taste, I say, I don't fuck just anybody. Pervert.

As it turns out, Gollum's fairly cool. Not that I've changed my mind about fancying her. I'd trust her with my stash but I know men I'd shag before I'd kiss Gollum on the lips. Let's just hope it never comes to that.

Once the screw leaves I kick my boots off, lie down. Got stuff to do.

I look over at Gollum, introduce myself.

Just killed three dickheads, I need a sim card, I say.

35

I've been in police stations before but not this one.

Shantelle rings the bell on the counter, gives me a hard squeeze and a kiss on the head, then she's gone. She doesn't smell like Mam, but she still smells nice.

I stand in front of the counter, look up at the big glass screen. All I can see is the tops of some heads.

Then a Ginga with freckles and glasses opens the flap, looks down at me and smiles. Alright there my love? What's up?

I don't know what I'm supposed to say so I say nothing.

She disappears, then a door opens at the end and she's in front of me with a man, a Baldy. They open a door behind me and we go into a room with no windows.

She sits me at the table and they sit opposite me. OK sweetheart, she says, take your time. Can you tell us what's happened?

To be honest I can't really believe Shantelle left me here instead of somewhere safe, but I'm not about to grass her, being how she let me watch TV and brought me M&Ms and looked so sad all the time. I look them straight in the eye. No comment, I says.

They look at each other, smile.

It's not an interview love, says The Ginga. We just need to know who you are. We just want to help.

She turns to The Baldy One. Try the beat officer, Mike. Someone must know her.

After a bit Baldy comes back in with a can of Coke and a cup, krinks his nose at me, smiles. Sorry love, he says, no straws.

I'm not a baby, I say.

I can see that, he goes. What school do you go to?

There's no way I'm telling them what school I'm at, what's the point? I'm never going back there. School's a total waste of time when you're my age, just leaves you no time to look after yourself.

No comment.

To be honest I don't think I can tell them anything. If I tell them about Nan they'll send for the Social. If I tell them about Mam, or Lise, or Donna, they'll still send for the Social. If I tell them about The Christine One and Fatso and the biting, then they'll totally lock me up. Probably forever. And I can't tell them about Shantelle and climbing out of the skylight after Daz went to work. I promised Shantelle and even though I wouldn't have if I'd known she was bringing me here, I can't go back on it now. Sometimes all a girl's got is her word, Donna says.

I hum the song in me head then I get an idea. They can't lock me up for wanting to see Father Tom can they? Not when he's a priest.

Can you get Father Tom please? I says.

I don't know Father Tom love. Who is he?

Are they stupid?

You know, at the church. He's the priest.

They look at each other. Appropriate Adult, says The Ginga. Just in case.

Everything moves pretty fast after that. Next thing I'm in a room full of toys with a mirror and no windows and the man has gone. A new woman who says she's called Sally sitting beside me.

The Ginga points to a TV on the wall. It's a camera, she says. Takes pictures of everything we say and do so we can remember it all. OK love?

I haven't a clue what she's talking about so I just shrug. No skin off my nose.

The Sally One asks me how old I am, what me name is, who me Mam is. Stupid things. I don't tell her.

Then she asks me what I like to play with.

I don't play with anything, I'm not a baby.

You asked me to do something, says The Ginga, when we were in the other room? Can you remember what it was?

Donna's right, I don't know how they ever catch anyone they're that stupid. Can't you remember? I say.

I can. I'm just wondering if you do.

She's talking rubbish now. Best not to say anything.

Can you say it again for me love? What you said before?

I say it slowly for her. I. Said. Can. You. Get. Father. Tom?

I've obviously hit the jackpot because her eyes totally light up and everything. Do you mean Father Thomas Doherty from the Sacred Heart?

At last.

Can you tell me what he's done, love?

Done? He's done loads, I says. He's always doing stuff.

I don't really want to say what the best thing is that I know he's done, because it makes me sound like a right baby, me wanting him to give Mam a message and him singing You Are My Sunshine just for me. I think of Sunita Clegg's face and a shudder goes through me. I'd never live it down.

I can't, it's a secret, I says.

Did Father Tom tell you that you had to keep it a secret?

I shrug. We just agreed. It's our secret.

Sometimes grown-ups tell us to keep secrets that we shouldn't really keep.

I don't really know what to say to that. What like?

I can't tell you that. I need to know your secret first, yours and Father Tom's.

Now I know for deffo she's stupid.

Well I can't tell you can I? That's what a secret means.

I'm sorry love, but it's really important you tell us what he's done first. We can't go arresting someone without knowing what he's done. If you tell us, we can do something about it. I promise he won't be able to get to you if you tell me.

Arrest him? Get to me? She's as barking as The Wiz, this one.

Look, I say, he only does nice things.

She tips her head, does a weird little half-smile, takes a deep breath.

Sometimes we think things are nice when they happen but they really aren't and they can leave us feeling bad, she says. We have to think really hard about how they make us feel and if it's bad, we have to tell someone.

Now she's doing me head in and I'm wishing I hadn't said a dicky. I look round the room but there's no way out without going right past them. Maybe I'll be stuck in here forever unless I can work out what she's after, and every little thing I say seems to make it all worse.

It'll feel better if you talk to me, love, I promise.

You're OK thanks, I'll leave it, I says.

36

I might never be going home, Christine says.

If I behave myself and don't run away and don't be rude and don't be all nowty, they're going to find me a Forever Family.

What's one of them? I ask her.

It's a family that will love you and look after you forever, she says.

No ta, I don't need another one, I've got one already, I says.

To be honest one is enough trouble as it is. I don't know how I'd cope with two.

She tells me that's not how it works, and I'd have the Forever Family instead of the one I've got now.

What? Like a straight-on swap?

Sort of, she says.

Can I choose them?

Not really, she says. They choose you.

How do I know I'll want to swap all mine if I don't know what I'm getting instead? I ask.

She doesn't say anything and I don't want to look ungrateful.

I don't think so. Thanks though, I says.

After The Chat I go out the front into the garden. Loads of trees and a rope swing, climbing frame and a slide. The babbas are in the sandpit by the hedge.

Why don't you go over and play with Sarah? says Miss.

I pretend I can't hear, sit down by the tree, even though the grass is still wet from the rain and turns me bum cold. Me head's going bizzy again so I bang it back on the tree trunk. Not hard, just enough to stop the bizzing.

One two three, One two three, One.

When the bizzing stops I start wondering what Nan's doing. I daren't ask for Father Tom again, seeing how it just sent them all loop. I don't know why but everything went mad after that and I ended up here and now they won't let me see anyone sound.

I can't see Nan, Christine says, because she can't stop drinking and that makes her An Alcoholic and even though she knows Nan loves me it's Too Risky. I can't see Mam, obviously, because she went and died and left me. I can't see Kaheesha and Sanjay because I ran away once and even though I promised I wouldn't do it again Christine says that's not enough because I've made it Too Risky as well. And I can't see Donna or Lise or Sonn or Rio because they're not Proper Family, she says.

They are, I tell her. Donna's me God-Mam.

She says that doesn't count. Good job Mam and Father Tom can't hear her say that.

I can't even see Geet because it's Not Appropriate, so that just leaves nobody.

Christine's got a little painted Mr Nobody box plus a box for everyone I know with their names stuck on, a little slot on the top. When she gets them out I have to write things down and post them through the slots. For Feelings.

I just make them up in case it's a trick. If she thinks some stupid game is going to make me grass on everyone in the world she's got another think coming.

I think about the Forever Family and me heart starts thumping and me head goes bizzy again. Donna and Lise will probably definitely be coming for me, but they'd better hurry up by the sounds of it or who knows where I'll land up.

I go over to the sandpit and take the red bucket off baby Rosie, lob it over the hedge which sets her off whingeing. Crybaby, I hiss. Mard-arse.

I look over to the house but there's nobody looking. Only Miss bending down at the flowerbed doing the weeds. I get hold of Rosie's ear at the edge and pinch it hard so she squeals. I know it's wrong and I feel bad even while I'm doing it, but sometimes you've got to do a little bad thing, to stop a bigger one happening.

Miss comes trogging over in her crocs, bends down to Rosie, picks her up, sees the red on her ear and rubs it. Oh you bad girl Aurora, what've you done?

Me Miss? Nothing Miss.

She takes Rosie inside and I go back to the tree. That ought to do it. We'll see what Forever Family wants me now.

I'm about to throw the spade over after the bucket when I hear a low whistle from behind the hedge, two short and one long, like me and Donna used to do.

The hedge is thick with wire net behind and I can't see anything through it but someone's feet and the road.

I run to the gate but it's locked and I can't see over it.

I run back to the hedge.

It's me sweetpea, whispers Lise. Can you get over?

The gate's locked, I whisper.

Look round lovey. Is there anything you can climb on?

I look, but there's nothing. I run back to the gate and mess with the padlock, but it's fast shut. I can hear her on the other side and me heart's hammering.

Lise! Don't leave me!

I won't. Stand back and I'll kick it.

Then she must have given it a proper Karate Kid because the whole gate nearly comes off its hinges it crashes back so fast. Then Lise is standing in front of me with weird curly ginger hair and a bob hat on. I think me heart's going to jump out of me chest I'm so happy to see her.

She grabs on to me hand. Then I hear shouting behind me and we're running, running, running, me nearly pulled off me feet.

At the corner I see the car with both doors open and the engine going. Lise pushes me in the back and slams the door. Then she jumps in the front and we're off.

I look over me shoulder out of the back window, see Miss and Christine, standing in the road, looks like they're shouting. I give them a wave.

Oh My Giddy Aunt says The Driving One, and then Lise and her are both squealing, laughing. The Driving One looks over her shoulder at me, pulls the scarf from her head, gives me a smile. It's Geet's Mam! I'm not kidding, I never been so pleased to see anyone. Ever.

When we come off the dual carriageway Geet's Mam pulls over. Lise goes round and gets some stuff from the boot. She gets in again and passes some clothes over to me. A pink cardy and blue jeans.

Pink? I goes.

Don't mess me about Ror, she says, put them on.

Then she passes me a wig with a yellow pigtail. Make sure you tuck all your hair in. Your name's Josie. I'm your Auntie Jane, she says.

37

The sinks have all got mirrors and the light is so bright I have to squint.

I've had a wee, washed me hands with all the squirty soaps and had a go of all the blowers to see which is the best. Not much in it.

I lean against the wall and wait. The queue goes long and then short and then long again and the door in the corner's still locked. I go over.

Lise? What you doing?

The door opens quick, and she pulls me into the cubicle, shuts the door behind me, locks it, tells me to sit.

She's got no top on, just a bra. There's a bandage wrapped right round her middle and then she's got hold of the long end in one hand. I sit down on the toilet.

What you doing?

You'll see, she says.

After a few more wraps round her middle, she bends down to the bag, gets out a brown paper packet, tears it open. Money. Whole blocks of the stuff in elastic bands, tons and tons of it.

Dingers. Is that money?

Shhh, keep your voice down, she says.

She puts a block of money at her middle then wraps the bandage over it and right round. Puts another one next to the first and wraps it again.

After a while all the money is packed up under her T-shirt and she pulls her top down. She looks well fat and I giggle.

Not a word, OK? It's for spends. If anyone stops us, pretend you can't speak. Don't say anything.

Then I must've looked scared because she leans over, squeezes me knee. Majorca. We're going on holiday, don't worry, she says.

All that money just for spends? I ask her.

It's a long holiday, she says.

Out in the concourse the tiles are marble and shiny, noise everywhere. People rushing and pushing, dragging cases on wheels, the tannoy going non-stop. I try to follow Lise through the crowd, trip over a case. She pulls me up by the arm, Watch where you're going love, keep up.

I want to ask her to slow up but then I see them, the police. Lined up against a glass wall, dozens of people filing past. Out at each side there's one with a gun, the kind you need a strap and two hands to hold up. And Lise, pushing through the crowd, she's dragging me, heading right for them. Lise!

She's not listening, just drags me harder, Come on.

We get closer and through the glass I can see big machines. Eating people.

Lise! I pull me arm free and she stops. She follows me eyes. It's alright, she says, just metal detectors. Passport control.

The police though, I say.

It's OK, she says, they're special ones, always here. Airport police. They're not looking for us, it's too soon.

As we get closer I see the machines are just big gates and the people go through one by one, come out the other side in one piece, no problem.

Lise puts the passports and tickets on the high counter and the man looks at them, then looks down at me. I hold me breath.

And where do you think you're going young lady?

I look at Lise and she nods, He means the holiday.

Majorca? My voice is a squeak.

He nods, smiling. Smashing there. You have a lovely holiday sweetheart, he says, then he gives me a wink. Then he gives Lise the passports, waves his hand and we join the queue for the machines.

Take your shoes off, says Lise, put them in the tray.

When we get to the machine Lise puts her bags on the first tray and it jolts forward, disappears inside. I'll go first, she says, you wait then walk through.

She walks through a metal gate and out the other side. The woman in a uniform waves her past. Then it's my turn.

I step through the gate and there's a noise like a Ding.

Hang on love. The woman holds me by the arm, pulls me over to the side. Another woman comes up, a black stick in her hand. Lift your arms up, she says.

I look round for Lise but I can't see her. My heart thuds so loud in me ears I can't hear anything else.

Duhduhduhduh says the woman with the stick, her lips moving. Then she lifts me arms up and out, runs the black stick across them and me hearing comes back.

Ding.

I don't know what that means but I know it's not good. Me chest hurts. Could the Social have put a Ding on me somewhere to stop me getting away? No way I'm going back there. I get ready to run just as the woman grabs me arm.

It's the bracelet love, she says. You'll have to take it off and go through again.

I can't undo the bracelet because me hands are all thick so she undoes it for me, puts it in a tray and round the side of the gate.

Then Lise is back beside me, gives me a little push.

Go on now, go back through, she says.

I walk through again and there's no Ding.

Through the gates we get our stuff back out of the trays and I put me shoes on, hand Lise the bracelet.

It's fine, she says, you can put it back on now.

It's OK I've gone off it, I say.

More queues which take forever, then we're on to the plane, crammed into two tiny seats in between an old woman and man with a babba. Bloody hell, says Lise under her breath. That's all we need.

The plane starts to move. I can hear the engines and through the little window I can see the grass at the edge of the tarmac moving slowly backwards.

Then a waitress stands up in front, saying stuff and pointing.

Pay attention, says Lise, you need to know this. It's safety.

What for? In case we crash?

Lise is reading something on her phone, not even looking. We're not going to crash, she says.

My chest starts to hurt again. I watch the waitress, make sure I remember what she says, then get the card out from the pocket in front of me, start to learn it.

Suddenly the engines get louder and louder and the noise is like screaming, hurts me ears. Then a pull in me guts, like a weight being sucked down right through me and out the back and I'm pinned to me seat. I look over at the window, grass scudding by now, top speed. Lise!

This is the best bit, Ror, he's revving up to take off.

He needs to let that clutch out, I say.

The weight on me chest gets heavier and heavier until I think I can't breathe, then all of a sudden everything goes slack and me stomach drops out like on the big wheel. Then it all goes smooth and I'm tipped back in me seat.

Look, says Lise, pointing to the window. We're up!

I look sideways, see the ground disappear out of sight.

Lise! It's gone foggy! I reach for the card.

Lise laughs. You daft apeth it's only the clouds.

After a while the clouds melt away and the sky is pure blue, the sun bouncing off the metal of the wing so I have to screw up me eyes and squint. There's nothing to see now except sky but I can't take me eyes off the window. It's like summer, I say.

She squeezes me hand. It's always summer this high up, she says.

A warm feeling comes over me. Mam'll love that.

A bit later when the engine's just a hum in the background and Lise has gone off to the toilet I get to thinking about Donna, then Mam again. I try and see Mam's face but I can't, then it's hard to breathe and me heart starts to thud. Then clear as a bell I hear her voice in me head, feel her hand on me forehead brush the hair away like she used to, *It's OK love, she says.*

Lise wriggles back into her seat, gets hold of me hand and squeezes.

Don't cry sweetpea we're safe. It's all over now.

I feel tired. I think about what Nan's doing and who'll do The Complan, wonder whether I'll ever see Geet again.

Maybe not for a little while, says Lise.

Is Donna coming... on the holiday?

Lise smiles, pats her knee, I hope so. Now put your head down, get some sleep.

Then she's reading with the *Closer* in one hand and with the other she's stroking my head. I hear Mam's voice over and over, *It's OK love, It's OK love,* and things start to sway.

And then I must have fell asleep.

38

I look out over the court through the plastic screen.

I'm sitting in a long dock, a screw from G4S on each side, a woman built like a tank and a Scouser with a tattoo of a ship on his hand. All I can see in front of me are rows of benches, fat penguins in a line nodding at each other, standing up and sitting down, arms full of papers. Black gowns and wigs, they all look the same.

I spot Harriet from Jessop's, second row from the front. She looks back at me, gives a quick smile, blonde curls bouncing, nods her head towards the tall bloke in front of her adjusting his wig.

The courtroom is huge. At the other end there's a platform with a door on each side and a bench across it. In the middle I can see the top half of a big leather chair.

In front of the platform there's a table facing this way, penguin behind it, gown but no wig. He stands up and says something I can't make out and then everyone stands up. The woman screw on my left grabs my arm, pulls me up to my feet. The judge comes in from the side door, walks across the platform, sits down in the leather chair. She waves her hand and everyone sits down.

The tank pushes me back down. Piss the fuck off, I tell her. I look over to the visitors' seats by the side of the swing doors but there's no one I recognise.

The brief in front of Harriet stands up. He's saying something but I can't hear what it is. Then again, I don't suppose it makes any difference if I can hear what's going on or not – it's not like anyone's asking me anything.

There's a soft sucky sound as the swing doors close. I look up just in time to see Marta slide her tail into a seat by the door. The star.

Donna Jane Wilson, stand up, goes the judge.

The screw behind me grabs my arm and heaves me up to my feet. He touches me one more time, I swear I'll chin him. The judge looks straight at me and some of the penguins turn their heads to me for a neb.

Donna Jane Wilson. You have been charged with possessing a firearm with intent, threatening behaviour, resisting arrest and assault of a police officer. The trial date is set for the third of March. A pre-trial review hearing has been set for the twentieth of January. You will be remanded in custody until that date or further hearing. I'm adjourning your case until then. Do you understand?

I nod at her and smile. No Santa then?

A few giggles. The judge pretends she hasn't heard.

The clerk at the front stands up again says, The Crown against Kevin Whitehead, or some other poor sod.

Marta nods over at me and I manage a wink before the screws push me out and into the back corridor that goes down to the cells.

I ask if I can go to the toilet – dicky guts.

You can wait, says the tank.

I tell her I'm bursting and it'll be hours till we're back. There's a bog just down the corridor, I says.

I want to kick myself, pray they don't ask me how I know, but it turns out the rumour about screws and planks of wood is pretty accurate, as it goes. What harm can it do? says the Scouser.

They search me in the corridor outside the bog door. Then I push the door open and I'm in.

The light comes on automatically. Three toilets. I go for the middle one, look up. Above me I can see the ceiling tile is loose and there's a gap. I stand on the toilet seat, jam a leg against each side so I'm suspended, hope that crappy divider stuff holds. I walk myself up until I can put my shoulder under the loose tile, push it up. I get my elbows on the lip, then my legs go free and I heave them up after me.

I'm expecting a crawl space but it's more like an aircraft hangar. Wires feeding the lights, huge ribbed pipes everywhere, joists like walkways. Goes on forever and I can pretty much stand up.

I bend down, ease the ceiling tile back, snap it tight.

Beside me there's a bucket, a zip-up overall and a blue plastic hair cap inside. I put the cap and overalls on, grab the bucket.

Across the roof space I can see a yellow duster tied up to the pipes, then another, and another.

I make my way across the steel beams. At the last duster I pull up the tile. I look down through the gap and I can see a corridor, thick green carpet below me.

I stick my head through and there's no one about. A few yards each way and the corridor turns and disappears so I just have to risk it.

I let myself drop down through the gap. It leaves a hole in the ceiling but there's nothing I can do about that now but pray no one looks up.

I straighten up, put the bucket over one arm, adjust the hair cap and pull it down at the front. Try and decide which way to go. Christ, I can't just stand here.

Then I hear voices coming towards me but there's nowhere to go. I'll have to blag it.

Jen and Sonn's cousin Ali walk round the corner with Mina, overalls on, pulling a cleaning cart behind them. Jen grins out at me from under her cap.

I fall in step and we walk round the bend, smack into Wallace and Gromit waiting outside the toilet, kicking the carpet.

The Scouser smiles. Iya geeals. No rest for the wicked, eh?

Ali grins back at him, Yeah you're not wrong mate.

I do a Salford, nod without looking, Iyoh.

We walk past.

We're at the next corner as the Scouser turns to the tank. What the fuck you think she's doing in there?

Then it's all I can do not to run.

By the time we get to the fire exit we've got the giggles. I half-expect it to be locked but course it's not.

Ali and Jen park the cart, I push down on the bar and the sunshine hits me, day cold and clear, smells great. I take a deep breath.

Across the car park, security hardly looks up from his paper, flicks the gate switch on autopilot. See yer ladies, he says, without looking up.

The gate takes forever to slide open and even though it's cold, I'm starting to sweat.

When we step through and away, I can't really believe it. The gate slides shut behind us.

We turn right up the street.

Parked up ahead there's a dark green lorry, engine running, driver in overalls and a cap messing around with a tailgate. As we get nearer, she pulls it down, steps aside.

Ali and Jen keep on walking between the lorry and the wall.

I catch sight of Mina's face, turn to give her a hug. She buries her face in the crook of my neck. I'll miss you, she says.

Don't worry, I'll be in touch, I say.

She looks up at me and smiles, eyes shining. You don't mean that, but it's OK.

She's probably right. What is it about this woman still makes me feel like I'm a first class shit, even when I'm saying and doing stuff I'd never have dreamed of doing before?

I kiss the top of her head. Gotta go. Thanks for everything babe.

She pulls away. Ahh get lost now, she says, you be safe.

I watch her run after the others until she's well past the lorry...

Then I walk right on up the tailgate, plastic bucket and all.

When the tailgate closes behind me it's pitch dark. I step forward, trip over something. Down on my knees I feel around. A holdall.

I feel the engine rev, then a jolt and we're moving away.

Slowly things take shape in the blackness. High up there's an air vent. I reach up to slide the clip. The grid swings open, letting in tiny strips of light. The lorry shudders down through the gears, dust dancing with the movement. I make out the bike secured to the far side of the lorry with straps, a single mattress strapped up alongside.

I open up the holdall, scrabble inside, take out a pair of jeans and a shirt, my leather bike jacket. Under the jacket is my phone and my knife. In the pocket is a wad of money, my legit passport and my UK driving licence.

I get changed, ball up the overall and cap, shove them back in the holdall, put the knife and cash in my sock. I put the phone in my top jacket pocket. I'll keep it till I get the clean one, transfer the contacts.

I let down the mattress and stretch out, too wired to sleep. For some reason I get to thinking about Louise, how I tret her so bad just because I didn't love her, how she didn't deserve it, not after two years. She was always there in the background, even though I'd leave her standing at the bar to work the room, sometimes not even go home. How I'd call round the next day, sheepish, and her eyes would be puffy from tears and I'd pretend not to notice. And the last time, how she cried in my arms and all I felt was trapped. Never gave a thought to how she might be feeling, couldn't wait to get away.

I was reaching for my pants. For God's sake Lou stop crying, it's pathetic.

What do you expect? she says.

Why don't you ever just get angry? I can't stand it.

Angry? What's the point? You can't deal with anyone else's feelings.

What's that supposed to mean?

You'd just have left me.

I'm leaving you now, so what's the difference?

Why d'you have to be so cruel? she says. Just because I'm not Carla.

I look at her. What the fuck are you talking about, not Carla?

She gives a short laugh, hard, hollow.

You're the only one who doesn't see it, she says.

It must be hours later. I wake with a start. The lorry swerves sharp to the left and brakes, tyres squealing, then we come to a dead stop. Then I'm straining my ears, heart going like the clappers, but there's only the sound of a car whizzing past, then the rattle of a lorry. Must be at the services for the changeover.

Then I realise. There's no light at all now coming in through the vent so it must be dark outside, means no lights out there which means we're not at the services we're in the middle of nowhere. Which means there's only one other option and it comes with a uniform. Fuck I wish I could see.

I hear the front cab door slam shut, realise I'm holding my breath. I get on to my feet, feel my way to the back of the hold, crouch down by the bike.

A bang at the back doors and I hear the bolts sliding back as another thought hits me. Christ, the driver. Those doors are going to open and I'm going to be staring down a Darts nine millimetre with nowhere to go. I've underestimated Danny, or Kim, or someone. What the fuck was I thinking?

I can hear two voices now, maybe three.

There's no way I'm going down without a fight. I pull my blade out of my sock, offer up a prayer for whoever remembered to pack it, flatten myself against the wall of the lorry right up beside the door. They'll expect me to be as far back as I can get, which means if I'm not where they think I might get past, get away.

The door starts to open. I kick it hard and wide with my foot, catch the fucker behind it, hear a yelp as sheet metal connects with bone, see a torch drop to the ground. I don't hang around to count how many there are, leap as far as I can, out into the night. Now I thank God it was dark in there. If they had a torch, I'll be the only one who can see.

I hit the ground running, a layby. To one side there's a hedge and a ditch, behind it the trees.

A woman's voice behind me. Donna! Where the fuck are you going?

I glance back across my shoulder, skid to a halt. One woman sits on the ground holding her face, shakes her head at me. In front of the lorry, a beat-up old Luton.

My driver lifts her arms, palms wide, says again, Where are you going?

My fucking face, says the one on the ground.

I walk back over, blade still in my hand because you never know.

Changing lorry, duck, says the driver, tucking her shirt in at the back, didn't they tell you?

I look around, Yeah? So how come we aren't we at the services?

She grins. You want to be on *Crimewatch*, babe, do a turn for the cameras, feel free to ride back to the services. But you're on your own with that one. A layby is way safer.

I weigh them both up. Could be on the level.

Where are we?

Just outside London, says the driver. Need to change here.

I need your names and your contact, I say.

No names, no ID, says my driver, we was promised.

I grip the blade in my hand, raise my eyebrows.

Leanne, she says with a shrug. Run haulage in Stoke, took my orders from Crewe.

I look at her properly now, dark hair pulled back in a ponytail, eyes friendly, hands rough as you like. I wave a hand to where the one on the ground is still prodding at her nose.

I look down. Long red curls under a baseball cap, a million freckles, smear of blood on her face. Who's she?

Karen, she says, standing up. Walthamstow Rugby Club. Your lift to the south coast, she says, or I was. Any more tricks like that, Jackie Chan, and you can fucking well walk.

I weigh it up and nod. Open the van up, I'll get the bike.

In the lorry I put the knife in my belt and strap the bag tight to the bike, while they let down the ramp. Just push it down, says Leanne.

I take no notice and start up the engine. I jump on, pull the throttle right back, jam my foot on the accelerator, shoot out over the ramp. Whatever their names are, they jump to one side just in time as I fly past, skid into a turn and face them, No offence ladies, I just can't take the risk.

Then I'm out past them and gone.

39

After twenty minutes across country I feel safe enough to pull over, get out the map and the torch.

I follow the A-roads and my nose until I'm well clear of London, cut across to the A22 and head down for Eastbourne, making reasonable time because it's dark. The fuel gauge is low so I pull over, top up from the spare gallon I keep strapped to the back. If I have to refuel again I'll find a parked car without a locked petrol cap, use the pipe. Can't risk a garage and the CCTV.

The land seems flat to me, no proper hills. I cross the A27, see a signs for Brighton, remember how we always swore we'd get there some day, for Pride. Never did though.

Down through Eastbourne I head for the front. Morecambe with a makeover, everything white. I take the coast road as it turns, climbs away to the cliffs. In my mirror I watch the lights of the town fall away, tiny sparkles from a ship on the sea.

When I take the turn for Beachy Head it's nearly dawn, my arms and legs frozen numb with the cold. At the brow of the hill I turn off left, follow the road away and round across the flat of the fields. The wind coming off the top hits the bike like a brake. Further on there's a phone box in the middle of nowhere, a sign on it that says Samaritans Call Here.

I pull up and take off my helmet, take off my gloves and rub my hands for the cold, turn off the headlights, let my eyes adjust. I look up and catch the dawning, light spilling slowly in from the east. At the cliff edge gulls are calling and circling, long tufts of grass whipped around in the wind.

The grass is short here, deserted, a wide plain to the edge of the cliffs, no fences. Across the field behind me what looks like a pub, silhouetted in the half-dark, no lights on. In front just the cliffs, the birds, and the sea.

No point marking time. I give the bike a last check, turn over the engine, climb on. Then I hear Carla's voice, clear as day. *Wait till the sun comes up*, she says.

I lean forward, put my cheek against the top of the tank. The metal is warm and smooth, smells of everything we've ever done and all the things we never got to do. I feel the engine throb against my cheek, gives me some weird kind of comfort. Then I'm stepping out of my skin and watching someone else, someone small and lonely. Somebody no one will miss.

A ray hits the cliff edge, turns the white rock rose-pink and she'd like that.

I give the bike a last pat, take a deep breath and circle wide for the turn, line her up. Then I pull back the throttle, let her go. The roar of wind in my ears and I'm bouncing over the tufts, the grass spinning past. I keep the gear low till the engine's screaming then double declutch, and she's flying over the grass to the edge.

As I see the edge I throw myself sideways and the bike

shoots out over the cliff without me, fifty feet out and still climbing. She seems to hang in the air for a moment then plunges straight down out of sight.

I crawl to the edge but there's nothing to see, only the rocks below and the waves. Must have sunk like a stone.

I take off my leather jacket and check the pockets. Driving licence, passport, Artemis card, the phone. I put the licence, the passport and the card back in the jacket, throw it over. It floats like a bird then falls soft to the waves. I watch it flow backwards and forwards in the foam until finally it disappears. I know it'll wash up again on the rocks, even the bike will I suppose, eventually. See ya Donna, I say.

About now I should say a prayer or shed a tear or get mad or something but that's not my way, never has been. Did all that before when I made my decision. When you know you've got to let something go, best grieve it first, Dad used to say. That way when it's gone you can get on, no loose ends.

Then don't look back love, he said. There's no point.

And there's me, I always thought he was talking about women.

40

Back at the road I get the bus west along the coast.

Even though it's cold, things look clean and light here somehow, smell dry. Makes you want to stretch your legs out and breathe in. I'd have to say there's more sky here than at home. Through the bus window the winter sun makes a square on my jeans.

I watch the fields and villages go past. Bungalows and spiky plants everywhere, gardens and spaces between them and a place with so much money you'd think they would want a house with an upstairs; they can't all be disabled.

Newhaven, middle of fucking nowhere, nothing there but a harbour and the ferry as far as I can see. I get off at the bus station, look round for the caff. Across the main road and past the harbour the sea winks cold and slate-green, seagulls crying and swirling all over the place. I don't know how people live with that noise.

Inside the caff it's warm and steamy, scuffed pine and plastic sauce bottles. Stinks of Flash and cooking fat, condensation running down the insides of the windows. There's a plastic flower on the middle of every table so I guess someone tried. A couple of tramps with mugs of tea.

The girl behind the counter looks up, home-made tattoos and a lip ring, bright orange hair pulled up in a pineapple. Looks about twelve or maybe I'm just getting old.

I ask for hot chocolate. I'll bring it over, she says.

When it comes, there's a mobile number written on the till receipt wedged under the mug. The till receipt says £1.80 which must be a mistake. I leave a quid on the table and head for the door.

Away from the bus station I find a phone box. That's the other thing about this place, phone boxes that work. I dial the number and a woman answers, tells me to go to Unit 13 on the dock.

At the unit everything's locked up, no one around.

Then I hear a whistle.

There's no one about this far down the quay except a fisherman bent over, looks like he's mending some pots.

I walk over.

He's a she. Hard to tell with the waders and the cap and how she doesn't even look up when she says low and lazy, Ju Donna? You late.

She's twenty-five, maybe thirty, and wiry, eyes the same grey-green of the sea, lashes rows of dark feathers on tanned skin, looks Spanish. Chin looks like it's carved out of rock. eyebrows black and bushy nearly meeting up in the middle. Lise would have a field day plucking those buggers out. On the ropes her hands shuttle back and forth, palms muscled and broad but they got shape, nails rimmed with black. Wouldn't get many takers down Canal Street on a Friday night in that state but I reckon she'd scrub up pretty well.

When she stands up she's taller than me and solid. I follow her past the sheds and round the quay, dodging pots and boxes and piles of stuff wrapped in tarpaulin. Walks pretty fast for someone who talks so slow.

We come to stone steps, steep and down to the water.

I stop at the top and look down at the boat, Are you fucking kidding me?

At the bottom of the steps there's the kind of boat I wouldn't climb in to cross the rezzer at Debdale on a calm day, never mind the Channel in December. Looks like something out of Shiloh's story book, little cabin up top, deck crammed with all sorts, only about three feet between the deck and the water. The Little Boat That Could. Christ, I hope so.

My señorita says nothing, starts untying the ropes.

When she's ready to cast off she looks up at me, steady.

Ju need to hurry, she says.

I spew my guts inside out for four hours straight. Ms Personality up on the wheel doesn't smile once the whole time, and says even less. I don't remember exactly when I stop heaving but I know it's way after there's anything left to come up.

Eventually I slip down from the rail exhausted, lay my head on the deck.

When I wake I'm frozen solid, the moon picking out the frost on the rails and the tarp each time there's a break in the clouds. Otherwise there's just blackness, the sound of the engine, the rock and slap of the water against the hull.

I haul myself up, duck my head into the tiny wooden shelter that serves as a wheelhouse. The digital clock says 18:05. Where are we? I say.

She stares straight ahead.

I'm pissed off. Look love, I know the whole silo thing is important but this is ridiculous, we're on the same side. I'm not asking for your bank account details. Where the fuck are we?

She reaches down, flips up a screen in the dash. A neon digital map shows the Channel, the coasts of England and France on each side. Between the coasts the map is crammed with teeny bright triangles, seems like every kind of colour, pointing in every direction, all moving. I realise they're all boats. Looks like the M602 in rush hour. She points at a tiny triangle pointing south, three-quarters of the way across.

That's us?

She shrugs, as if it might be, might not.

I look out across the wheel. Can they see us?

I hope so, she says, without a hint of a smile, takes one of those tankers three miles to brake.

I don't know whether that makes me feel better or worse. Better because there's so much traffic out there that they won't be looking at a tiny fishing boat in range of the coast, will they? Worse because I can't see how we can get to the other side without hitting something. I just hope it's not a tanker.

I duck back out on to the deck. I'll let you concentrate, I say.

Later I watch the dark shape of land appear against the night sky. Every so often a cluster of lights on the shore, tiny as pinpricks, that loom and disappear with the swell of the sea. One light is different from the others, flashes every couple of seconds. Buggered if I'm going to ask her about it, let her treat me like I'm stupid.

The engine is a slow throb now and I pull myself together, stand up over the rail, icy steel burning my hands. I lean over the keel, wash my face, rinse my mouth and spit, water salty and freezing. My jeans are crusty and damp.

Where are we now?

She rolls her eyes, reaches under the tarp for a plastic bag, unwraps it. Tears off some bread and throws it towards me. Eat now, she says.

She needs to stop being so twatting rude. I swear to God if I could work a fucking boat I'd knock her spark out.

She breaks off some hard cheese and hands it to me, hunkers down. Reaching behind, she pulls out a flask and fills two plastic cups, hands me one. I put the cup to my lips, sweet and milky, the best coffee ever. Then I'm watching her eat, spearing small hunks of cheese with a penknife, tearing the bread into pieces with grimy fingers, dipping it into the coffee then up to her mouth. I must be staring because she looks at me sideways.

Eat, she says, and waves at my bread.

The radio crackles and I jump.

She strides over towards it, presses a button. A woman's voice talking twenty to the dozen, a strange language, hard, doesn't sound Spanish, fills the night.

My girl turns the radio down, her back to me, talks quickly and low into the handset. When she turns back to me I try to read her face but it's smooth with her secrets.

My guts twist. What is it?

She shakes her head. Nothing.

An hour or so later we pull in at a tiny inlet to wait for the light. We sleep half-sitting, huddled under the tarpaulin between the creels on the deck, as distant from each other as the stars.

I lie awake, listen to the slap of the water against the boat, think about Ror and how she'll be when she sees me. Not that I'll see anyone for a while – I can't risk it. If anyone is tailing me I'd just lead them straight to Ror. They'll stay where they are for a month or two then we'll meet up on the mainland, decide where to go from there. Lise thinks we should go long-haul for security but I'm set on the Costas for safety. The law can follow us anywhere but we got links to every second person in the Costas and that's got a security all of its own. Proper home from home to be honest.

I think I hear her cry out. I look over but her face is smoothed out in sleep so maybe I'm hearing things. I watch for a while longer, wonder where she comes from and whether she always sleeps curled up tight like that, so alone.

When I'm sure she's asleep I shift position against my bag, take out my phone and turn it on and there's a signal. I transfer the data off the sim on to the phone, drop the used sim into the sea. I reach a clean sim from the bag and put it back in the phone.

I'm scrolling through the address book deleting anything that I don't need when I come to Louise. Then it's not that last time I remember. Not the screaming and raging or that ugly pot statue she made me get her in Crete. Venus-something-or-other, hitting the doorframe and just missing my face. Not even the sad quiet sobbing when she knows I won't stay.

It's the moors I remember, a while after we met. Climbing the slabs at the top, scrambling over the rock, her scraping her arm. Then us running down full pelt from the Tor like mad kids holding on to each other, falling over ourselves in a heap on the peat.

We lie for a while, me back on my elbows. Then she leans over, hair everywhere in the wind, lifts her face up to mine. She looks beautiful. What? I say, laughing down at her.

I love you, she says. Do you love me?

I fuck you, don't I? I say.

But she's not laughing.

I get up and brush myself off. Don't be stupid, Lou – that's just something people say when they want something from you.

I see her flinch and her face closes down, and for some reason that makes me feel better.

Whether I loved her or not, she didn't deserve that.

Then I think about Mina the last time outside the court, the smell of her hair. *You don't mean that.*

It's a clean sim and I'm practically in France so what can it hurt? I find the contact, key in the text. I'll be in touch Mina, I promise. I'll miss you too. Then I press send.

I'm surprised how much better I feel. *Everyone's got to grow up some time*, says Carla with a grin.

At first light she's up, rinses her mouth with seawater and the sound wakes me. Everything is still, dawn creeping across the horizon touching the mouth of the bay. I lick my lips and taste salt. Things feel new somehow, bright.

A white bird circles round off the headland then goes down like an arrow, straight into the sea, looks like it knows exactly what it's doing. Then comes up with nothing. Missed it, poor bastard.

Señorita follows my eyes, shakes her head. Gannet, she says. He never miss. Eat the fish underwater before he come up.

Underwater? Why?

And then, for the first time, she grins. Nice teeth, pearly white and even between chapped lips. Something in her smile reminds me of Mina, the stab in my chest taking me by surprise.

She shrugs. So no one else take it, maybe.

Then there are dozens of white birds in the air, rising out from the cliffs and up from the sea. They swirl and dive, swirl and then dive, together. I watch the water churn in the wake, think about everything that's gone, washed away behind me like the froth by the ocean. A new start, just what Car always dreamed of for Ror, and the cold hand that's been clutching my heart ever since I can remember starts to loosen its grip.

I ask her where she comes from. She screws her eyes against the headwind, pulling the rudder a quarter-turn. San Sebastian, she says.

You're Spanish?

She frowns and snorts. No Spanish. Basque.

San Sebastian is Spain, I say. Even I know that.

She flashes a smile, bright against brown skin. San Sebastian in Spain, yes, like Belfast in England.

She's lost me now, or maybe it's the language thing, so I give up on the geography lesson. If Ror was here she'd likely be able to sort it all out but she's not.

She wipes her face against the sun, pulls her long-sleeved shirt over her head with one hand, the other on the tiller.

Her shoulders are smooth mahogany.

You got family? I ask.

She shrugs, doesn't answer.

You got a name then?

Then her eyes are narrowed, looking straight ahead as if she's seeing something on the horizon.

I follow the eyes. To one side the coast of France, nothing up front but gulls and the sea.

We pull into Port-en-Bessin and I make a dash for the toilet block. I'll be honest, when she showed me the bucket under the tarp I knew I'd rather drown than shit in that with her watching. The harbour is tiny even compared with Newhaven, and it's pretty. Little houses like rows of painted crooked teeth straggling down to the dock. Only one or two fishing boats moored up but I bet it's packed in the summer.

I get back to the boat and I'm just about to climb on when she takes out a thin polythene package, throws it over to me. I catch it. Then she throws my holdall on to the wooden platform where I'm standing, starts to cast off. No instructions, no explanation. Bollocks all.

Where you going? Is this it?

Adios mi camarada! She nods her head at the packet. Ring the number.

There's supposed to be advantages to not knowing the next leg in advance, like you can't give something away by mistake if you don't know it. I signed up to it but there's a definite down side.

I tear open the plastic. Inside there's a passport and driving licence with my photo and someone else's name, a new phone, two new sims and some cash. On a scrap of paper there's a phone number.

I look up to say what the fuck, or thanks, or something anyway, but she's already chugging away from me, heading for the mouth of the harbour.

I watch her back as she stands on the deck, feet planted wide, One arm up, ta-ra, and no looking back.

Adios, I'm thinking. I fucking knew she was Spanish.

I head up the dock for the gates and I'm still pissed off. Good riddance, miserable Spanish twat.

I'm busy imagining I'm going to get something decent to eat, maybe even a shower, the sun on my face like warm breath. I touch the paper in my pocket, think what Lise is gonna to say when she hears me, squealing all over the place like she does. How it won't be long before I'm hugging Ror and swinging her round.

Then I'm grinning at Carla. We done it baby, I goes.

So I'm practically skipping when I look up and see them. A line of six men, four in in uniform, hands on their holsters, walking right towards me.

Epilogue

They say the first three months behind bars are the worst but let me tell you nothing is ever going to be as bad as that very first moment – the one where you look up and see four French police officers and two smug-looking border twats, hands on their pistols, walking straight towards you just when you think you're home free. You know, that exact moment when everything you ever hoped for goes to shit. After that it's just a matter of adjustment.

Can't blame anyone else, brought it all on myself with the text. Takes microseconds for a text to be flagged up on the Serious Crimes Special Technology doodah if they really want to catch you. My brief says these days just turning on a phone can be enough. And it doesn't matter if you're in France or Timbuktu if they know who you know and who you're likely to ring. You can't be a minute out of date with this shit or you're shafted. Might as well have sent up a flare with my name on it. That'll teach me to go soft.

Mind you, Mina was impressed so it's not all bad.

It fell apart for a while in the east after Daz and Tony were hit, until Danny pulled it back together, took over the Darts. I keep my ear to the ground, doesn't do to lose touch.

Mike went down for thirty-nine years minimum this last April, Big Tommo for thirty-five. Threw the book at all nine of them, even though everyone knows Mike had nothing to do with those two murders. I'm not pointing the finger but they want to look north. Tried them all over in Liverpool, Gartside shitting himself he'd have no witnesses left if he paraded them at Minshull Street or Crown Square. For a while the whole town went crazy, half of Greater Manchester's Finest leg it into the witness protection programme, gives evidence in secret, never comes back. Word on the street now is there was a grass or an undercover on the inside, maybe both. Maybe Daz and Tony were in on it. Me, I wouldn't know about that. Strange how these rumours can take hold once they start.

Danny keeps my patch going for a percentage, washes the money, gets it out to Lise every couple of months for their keep. Spanish school fees are sky high these days no kidding. Danny wants us to branch out, legal highs, but I told him there's no way I'm selling that shit, who knows what might be in it? I'll stick with the real stuff, tried and tested – you've got to have some sense of responsibility. It's a bit of a pisser letting Danny take the cred for Tony and Daz but I'll get the chance to update my CV sooner or later, no doubt about it. I keep a hold of the forensics in case he changes his mind. I'm not an idiot.

Mina comes in to see me when she can, brings me in a clean sim now and again so I can speak to Ror, hear what she's up to, how she's grown. Last time there were photos – Lise with her freckles all joined up and laughing, smoke from a barby in the background, Ror brown as a nut and doing a handstand, Sonn teaching Rio to dive in the pool. Fair made my eyes sting.

Father Tom came to see me yesterday. Thinks I should grass everyone up, reckons I can get some kind of deal, be out in a year, no sweat. I told him, forget it. Three and a half years is pretty lucky all told for possession of a firearm and resisting arrest, seeing how I kept shtum and they couldn't make anything else stick. And this way once it's all over me and Ror are home-free, no looking over our shoulders for the Social or the police, no point taking a shortcut if leads straight to fuck all. And when I think of Ror kicking about in the sun laughing, learning to swim, I'd do it all again in a heartbeat.

Carla comes to me in dreams on and off and we still get up to all sorts. I reckon when someone dies there's this whole other world going on right alongside, we just can't see it unless they want us to. I used to lie on the bunk for hours trying to sleep, willing it to happen. Just to get to her, you know, just to see her face. Now I don't bother so much. I know she'll come to me when she's ready, when she feels like it, and that's just the way it's always been.

And hey, don't even think about feeling sorry for me. Locked up with three hundred lonely women, how hard can it be?

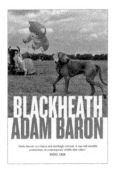

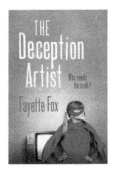

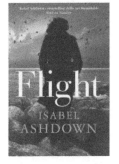

MORE FROM MYRIAD

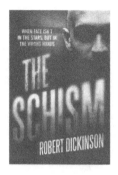

myriad m∞

Sign up to our mailing list at
www.myriadeditions.com
Follow us on Facebook and Twitter

Jules Grant was born in Scotland and grew up in Manchester. This is her first novel.